AD LUMEN PRESS

American River College

Tina Goes to Heaven

Tina Goes *to* HEAVEN

a novel by

LOIS ANN ABRAHAM

Ad Lumen Press | Sacramento | 2016

The following extracts used by permission:

Terry Pratchett from *Interesting Times* (London: Victor Gollancz, 1994) by permission of the publisher

Dorothy Bryant from *Writing a Novel* (New York: Ata Books, 1978) by permission of the author

James Brown from *James Brown: The Godfather of Soul* (James Brown with Bruce Tucker. London: Head of Zeus, 2014) by permission of the publisher

For information address: Ad Lumen Press
American River College | 4700 College Oak Drive | Sacramento, CA 95841
www.adlumenpress.com
Part of the Los Rios Community College District

Library of Congress Control Number 2016017610

ISBN 978-0-9911895-8-8

1st Edition | 1st Printing

Tina Goes to Heaven

Prologue

THE SWEDES HAVE A word for it: *hortur*, a whore's luck.

But really, being a whore in the first place is unlucky, and any luck after that likely to be fleeting, a brief postponement rather than the actual avoidance of trouble and pain. If you come into money, it's quickly stolen. If you make a friend, the friend robs you and disappears. If the sun shines down on you, it reveals the extent of the damage, showing what you have become and what is left to sell.

The definition of *hortur*: the good fortune of having your body used by an attractive customer instead of an ugly one. As though desire were any part of the equation.

There is no way to be careful enough, let alone lucky enough, to stay okay. You are paid to be invaded, possessed, and dispossessed. You are pierced and bruised, raped and robbed, discarded and scorned. You are forty times more likely to die this year than your sister who is not a whore. You are forty-six times more likely to be murdered. In that matrix of harm, luck is hard to feature.

Maybe a whore's luck means not getting hurt too bad tonight. There is a word for it in Swedish, but the word is meant as a joke.

1

Hell is pretty bad, but you get used to it. Then it gets worse.

—*Anonymous*

The party for Freddy Napoleon's thirty-third birthday was meant to double as a send-off for his trip to New Orleans to do business with the Ortega family. It went bad before it was halfway through, in spite of all Tina's planning and careful attention to detail. As Freddy's girl, she had made all the arrangements, rented the Hot Parrot Club for the night, and invited the right important straights and musicians along with Freddy's usual big customers, contacts and associates. This had required some very careful visits to the hangouts of dangerous men who sold or bought the coke that was Freddy's main business, men who might be high or crazy, men with hair-trigger tempers, lounging cruel-eyed in restaurant booths or in the backs of luxury cars, surrounded by their violent reputations and their violent men. They probably would have hurt her if she wasn't Freddy's or if she hadn't had one of his guys with her. Then she would slip away, putting a check mark next to their names on her invitation list.

It had to be a good party and Tina tried to think of everything, all the treats and special touches Freddy would only notice if she forgot something. Using the worn-out, cheap-looking girls who already worked for Freddy would have been like serving leftovers, a sign of disrespect. The life was hard on whores and Freddy didn't have the energizing arts of a really good pimp; he tended to focus on the drug business, which required fewer people skills—buying and selling, intimidation and violence. The whore business was a sideline to supply himself, his guys, and his favored associates with pussy. So for the party, Tina brought in a variety-pack of different types of girls from Nevada to dress the place up and slip into the back room with any guest important enough for special treatment. They were expensive, but it was important to show the guests that Freddy could take care of his people. She insisted that Freddy's guys—T-Wah, Hoppy, Geron, and Brad—bring their own dates so they wouldn't wear out the hired talent.

Tina enjoyed the whole planning process, but especially the phone calls, admiring the crisp, professional way the caterer, florist, and other providers answered the phone: "River City Florist, this is Shannon. How can

I help?" "Puffer Bakery, Rick speaking." "Casablanca Escort Service, what is your pleasure?" It made her own usual greeting, "Yeah?" seem pretty lame, so she experimented with ways to answer that would mirror the calm, surface respect she liked so much, when the various businesses called back to discuss the details, make changes, or confirm her careful arrangements. "Napoleon event, Shatina speaking," or better yet, "This is Shatina Martinez, Napoleon event coordinator." She thought it might be impressive to use her full, formal name, Shatina Winona Mai Martinez, but in the end, she settled on a snappier, more business-like version: "Napoleon party, Tina Martin speaking." She liked the anonymous, white sound of it. She could be anyone, and the caller wouldn't know. It felt safe.

Tina had set the menu with Freddy's favorites, including a long buffet table crowded with all the sweet and greasy things that Freddy liked: baklava, cream puffs, donuts, zabaglione, along with the usual Chinese takeout, pasta, and deli meat they all liked, the comfort food of mobsters and thugs. The purple strobe light show, the light sticks, the streamers, the disco balls, and the glitter spray were a great success. All the girls looked fabulous and inviting. Tina herself wore a silver satin dress that blended with her shiny brown skin and kinky yellow hair to make her look like she was made entirely of metal, a very sexy cyborg, designed to please. Long gold hoop earrings and slender gold bangle bracelets added to the effect. It was all to make a show for Freddy. It was Freddy's party.

The guns were tucked away where casual guests wouldn't stumble across them, but near enough to hand that the guys could get at them if something went wrong. There was enough coke and ecstasy to keep things moving, but not enough to have to cope with an OD, although you never know. She would have to keep an eye on it. The music was live and hot, the musicians professional enough to play the music and stay out of trouble since Tina was paying them with cash instead of product. Hoppy was posted to keep the guests from lifting presents from the table where they were stacked, awaiting the attention of the black-clad birthday boy. Tina had bought Freddy a Japanese robe, red silk with black dragons, admittedly with his money but that was the only money she had. She thought Freddy would probably leave the robe in her apartment, and she looked forward to wearing it when he wasn't there. Her only worry was that it might strike him as gay, so she had Geron and T-Wah go in on a samurai sword for him to open first.

She knew from experience to be careful, not to go too far and make Freddy uncomfortable. Everything was about Freddy, and there shouldn't be anything he didn't like. So when she bought masks at the party supply store, she made sure some of them were fierce demons and monsters (for Freddy and his main guys), and some of the others were cartoon characters like Bart Simpson and Mickey Mouse for Freddy's lower subordinates with a mix of other masks for any guests who felt like masquerading. Freddy had to maintain his position, even in a carnival. Freddy wore the red devil mask she had set aside as the scariest one though he tore it off when it got between him and his food.

The masks were a big hit. Even the hip new city councilman who had begun the evening on a very cautious footing eventually succumbed to champagne and weed and the thrill of sex in a Marilyn Monroe mask with tall, black Sabrina, her contemptuous face hidden behind Richard Nixon's. Meanwhile, Geron was showing the councilman's little blonde wifie his tattoos and piercings in another private room. All was going well and Freddy seemed darkly pleased, sitting in the center of the room surrounded by nervous well-wishers and underlings, which meant Tina could finally relax a little.

Tina had belonged to Freddy for almost eight years, and it had been good enough. He was less demanding than Mickey had been and not as crazy as Lalo, though she missed the fancy restaurants Lalo had taken her to. And she missed his crazy laugh. But being with Freddy was better than trolling johns at conventions and hotel lobbies like her early days. Freddy liked her odd mix of kinky hair and caramel skin and Indian eyes. And he more than liked her generous, soft-lipped, well-muscled mouth. He had more money than Mickey or Lalo and a relaxed style that made it easier to anticipate what he wanted. Lalo used to pull down his pants and say things like, "Hey, Shatina, come over here and take me to heaven!" Freddy just grunted.

So maybe Freddy wasn't relaxed so much as consistent. He was not imaginative in his vices, which made things simpler. She felt lucky to have found him when Lalo got sent away, and lucky that he seemed to like her close by whether he was partying or doing business. He called her his lucky piece. He might even have her sit on the bed with him while he had one of the other girls, though mostly it was just him and her. She helped him count the money and the bags and soothed his anger when either one was short, giving him her calming mouth, since that's what he liked and what she was particularly good at. She had seen Freddy beat the whores bloody, but he had treated Tina good, except for the one time he had slapped her for smiling at the wrong time. She liked to think that she was his girlfriend, though she knew that wasn't strictly true.

Freddy had rented her a pretty nice apartment with classy furniture: an enormous black bed with a red velour comforter, a wet bar for mixing his drinks, soft, bulging couches and chairs covered with smooth black leather. He had his own place, but he sometimes chose to sleep at the apartment where Tina was, where he entertained clients and collected from the runners and bagmen and sometimes the girls, who had to find their own places to live. He fucked her sometimes, but mostly he just wanted blowjobs. Her unprotected childhood had honed this skill, and she was proficient, judging the right degree of suction and pressure, the effectiveness and timing of various tongue moves, how to use her hand to keep the dick out of the gag zone without seeming at all unwelcoming, and how to hold the cum in her mouth for a second or two before she swallowed. Snotty consistency, salty, with a hint of bathroom cleanser thrown in to confuse the palate, but once swallowed, gone with very little aftertaste. Unless she had to do a lot of guys.

Sometimes Freddy would have her take one of his guys or a business associate into the bedroom for some head, but Tina didn't mind that much. They were often quicker about it than Freddy was. And besides, blowjobs were her forte. That was how she had managed to end up in this cushy spot with a life of partying, shopping, and blowing Freddy and his friends. She would rather blow a guy than get screwed anytime. For one thing, it was quicker. And it tended to hurt less. Tina would do almost anything to avoid getting hurt. It's why she never smoked, hated needles, why Lalo used to make her eat jalapeños for punishment or a joke.

The first problem that arose at Freddy's birthday party was caused by Brad. He had brought Monika as his date. Brad liked Monika. Tina liked Monika too, but knew it was a bad idea to bring her. Tina and Monika had been pals for a while, sharing the apartment and Freddy, even pretending to be sisters, but Freddy stopped that by sending Monika out to the motel strip to turn tricks, and Tina hardly ever saw her anymore. She wouldn't meet Tina's eyes as she sidled through the door behind Brad. She was skeletal in her dirty blue cami and a stained denim mini-skirt. The flesh on her arms had a waxy look, as though a thumb pressed there would leave an imprint that would never fill in. She seemed more like Tina's grandmother than her sister now, eyes marked with blue circles and the grooves down her face so deep she looked like she had been painted with ugly brown stains. Her chest was sunken, her stomach swollen, her mouth starting to cave in around the missing teeth. That was the crack, probably.

When Freddy spotted Monika snagging cheese puffs at the buffet, his face got uglier and he sent T-Wah to roust her. She saw him coming and slipped out the door like a silverfish down a drain. Brad was busy casing the room and didn't notice, but Tina saw her go. Freddy made Brad wear the Bart Simpson mask as a punishment for being such a pussy, but Brad just put it on and went around saying "Cowabunga, dude!" until enough people told him to shut up.

Brad was the guy she knew best; they had lived in the same foster home twice, and she remembered him as a little blond angel of a boy who had followed her around chattering and slept next to her, his feet twitching as he ran or fell or struggled in his dreams, until she slid her feet under his to steady him, and he would almost wake and then sleep again, unmoving. She had carried him on her hip when he was tired, and made sure he got a share of whatever there was—candy, T-shirts, toys. She defended Brad when she could, when the attacker was not much bigger than her, was unarmed, not the foster mom, who would be harder to placate. She learned early to use her mouth when necessary to buy a peaceful moment for Brad and the rest of the kids.

Then Brad had been moved, she had been moved, and the move after that she found Brad again, by this time a cocky 12-year-old who stole her food and ignored her when other guys were around, but who seemed to like her and promised in private that he would back her up, though that never actually happened. Later she was the one who got him the job with Freddy, and she hoped he wouldn't do anything stupid, and if he did, she hoped Freddy wouldn't blame her. Anyone but Brad would have known it was unprofessional to bring Monika to Freddy's big event. Even Monika knew it, but she was used to taking chances, hoping her luck would hold.

The second spot of trouble came when the councilman and his wife Patti, both intoxicated and rosy with guilty secrets, took their leave a little early. Patti, a practiced politician herself, sought out her host to say goodbye and flatter, and then turned her attention to singing the praises of her hostess who was leaning against the wall, keeping an eye on the caterers and the musicians and the level of alcohol in the bottles behind the bar.

"I was just thrilled when Van told me we were invited to one of Tina's parties. Tina is a bit of a legend as a party-giver, you know. I just knew that anything Tina set up would be spectacular, and this was just darling. You must have worked like a dog to make all this," and she swept a wavering arm around to indicate the squirming mass of celebrants, "actually happen. Oh, Tina, next time I plan a little get-together, I'm going to give you a call and pick your brain."

Every time she said "Tina," Tina flinched as though a little puff of toxic gas, released from between Patti's tongue and hard palate, was hitting her in the face. She looked down at the floor at the way her satin party shoes gleamed in the darkness. She could feel Freddy congealing where he stood. It was Freddy's party; it was about Freddy. Tina was nothing. Tina was less than nothing. Freddy was everything.

Tina wanted to throttle the fucking bitch where she stood, and was careful not to look at Freddy until the guilty two, united by their mutual ambitions and their individual secrets, had weaved their way through the crowd and out the door to a waiting taxi, to be taken home to their upscale downtown condo, where nothing so exciting ever happened, not even when they were both topped up with expensive wine.

"God, what a stupid bitch!" Tina was hoping to patch this up, but Freddy shoved her roughly aside and headed back toward the buffet table to assuage his hurt pride and to order up revenge. T-Wah met him there, and they conferred as Freddy started building another plate for himself, carefully segregating the sweet from the savory, so that the Napoleon pastries were separated from the egg rolls by the delicious ambiguity of sweet-and-sour pork. Freddy's face was dark, lightening up into a mean satisfaction only after the sugar had taken effect and his will had been made reality. The councilman was going to find himself short of weed and girls for a good long while.

The real disaster, the big one, came with the fireworks, the finale, the height of the evening. Tina had arranged with the Truchas Brothers Pyrotechnics, Catering, and Big Top Company to set up a display on the roof of the warehouse across the street, so at midnight everyone could crowd onto the balcony and watch Freddy's name in fireworks. It was the kind of thing Freddy liked best. After a tense wait, the words across the opposite building spelled out

FREDDY NAPOLEON

in sizzling red letters. The crowd drew in a unanimous breath, let out a collective oooh, and Tina saw Freddy expand and look around at everyone admiring his name. It was unprecedented, not something anyone had seen in the gangster movies they watched with such admiration. It was an effect that Tina alone had dreamed up, just for Freddy. But then the letters sputtered and some went out until it said only

F ED OLEO

which remained there while squibs and rockets squealed and boomed, plumes of red, purple, gold, and blue arcing through the sky. But Tina heard, and knew that Freddy heard, the various guests mouthing the word "oleo," even though no one would dare to say it aloud. They didn't know how they knew, but they knew it meant something fat.

There was a stifled giggle among the murmurs, and Tina would have smacked the giggler if she had known who it was. It was more than disrespectful; it was another blow to Freddy's pride, and Tina had seen guys seriously damaged for a less public slight. No one disrespects Freddy Napoleon and lives. That's what Freddy always said, and it appeared to be true. She remembered the broken faces and the gurgling noises that had come from the crushed mouths of the two guys at the Sixty-Nine Club who had looked at Freddy sideways and then laughed. She remembered bloody fingers holding to the doorframe, a black coat flying out of the speeding SUV like an injured bird, and the scream that had trailed behind it like a ghost anchor that would not hold.

Tina tried to cover the moment by starting the happy birthday song, but most everyone was too drunk or stoned to follow along. That led to more giggling, and anyway, it was too late; the damage was done. The look Freddy gave her, his oily, round face lit by the red flares, his snake eyes dull black in spite of the exploding lights, told her that it was more than a failure; it was a betrayal of the worst kind. Freddy would not forgive her. Not even a new whore, not even one of Tina's blowjobs, was going to smooth things over. Freddy would take his revenge.

"Party's over." Freddy sounded like he had thumbtacks in his throat. He nodded at his guys to clear things out, and in three minutes, the club was empty of party-goers, catering staff, and entertainers, except for the bass player hauling his burden out the back door, glad of the early release so he could get home and check up on his girlfriend. The room was quiet, with only the faint click of one of the disco balls as it turned on its axis. The food tables looked ransacked and ruined, the gifts piled high, unopened. T-Wah, Hoppy, and Geron stood with their backs against the wall, lounging but ready. Brad stood next to them, but his face was blank in a different way, like he didn't quite realize the party was over.

"Brad drives me home, then takes us to the airport in the morning," Freddy said. "I got two guys meeting me there. You guys stay here. Fuck Tina and let her walk home." He didn't even look at her. "She's going to make me some money from now on, instead of sitting on her skinny old ass. I want her out there selling pussy when I get back. Welcome to the mean streets, bitch." He turned away, leaving Tina in dismay, her mind working but slipping against this new reality, grasping at nothing, falling backwards down the tractionless slide of fate.

"Freddy," she said, but she might as well have called out to a stone.

Brad giggled, pleased to be the driver for once. He usually had to sit in the back so he bustled out feeling important, looking back at Tina to see if she saw how well he was doing. T-Wah, Geron, and Hoppy also looked at Tina. She had been their friend, their comfort, their den mother, and their ward, and she tried to remind them of that, but they weren't listening to her at all. They were all stones.

"You heard the man," T-Wah said. "Let's us fuck Tina and get out of here."

"Everybody have to fuck her?" Geron was a little tired, having been out most of the night before collecting money and threatening slackers. He wanted more than anything to get home and sleep.

"Freddy say we fuck her, so we fuck her." T-Wah pushed Tina into the side room, sweeping ashtrays, dirty plates, and half-filled glasses from the table onto the floor to make room for her.

"C'mon, T. You know Freddy's just mad tonight. Tomorrow he's gonna be madder if you fucked his exclusive girl, you know that's true."

"Never been exclusive, Tina. Not his girl no more, it sounds like to me." T-Wah hiked her silver party dress up a few inches, pulled her panties off and his pants down. She had done T-Wah before, but not very often, and not like this, for punishment. "Sounds like you graduated to Freddy's full-time whore."

Tina was fairly used to doing things she didn't like to do, so she accommodated T-Wah as best she could. She knew if she tried to fight them, she would lose, and she would get hurt, and she would never find a way out. As long as she played along tonight, she would have tomorrow and the next day to figure it all out. She tried to make the right moves and the right noises, needing to get it over so she could think. The edge of the table dug into the backs of her legs, and she wished her feet reached the floor to get a little purchase, to have some way to steady herself against this heaving and pushing and grinding of flesh. He smelled of lavender and cigarette smoke.

T-Wah was quick, having been on duty with Freddy instead of partying for hours and drinking like the others. Hoppy was slower and rougher. Tina was beginning to get sore, and there was still Geron's turn coming. She talked him into a blowjob, which he liked better anyway, but he twisted his hand in her hair and tightened it enough to hurt, just to show they weren't friends anymore, that he was stone, and she was soft flesh. It made her sorry she had gone to his sister Juanita's funeral with him, and then cooked him Juanita's recipe for fried chicken afterwards. But however uncomfortable it was to do these three guys in a row, she knew it was a lot easier and a lot safer than being a street whore was going to be. After all, these were guys who liked her.

Maybe they used to like her, but once they were through with her, they packed Freddy's presents into T-Wah's car and drove off, leaving her to walk home through the dark city. She found a long, black coat in the cloakroom and stuffed the pockets with party favors and the least sticky food offerings since they would only get thrown out. Then she wrapped the coat tightly around her like a new, unbroken skin and started walking, only twenty blocks or so but in high heels that were raising blisters. The backs of her thighs were starting to really hurt, and she felt stretched and bruised. A few cars slowed down as they passed her, and she tried to imagine what it was going to be like to get into a dark car like that and put herself in the hands of a stranger, how he might treat her, what he would want, how she could get the money but still keep from getting hurt too bad, from getting sick, from going down into the darkness the way Monika had.

Some girls were so tough most johns wouldn't mess with them. Tina wasn't that tough and she knew it. She didn't think she could get that tough in the time she had before she was out there. She thought she would probably break and someone, Freddy or a john, would kill her, or beat her and leave her to die. Or she would die from misery, though she knew it wouldn't be that simple. She hurried home through the damp, dark streets towards the safety and refuge of the apartment, still hers until Freddy came back and threw her out. She needed to cry just enough to clear her head.

2

Finally, remember that detailed planning is of great value, but only if you understand that it does not work.

— *Dorothy Bryant*

TINA AWOKE IN THE early afternoon, her hands tucked carefully under the pillow as she had been taught by the nuns at St. Nicholas Children's Refuge when she was six, feeling sorc but ready to be hopeful. She stood in the shower letting the warm water stream down her body, wrapped herself up in the white spa robe she had always kept for Freddy's use, and then made coffee and sat down at her kitchen table. She picked up the lined yellow tablet and ripped out all the sheets she had filled planning Freddy's fucking party. The club, the catering, the girls, the guests, the fucking fireworks. That straight bitch was right; she had worked like a dog.

Jesus, she didn't want to work the streets for Freddy. But she knew when she really thought about it that it was bound to happen sooner or later. He had been looking at her differently for a while, like he noticed that she wasn't the fresh goods he had commandeered eight years ago. She didn't think he realized that she was so close to his age, though there would be no birthday party for her.

She knew Freddy would be extra mean to her since he was looking to punish her for the fireworks mess, so she couldn't even hope for a prime location. Whores don't last very long unless they are lucky, and she had seen how girls like Monika turned out, how bruised, how ruined. She had seen the scars and the way their eyes turned dull and hopeless, like there was nothing left to try for. There had to be a way to solve this. She had a few days before Freddy came back to figure it out. She began to write in her bold but tidy handwriting.

1. Kill Freddy

It seemed like a good idea; she could hardly be Freddy's whore if Freddy was dead. And he certainly was asking for it. She had a gun Geron had given her stashed in her underwear drawer along with a box of bullets, though she had never loaded or fired it. But it would feel terrific to see Freddy's fat face with fear written across it. The problem was that Freddy would be hard to kill. First, she'd have to get past T-Wah, which would be almost impossible. She couldn't pause to enjoy the moment or Freddy would take the gun away and beat her to death with it. She had seen this happen in the movies, and she had seen Freddy in a rage, though not at her. Better to shoot him in the back. But then she wouldn't see his face, would she. And T-Wah would feel honor-bound to kill her either before she could shoot Freddy or afterwards. And she still wouldn't have any money or any way to live. So killing Freddy would be a pleasure and a satisfaction, but not a solution to her difficulty.

2. Turn Freddy in to the cops

Tina wasn't sure she had witnessed enough crimes to merit much protection from the cops. The only murder she had actually seen was when the guys pulled Ricky Dick Rivera into the SUV, beat him bloody, and then threw him out on the freeway. Freddy hadn't even been there, though the guys only did what Freddy ordered. And she wasn't sure Freddy was a big enough fish to get anyone excited about catching him—it was mostly drugs and whores. If it wasn't him, it would be someone else. On the other hand, it would feel good to see his face in court when she stood up in a demure but sexy little dress, maybe black with a white collar, and he realized who was sending him away. Of course, Freddy had some business associates in the PD and a very fancy lawyer, so it might not even be possible. And again, no matter what happened to Freddy, T-Wah would shoot her and there wouldn't be any money. They probably didn't have witness protection for girls like her anyway.

3. Find another guy

It would have to be someone who wasn't scared of Freddy, because Freddy would not let go, not when his pride was involved. And his pride was involved in everything. Maybe she could find someone who would kill Freddy for her, and maybe T-Wah and the other guys as well. That's a lot of trouble to go to for a blowjob, however expertly administered. So someone very crazy. Not good. Or maybe someone powerful, but someone like that could have pretty much any girl he wanted. And he would probably want a younger girl than her. Probably a lot younger. Almost certainly. It would only be a temporary solution anyway. She would definitely be too old soon enough, and she was sick, she realized, of blowing guys. She wanted to do something else for a change.

4. Start a foster home

This was more like it. She knew what kids needed and how to make them feel okay. She could protect the little kids from the mean ones. Better yet, she could refuse to keep anyone mean. No one would have to do things they didn't want to do. No blow jobs, no hand jobs, no man of the house. If she had to have a guy there, she could try to get Brad to help her. She didn't think he was into little kids. But they wouldn't let a girl like her have a foster home. You probably had to already have a house somewhere. And Freddy would still find her and have T-Wah shoot her, probably in front of the kids. And it would take money to start up. Money, money, money.

5. Nuns

At least it wouldn't take money. You probably didn't have to buy your way into a convent. And some of the nuns, sister Mary Helen for example, had been very sweet, smiling at her and promising her that if she was good, she would go straight to heaven when she died and be with Jesus. It had seemed unlikely to Tina that this would actually happen, but it was a nice thing to say. So maybe the nuns. Freddy probably wouldn't shoot her in front of nuns. Maybe Monika could go to rehab and then come with her and they could be roommates. They could do something together back at

St. Nicholas, like look after the littlies or mop the halls. Tina had been to confirmation, but she didn't think she was Catholic enough to qualify. She hadn't been to mass or confession for close to twenty years, hadn't given it a thought. But she could always lie about that. Still, they would almost certainly boss her around, which could be hard to take, and there wouldn't be any dancing. And Sister Angela had been a nasty bitch, having put Tina on detention for painting her fingernails red with magic marker. She'd probably end up having to blow some fucking priest. Being a nun would have to be a last resort.

6. Run away

It would have to be somewhere far away, like Ohio or Alaska. She would have to move fast to get gone before Freddy came back. Then there was the problem of what to do for money when she got there. It was the damn money again.

The real problem, it seemed to her, besides the undeniable fact of Freddy and his guys and the guns, was not enough money to do anything. She was willing to use her mouth if she had to, but that wouldn't bring in enough. Even if she stayed clean and lived straight, she would never earn enough doing blowjobs. It was all about money.

She started another page, listing her working assets, using bullets instead of numbers.

- *Brad, maybe. Would have to work him.*
- *Monika. Too jacked up?*

Tina found her purse in the closet and rooted around in it. $515.00 and some change.

- *$515.00 start-up*
- *Gun and bullets*
- *Spare keys to Escalade*
- *Two days before F. gets back*

She needed a plan.

Sometimes a new idea comes to the seeker in a vision, a blinding, compelling flash of possibility, whether as a single image that implies the moving parts, a silent, vaulted sanctuary where peace is captured, or as parts coming together to form the whole, joists rising in the air to build a cathedral. Let's make a pyramid. Honor thy father and thy mother. A double curved helix that contains everything it takes to make life.

Tina's plan came to her in a voice that said, "Banks have money. Why not rob a bank?" She thought about it for a couple of minutes, realizing that it would be a lot like planning a party. What was already there, what to bring, how to control the crowd, how to avoid, she hoped, disaster.

The hard part would be figuring out where she could hole up until things cooled off. Not the city or the suburbs. Not Reno or Vegas. Not even Tahoe. It had to be right out of Freddy's world, somewhere not even the cops would look. And not anywhere you had to fly, or they would catch you at the airport. In the mountains, she thought, and she remembered how lost she had felt at the Red Robin Camp, how the rest of the world had been so hard to remember. It had been scary then, when she was seven, but she thought the mountains would be a place Freddy would just drive through on the way to Reno and the cops wouldn't think of. And she was not seven anymore.

She needed an accomplice, so she called Brad's cell. After listening to the loud but indistinct rap music on the recording, she left her message, counting on the likelihood that Brad was fucking up somehow. Brad was the kind of guy who always had something to hide.

"Hi Brad, it's Tina. Listen, Freddy found out about what you've been doing and he's really mad. Geron came by and told me. So come see me right away, okay? Bring the Escalade. It'll be okay. I'll help you. I have a plan." Then she texted him, just to be sure, and he answered. "K."

Tina began a new list.

- *My gun and bullets (have)*
- *Brad's gun and bullets (Brad has)*
- *2 masks Devil and Bart (have)*
- *2 Hello Kitty backpacks (get from that accessory place at mall)*
- *2 strong brown paper bags, doubled (behind fridge)*
- *2 big coats with pockets (mall)*
- *Freddy's Escalade (Brad has)*
- *Quarters for parking (top drawer)*
- *Camping things (buy)*

Brad showed up within the hour, with chocolate-sprinkled donuts and a hot chocolate.

"Damn, Tina, how does Freddy know about the Bjorn brothers? I only borrowed a few grand, and it's not hardly even late yet. Jesus, Tina, he's going to kill me. I mean that literally. He hates it when you borrow from someone else, but he wouldn't give me the money, so what was I supposed to do? Can't you talk to him for me, Tina, kind of pay the way?"

"I could try, but you know how Freddy is. He's really intense about stuff like this. And everybody knows about the Bjorns, Brad, not just me. Geron saw you and Peewee or someone talking, so now everybody knows. You need to get out of here." Tina waited and let Brad stew until his eyes jittered and his forehead popped with beads of sweat and he seemed desperate enough. "I'll help you," she said. "Freddy's kind of mad at me, too. But we need cash, right?"

Brad was shaking so hard his hot chocolate sloshed onto the table. He set it down and rubbed his face, hoping that things would get different, that Tina would carry him.

"It's okay, really," she said, mopping up the spill. "I've got a little project figured out that could land both of us some money. Big, Brad. Like really big. But I don't know, man, it's going to take some balls to pull it off."

Brad shoved what was left of his hot chocolate across the table to her, as a gesture of good will. He fixed his eyes on her, his only hope. She sipped the lukewarm offering thoughtfully and went on.

"Remember that movie we saw on TV? Where that big team of guys with explosives ripped off that bank? You know, with that weird guy in it, the guy with the googly eyes? That could be us, only there were too many of them, so they got caught and we won't."

Tina showed Brad the bank-robbing list and got him interested in the details. She had been sure he was in some kind of trouble she could tap into. There was always a way to work Brad. The only part of the plan he balked at was the Hello Kitty backpack, arguing for a Bart Simpson one, but Tina pointed out that if he really wanted to wear the Bart Simpson mask in the bank, it would be stupid to be seen with a Bart Simpson backpack later. Brad countered by saying that a guy wearing a Hello Kitty backpack would be way obvious something was off, and Tina agreed to make it Spiderman instead. She went back and amended the item to read "2 backpacks, Hello Kitty & Spiderman." They were working well together.

"How much can we get, do you think?" Brad was thinking of how ugly Freddy had been when he asked for an advance. He thought he was going to get killed right there. But it was nothing compared to how mad Freddy would be knowing that someone else owned a piece of him. "What's the split, Tina?" He was ready to argue. Freddy always shorted him compared to T-Wah or Hoppy. Even that bastard Geron, who only had one eye, got more than him. Brad's feet were doing a little tappy dance on the floor as he began to get excited. This could so work.

"Fifty-fifty, what do you think?" Tina saw that Brad was still nervous, but then he was always nervous; that's one of the things that made Freddy treat him so bad, that skittish unpredictable Brad thing. Could Tina depend on him to keep it together tomorrow? Robbing the bank was probably stupid, so that wasn't a problem. Brad would be fine with it, she figured. He didn't have enough sense to be afraid of long-term risks.

She would just need, as always, to keep him focused on the goal instead of dashing off in weird directions.

"Why do we have to do the camping thing? I never been camping ever. Why don't we go to Reno or Vegas and blend into the crowd, like?" He was pacing the floor, untied shoelaces flapping with each step.

"We go camping because no one will look for us there. I went to a summer camp once; it's nice, you'll like it. We'll take some pot to mellow out with." Tina added to the list: *pot*. "We can't go to Vegas right away. We have to let things die down. You know Freddy, how he always says no one crosses Freddy Napoleon and lives. He's going to be looking for us, and he's got lots of contacts in Vegas. He'd find us for sure. Plus we have to save Vegas for when we need to trade the bank money for clean bills."

"Why can't we fly to somewhere—like Brazil or Hawaii—where Freddy wouldn't find us and then we could spend the money? How long do we have to live in the camping place?"

The problem was that Brad had always been afraid of buffaloes, even though he had never seen one except in a picture book and sometimes on TV. In his dreams, he still found himself running, running, but the heavy thud of the buffalo only got closer and closer, hot breath steaming down his neck, smelling like a wet bed, until he was finally able to wake up, have a hit of something, and go back to sleep.

"Are there any buffaloes out there?"

"No buffaloes," Tina said reassuringly, although she had no idea where buffaloes were. They could be anywhere for all she knew. What she did know was that Freddy would be looking to kill her, fast or slow, when he got back, so she worked Brad a little more, reminding him that when they had the money, he could go on his own, be the big boss for a change, have his own guys around him, have girls to do whatever he wanted, have everything Freddy had.

"We're gonna have to lay low for a week or two, Brad. Everybody's gonna be looking for us, not just Freddy but the cops too. We'll hide out and have a sweet time on what's left of the money Freddy gave me for the party, then we'll trade out the bank money in the casinos and do whatever we want."

Tina added *full tank* to the list. Then she turned her attention to writing out the plan:

- *Buy camping stuff & leave in SUV - Brad*
- *Buy backpacks & trench coats - Tina*
- *Gas in SUV - Brad*
- *Bring paper bags, masks, guns, ammo from apartment - Tina*
- *Put paper bags, masks, backpacks, guns (loaded), into coat pockets*

- *Memorize what is in each pocket - Brad*
- *Park around corner from bank, leave unlocked. Pay parking meter, if any*
- *Pull out masks and guns and bags inside bank*
- *Scare tellers and bank manager, don't let them push alarm button*
- *Make people empty their pockets (money we can use right away)*
- *Money goes in paper bags*
- *Manager to safe for big bucks - Brad*
- *Keep everyone on the floor - Tina*
- *Paper bags in backpacks*
- *Masks and coats in trash*
- *Drive up I-80 to Hwy 20 to camping place where SUV is off the road*

Tina started to make a camping list, starting with "set up tent," but Brad was already uncomfortable with all the things he had to remember, so Tina walked him through the shopping list several times, gave him the wad of cash, and then sent him out to fill the SUV, buy camping supplies, and come back.

"With the change, Brad, bring back the change. And come back right away."

Pulling Freddy's gym bag from under the bed, she packed the pot, some clothes and clean underwear, red nightshirt, makeup, mango-cucumber moisturizer, and her toothbrush, then walked over to the mall to shop for backpacks and coats, carefully averting her eyes from the clothes in the display windows. She had to stay on task. Once she had the money, she could shop as much as she wanted.

Tina was excited about the plan. She knew it was risky, but she couldn't agree to suffer on the streets. She never wanted anyone's dick in her mouth ever again. The energy fizzing through her body made her feel like dancing. She was wound up, ready to take a flying leap somewhere. Over the rainbow, maybe, like the song.

3

You can't really steal anything; you can only take things without knowing what the price will turn out to be.

—*Anonymous*

THE BANK ROBBERY WENT exactly as Tina had planned, right up to the moment when the old man had the heart attack. That had not been part of the plan. Tina and Brad had put on their trench coats as they walked into the bank, pulling first the masks from Freddy's party out of their left-hand pockets—red devil for Tina, Bart Simpson for Brad—and when those were firmly in place, guns from the right-hand pockets. The child-sized backpacks were folded up under the guns, hidden from view so that the money from the paper bags Tina carried could be concealed for the get-away. All as planned. Both Tina and Brad had seen a lot of bank robbery movies, so they knew they had to yell and call people motherfuckers and threaten to kill them. Brad would have liked to jump up on a desk or vault over a counter, but he wasn't sure he could jump that high and he didn't want to look stupid on his big day.

The bank's customers had seen the same movies, so it all went pretty smoothly. Disarm the security guy, tellers out of the cages, everyone on the floor, face down, arms spread wide, don't be a hero. Brad was confused when the manager he was supposed to take back to the vault was out at a corporate meeting. He said it was totally fucked up, but Tina told him to take the head teller instead. It didn't seem quite right, it wasn't in the plan, but he didn't argue after his first protest. Tina guarded the customers and the rest of the tellers on the floor. She also pulled money out of a few purses and billfolds, all the time yelling that if anyone moved, the shooting would start. She collected cell phones and slid them across the room, seeing how far she could make them travel across the slick, shiny granite.

Tina could hear Brad yelling at the head teller in the vault where the big bucks would be. She hoped he would remember to only take the paper money. You never knew with Brad. Just as she realized with some irritation that what Brad was shouting was not to hurry up, motherfucker, or he would shoot, but "Cowabunga, dude!" she noticed that the old Mexican-looking man who had been at the end of the line was wheezing, his hands under him against his chest. She saw that his face, pressed against the floor, had turned a bad shade of gray, like an old dishrag in a crack house. For a moment, she forgot to yell. Looking around, she spotted a woman in a pink scrub shirt with a lollipop print, her hands trembling visibly at the ends of her outstretched arms.

"Hey, you in the pink thing, are you a nurse? You in the lollipop thing." Tina prodded her with the barrel of her gun.

The pink lollipop lady left her face down.

(It was not a good day to die, not for her. She was engaged to be married in three weeks. She loved her fiancé very much. They were going to honeymoon in Thailand. They had made an offer on a condo. She had four younger sisters she loved, one about to graduate from nursing school, one pregnant. She was much friended on Facebook. Her amusing animal story blog site had received over twelve thousand hits in the six months she'd had it up. It was a good day to keep living.)

She shook her head. She was not a nurse.

"What are you?"

"I work for a vet, a veterinarian. I help with animals. Please don't hurt me."

"Come look at this guy. Get up, Lollipop, or I'll shoot you. Get up and come look at this old guy!"

Lollipop eased up from the floor and crawled cautiously to where Tina the red devil was kneeling next to the man now gasping and moaning, his eyes squeezed shut as though in an attempt to block out light or pain or both.

"Why is he that color? Is he faking it?" the devil asked in an ordinary, non-bank-robbing voice.

"I don't know. I just see animals all day and they mostly stay the same color. Because of the fur. Sometimes a cat with pink lips can look kind of pale like this. I can't help it. I don't see people. I think he's probably sick, though."

"Okay, Lolly, help me roll him over and then get back down or I'll start shooting. Ready? One-two-three, and over!"

The old man gasped as they rolled him over, and he settled on his back like a landed fish, trying to curl around the pain, trying to breathe. Tina took his hand, so cold and clammy, and smoothed his forehead, because that's what they do when someone's sick.

"Anybody moves gets a bullet in the head—stay the fuck down!" she yelled at the room, then looked down at her patient again. Beads of moisture twinkled in his gray moustache.

"I'm dying. Please help me," he pushed out between gritted teeth. When he opened his eyes and saw the face of the red devil mask looking down on him, he began to cry in earnest. "*El Diablo*! Help me, sweet Mother of God, *Santissima*, help me! *Lo siento, perdóname! Ayúdame, Santa Maria!*"

Tina knew what *diablo* meant. She had hung out for a few months with a biker club called The El Diablos and she remembered the picture on the jackets. So she knew what he was complaining about. She pushed her devil mask to the top of her head so she could see better and patted his chest. "It's okay, it's okay. I'll get you some help, buddy."

He was gazing at her with parted lips, still pallid, but his breathing eased and he quit that whimpering that seemed to come from his throat instead of his open, gasping mouth. She had planned this to be her lucky day; she wanted luck for everyone—Brad, the lollipop lady, this guy. Everyone except Freddy. She patted him again and waved Lollipop back to resume the position.

She was holding his hand when Brad came bounding out of the vault, laughing and shoving the teller in front of him with the nose of his gun, the paper bag plumped up with the cash.

"Jesus Christ! Put your mask back on, Tina, what's the matter with you?" Brad didn't get many opportunities to advise caution. He was the one always getting bossed around, so it felt good to lecture Tina. It made him feel in charge. Even he knew better than that.

And, after all, she was just Freddy's girl. He was a soldier, one of Freddy's guys, a regular pro.

"Get me one of those phones. We need to get an ambulance!" Tina pushed her mask back into place. She figured the old guy probably wouldn't live to be a witness, let alone remember what had happened to him or what she looked like. She hoped no one would remember her name, blurted out by Brad.

"Are you nuts? We're robbing a bank here, not running an ER!" This was the wrong movie, not in the plan she had drilled into him. It was totally fucked up—first no manager, and now this.

"Yeah, *Bart*," Tina said, trying to impress on Brad the importance of not using each other's names. "I pretty much know what we're doing. Get me one of those phones."

She punched in 911 and explained the man's condition—down, breathing, talking in Spanish so you can't tell if he's making sense or not— and gave the bank's location to the machine-like dispatcher, who told her help was on the way and to stay on the line. Tina promptly turned the phone off and slid it across the room, making a bank-shot off the sole of the security guy's shoe.

Tina and Brad walked away from the bank, Brad practically dancing on his toes, trench coats and masks discarded in a trash bin along with Tina's gun, which she didn't expect to ever need again. As they crammed the paper bags into their backpacks, job well done, Tina could hear distant sirens. "I think this is going to work," she said.

In fact, the bank robbery had gone right, as well-laid plans sometimes do. The getting part was over. But the get-away can take longer. It stretches from this moment to the moment when memory finally fails, from this sidewalk down which they step to the unknown horizon that moves away and never stops. They weren't just fleeing the scene of the crime—they had both done that before or they wouldn't be here. The real getaway would be escaping from the whore's luck that had placed Tina under the protection of the heavy, punishing hand and implacable will of Freddy Napoleon.

4

Whatever happens, they say afterwards, it must have been fate.

—Terry Pratchett

Tina was pleased with how well the bank heist had gone, like it was a good sign, but after a few miles on the freeway, she was less optimistic. Brad was so excited, his eyes glittered and shifted, and he couldn't stop talking. "Did you see that motherfucker with the briefcase? I thought he was going to shit! Woo-hoo! Brad and Tina! High five!"

"Keep your hands on the wheel, yeah? We did good, now we just have to be lucky."

Brad's face fell. He had never thought of himself as lucky. Unappreciated, good with the ladies, ready for action, maybe, but not lucky. He went on, though, trying to prolong the high. "We really did it! We planned it and we pulled it off! Woo-hoo! We rule! Brad and Tina!" His enthusiasm was a little forced, and he stepped on the accelerator a little harder, to ramp things up.

Tina knew that she had to get him out of the driver's seat because there was no way he would slow down, even if she begged him to. For Brad, speed meant thrills, escape, freedom. Still, Brad could be touchy. You had to play him, even when it was a matter of common sense. Especially then.

"Pull over at that gas station and I'll get us some beer and Cheetos. We need some eats!" She made him get out and go in with her, not wanting to leave him alone with the money. There was no telling what he would do. And she wanted the driver's seat empty when they got back. Then it was simply a matter of phrasing. "Here, Brad. I'll be your driver like you do for Freddy. You enjoy yourself. Lay back and see what it feels like to be the big man. Good work! Okay, high five! Brad and Tina rule!" Whatever.

An hour later, after Tina had given him a little hand job to calm him down, Brad dozed. She had been afraid that he would climb into the back and play with the money, throwing it around in the car, a snowstorm of fifties and hundreds, all over the front seat, blocking her view, flying out the windows onto the asphalt, gone forever. The vision was appalling enough that it was worth driving left-handed for a while to distract him.

Then I-80's straight freeway gave way to Highway 20, a narrow road lined with big Christmas trees, really big trees that crowded the road and massed against the near horizon at the top of the ridge. They were bigger than she'd expected, and it made her nervous. This had to work; she hadn't had time to think up a Plan B. She wasn't used to driving this fast with only one lane each way and no divider, and she flinched every time an oncoming car brushed past. She tried to keep the SUV in the right lane and scan the green blur for a good place to camp. The occasional cabins she saw on either side of the road all seemed likc places people were already living, and the many rocky little driveways leading off into the deep forest were marked by huddles of mailboxes, marked with their owners' names in sloppy printing.

Of course, she wasn't looking for Red Robin Camp where she had been sent as a child. She had no idea where it was, and it was just for groups of kids anyway. But there had to be other places where they could rent a place or put up the tent she hoped Brad had bought and hang out for a week or two, smoking pot and doing whatever else there was to do. There must be things to do at a camp. She could remember being urged by a large girl to swim in the terrifyingly cold water of a lake, singing in the firelight that made the unfamiliar faces of the other campers even stranger, and making a friendship bracelet she didn't know what to do with and had thrown away on the last day. These were not reassuring memories. She couldn't see her and Brad doing anything like that. She was glad she had thought to bring the pot, a party in itself.

The Happy Trout Fishing Resort Camping Café sign almost got away, but Tina caught sight of it through the trees, and slowed in time to make the right turn over the narrow wooden bridge that spanned a culvert, right again, down a bumpy dirt road, and a stop at the railing in front of the café. Brad woke up and they sat in silence looking at the white board building, peeling paint, a Coors sign in one window and a handmade sign reading "Office" in the other. It looked like a child's drawing of a house except that there were several vents on the roof in addition to the chimney, and no sun. There was no one on the porch, just some empty wooden deck chairs, and Freddy's Escalade with them in it was the only vehicle in the rutted parking lot. A scraggly flower garden girdled the porch, sporting a few dried-out daisies, a vigorous patch of weeds, and a pathetic rose bush with spotted green and yellow leaves, evidently attempting to die. The wooden front door was held open by a number 2 can filled with sand and cigarette butts. The screen door was closed, but through it they could see a lunch counter with a man behind it, his wiping motion repetitive and slow.

Behind the little café and office were a red pickup

truck with a dirty white camper shell, an old green VW van, and one of those silver trailers Tina had seen before, shaped like one of the cigars Freddy liked, only stubbier. Surrounding it all was a wall of trees, not close, but seeming to them both to be leaning, listening, unsafe. The whole place was s little run down but bare of trash, and the effect was eerie, as though a freak wind had swept through and taken trash and people, leaving the bare framework as some kind of trap for the unwary. But this was it, the place where no one would look, the place outside of Freddy's world. It seemed pretty sketchy as a hideout. Tina turned off the CD player and lowered the window. The forest was silent but alive, wound up like a cat poised to leap. Tina had serious misgivings. Brad freaked.

"Why does it smell like air freshener? Where is everyone? I don't know how to do this, Tina! Tina, I never been camping before. I don't know what it's supposed to be like. Where is everybody? What am I supposed to do? Why is it so freaking quiet?" His pale face was drawn tight, pulled back at the cheekbones, and his voice squeaked with fear.

"It's okay, Brad. Go into the office and ask where we can put the tent up. It's probably like getting a hotel room, except there's no room. Register us as Mary and Joseph Smith, or something like that. Made up. Give them the money for it. If we don't like it here, we'll find another place somewhere tomorrow." Tina pulled him around to face her. "Brad," she said. It was hard to get his attention when he was freaked out like this. When he quit looking around wildly, she said, "We need to get started before it gets dark, Brad. Go."

"Why Joseph Smith? That's a real dork name. Why not something like, like, I don't know, something not so lame? How about Vincent?"

"Brad." Tina grabbed his shoulders and turned him again so that he was facing her. She could feel the nervous energy shooting around his body like a pinball, setting up an erratic tremor, even worse than usual. "Don't get fancy, Brad. Mary and Vincent Smith, then. But go and do this."

Brad yanked open the SUV door and lurched up the steps and into the place, the Happy Trout Fishing Resort, expectation of disaster written across his hunched shoulders. Tina waited, chewing on her thumb knuckle. Now that they actually had the money, and that had gone so well, handling Brad was going to be the big challenge. She wouldn't rip him off, easy as that might be, but she couldn't afford to leave him alone with the money or let him make any decisions with his addled way of thinking and his impulsive way of acting, made worse by the stress of the trees looming on all sides, the damp, breathing silence, the solitude, the unfamiliarity of this new world. She had to keep him out of trouble to stay out of trouble herself.

Coming out, Brad looked spooked, stumbling down the steps like a drunk. "Okay, we have #13, but he says there's no key. So it's not like a hotel room at all, like you said it was. He said it's a sight, whatever that is. He said it's downstream. But he wouldn't tell me which way that is, just put his eyebrows up and looked at me over his little glasses. God, I hate when they do that. Like I'm supposed to know. It's not like I live here."

Tina and Brad crossed a second, larger bridge over a small, tumbling river, just too wide to jump over, turned left at the T and followed the rutted road to the end without finding site #13. The numbers started at 17 and kept getting bigger. On both sides of the road, they could see campers and tents and people with children, doing things as though they didn't know they had no walls—eating at the tables, hanging things over lines strung between the trees, leaning into the trunks of their cars, pawing through boxes. They were so spread out, and so unguarded. It was unnerving.

Tina did an awkward turnaround, bouncing sharply over a particularly big rock at the end of the road, and then they headed back the other way, evidently downstream, to where their site lay—#13, a large open space of dark dust separated from the next site by a few of those same tall Christmas trees that seemed to be everywhere. They stared for a moment at the rusty barbeque, the cement slab and the picnic table, an empty trash barrel chained to its leg. Traced in the dirt was the outline of a tent. Evidently, this was where the tent was supposed to go. Tina got out and stretched, but Brad had to be coaxed out of the SUV.

He was unnerved by the lack of walls and felt like he had to glare at anyone he spotted through the trees. They were all acting like they were ignoring him now, but what was going to keep them from moving in on him when his back was turned? He had wanted to get back in the SUV and stay there, but Tina wouldn't let him. And then Tina made him leave his gun in the glove compartment instead of wearing it where it would show, which totally didn't make sense. It was practically asking for trouble. But she wouldn't give up.

"C'mon, Brad. This is when we look at all the stuff you bought—the tent and sleeping bags and stuff. This is fun! Show me all the stuff! Let's set up the tent, Brad. Then we'll have a safe place to count the money, like you want to." Tina spoke softly so that the other campers wouldn't hear them. No one seemed to be paying any attention at all.

"Yeah, like anyplace here is safe." Brad slithered out of his seat, opened the back of the SUV, and began to unload the purchases he had thrown in the previous day, when all of this was still a vision in Tina's head, his enthusiasm mounting as he went. He liked buying things, and he really liked showing off. He liked being able to explain something to Tina, who was always telling him what to do.

"Look, Tina, this is the base camp Taj Majal model, like that place in Hawaii. It sleeps twelve, interior divider for privacy. Check it out. Color-coded for easy setup—the guy set it up right there in the store. It's a one-man setup. Mattresses and double sleeping bags. I couldn't believe the horrible little tight bags they tried to sell me—this is more like it!" Two compact collapsible folding loungers, two camp chairs and end table with drink holders, kitchen box with shelves built in, a collapsible folding table, a portable espresso maker, two red pillows with arms for sitting up in bed, deluxe camper-green pillows for sleeping, collapsible lightweight camping toothbrushes, one red, one blue, collapsible green cups, flexible green nesting plates, speckled gray bowls made of unbreakable plastic, map holder with belt attachment, Swiss Army knife, ultra-lite backpacks on aluminum frames. Brad hadn't thought of everything, but he had bought everything he had seen.

He started setting up the tent. "This little blue thing attaches to the other blue thing, like a click, and that way you have it right ways up. It's like a model airplane, but no glue. That's what the guy said. Oh wait, turn it over and then click it all the way around. He said to stake it down, but I don't see this baby going anywhere. It's easy, see? Hold this. Where's the blue cord-thing? See? Isn't this cool?" The tent went up with just a few beginners' learning errors. "I could totally see doing this another time." Brad was getting the hang of camping.

Tina was worried. She had never bought camping equipment, but this seemed like a lot. And she realized she had lost track of Freddy's money, their operating fund for the next few weeks.

"How much did you spend, Brad? Did you bring me the change like I said?"

Brad stuck his head out of the tent. "I don't know—it's not like I kept the receipts. Remember, I had to pay for this place, for all this dirt to put the tent on. It's weird—it's like being in somebody's backyard, only there's no fences. It's like being homeless, only with a tent and you have to pay—that's lame. But look at this—you collapse it and then it opens up again. And it's what they take on real mountains, like in the movies, the guy said. It's what they took to Mt. Ernest." Brad tried to fold up the toothbrush again, but it jammed.

"Brad, how much did you spend?"

"I had to buy stuff like you said, and anyway, there's almost like a hundred dollars left. Don't be so uptight."

"Oh, Christ." Tina sighed and surveyed the Taj

Majal. "Hold on—I'll see what I have."

It was not enough—$213 from the bank customers, $32 left over from Brad's shopping trip. Just under $250 to pay for the two weeks hiding out Tina estimated would be enough for things to cool off. What they had might cover three days and a tank of gas. Maybe a week, if they were prudent. Say three days.

"Tina, for fuck's sake, we just robbed a bank! We have thousands of dollars, if you would just let me count it!"

"Brad, I told you, we can't spend the bank money. We have to run it through the casinos. We can't use it until later, remember? Remember that TV show where it showed those cops keeping track of the numbers on the money? Remember how those guys got caught? So just let me think." Tina sat on the cold cement picnic table watching Brad play with the flaps of the tent and thought, her arms crossed over her chest, rocking slightly as though a motor was gently turning over in her brain. It would be stupid to spend the bank money. They would get caught and go to prison. She knew enough about prison to know that it would be better to try the nun thing, if it came to that. Not very different, but definitely better. But that didn't take care of Brad. He would still be running around yelling cowabunga somewhere, calling attention to himself.

While Tina thought, Brad busied himself

arranging and rearranging the furniture in the Taj Majal, moving the sleeping bags to the back, the camp chairs and portable table to the front for a dining and conversation area, which unfortunately half-blocked the entrance

Now that he had the four walls of the Taj Majal and an identifiable doorway to create the illusion of safety, he was relaxed as a three-year-old, happily stacking the all-purpose kitchen box on the collapsible folding table, picking it back up when the folding table collapsed into its original compact state, trying again, finding it wouldn't all fit, trying it again. "Here's the table where we can *count the money*, okay, Tina?"

"What was the guy like? The one who looked at you over his glasses? Gross? Okay?"

"Some guy." Brad was finding places in the kitchen box for bowls and plate. "What do you care?"

"I'm thinking we have to get some cash out of him, or at least some food for the next few days. All I can think of is to give him a quick thrill, and we'll be okay for now. Maybe set up something for tomorrow, too. Maybe he has friends who could use a little head. But was he gross? Did he seem mean?"

Brad was opening his Swiss Army knife. "Look, like a little corkscrew thing!"

"Brad, look at me! What was the guy like? Like a biker? Like Freddy?"

Brad flinched at Freddy's name. It seemed like Tina was trying to ruin the fun.

"I don't know, Tina. He was skinnier than Freddy. And taller. I was only there for maybe two minutes. Where do you want the kitchen? Could we actually cook something in here?"

"Brad. I'm asking about the guy."

"Okay, Tina, Jesus. He was like a science teacher, okay? Only with a white towel around his middle. He didn't have a gun, does that help?"

"A science teacher? So, he was clean?"

"Maybe a coach. Yeah, I guess he was clean. I didn't pat him down for germs." Brad snickered at his own joke, still moving the corkscrew in and out of the red knife handle.

"Okay, we need to do this before it gets too dark. You don't seem to have any flashlights in there. And I don't see any streetlights. Let's go and try to get food and a date out of him."

"And beer. Don't forget beer, okay, Tina?"

Tina had to remind herself that she could do this—line up the john, hook him, and get it over with—but do it nice because they needed more money than just one blowjob was worth. She had been thinking that she was through blowing guys, but she could do it, could lick her lower lip—lipstick in her purse—lick her lips and move her body around so that her tits moved in his direction, but mostly keep his attention on her mouth. She really didn't want to fuck for money. But she could if she had to. At least it wasn't fucking Freddy, that's the good thing, not Freddy. Just some other fuck.

Jesus, she hoped he wasn't twisted somehow. She had Brad to watch out for her, for what that was worth. She had to make sure he looked out for her, that he would help her if she got into some trouble. Girls got bruised and cut and burned sometimes by sick tricks, so she hoped the guy was a normal guy, a science teacher, a coach, not a biker, not a psycho. She would walk in and find the guy with the towel around his middle and get him interested, make the offer, go someplace private with him. Brad had to be watching her back on this. She would go with the science teacher and make it worth the money, play around a little, flirt, talk dirty, but get the money. She could do this. She was Tina, and this was *something Tina could do.*

They packed the uncounted money back into the SUV, not trusting the security of their palatial but unlockable tent, and drove back to the little café, stopping only to smoke a little pot, to chill out a little. It didn't work for Tina, who jittered in the shotgun seat, but Brad was mellow. Tina had let him bring the gun, just in case, so he was feeling confident.

"It's no big deal, Tina. It's not like you never done it before."

"Not like this. You have to keep watch, okay? And if I don't come out in fifteen minutes, or if you hear yelling or something, you have to come help me. You have to, Brad. We don't know this guy at all. You have to look out for me." Tina stared out at the porch, still empty. It was getting dark.

"What do you think?" Brad said. "I've got your back. Brad and Tina, right? High five!"

Tina gave him the high five, and then tried to shake herself up, to take on electricity, to assume the muscle alertness that says look at this, I'm the goods, how about it, big boy. I am the answer to your wettest dreams. She went up the steps, swung open the screen door, and set foot inside the Happy Trout Fishing Resort for the first time.

She heard the bright little bell on the door, but she didn't feel her fate closing in around her like a fist. And yet close it did, with a click more felt than heard, if she had been paying attention, like one blue thing clicking into another blue thing, for better or for worse. Everything she had done, been, thought, felt, imagined, wanted, avoided, believed, denied, and lied about funneled into this moment, this step. She could have backed out, but it would have been film rewinding, life unhappening, the butterfly climbing back into the cocoon and pulling it shut, and she was intent on solving the problem she perceived, unaware of the questions that needed answering: Who is this woman? What is she for?

The lunch counter was small, five stools long, and the three booths lay alongside the windows, two of them filled with men eating burgers and fries. Two tables in the middle of the room completed the layout. The other side of the room was filled with homemade wooden shelves displaying camping things—flashlights, batteries, toilet paper, matches, cans of food—all the things Brad had neglected to buy. It had been hours since the Cheetos she had bought to calm Brad down, and the hamburgers on the tables smelled so good it made her slightly sick. The man behind the counter wasn't scary at all. He was just a guy, like Brad had said. No tattoos of wounded women dripping blood, no Aryan Nation insignia, no skull earring, just a guy, maybe even a nice guy. Tina took heart and a seat at the counter.

"What can I do for you, ma'am?" he asked.

"Ma'am" was not a great beginning. Even "Miss" would have been more encouraging. Tina ran her tongue over her lips and looked deep into his brown eyes, where she could see by her reflection that she should have maybe done something with her hair.

"Maybe it's a question of what I can do for you, baby," she said. Maybe too much too soon? But you have to start somewhere.

He took a step back, puzzled. "What exactly do you mean? What are you selling? Because I'm not likely to buy anything, you should know that. No need for you to waste your time."

"What's your name?"

Bill pointed to his nametag.

"Well, Bill, I'm not really worried about wasting my time. I have all the time in the world for a man like you." Tina looked him up and down and licked her lips again. She hoped this would be quick. She was starving. He looked relatively young and healthy enough not to take forever like older guys sometimes did.

"Here's how it is, Bill. My boyfriend and I are running a little short of money and food, and I am willing to do..." Tina breathed in and out, letting the breath move her body towards him, as planned, "...almost anything to make a little cash and have a little fun on the side. You look like a man who likes a good time. How about I take you back behind the kitchen there and give you a thrill? Fifty dollars, and the blowjob of a lifetime—what do you say, Billy-boy?"

She thought he was hooked. He put his elbows on the counter and leaned forward until his face was only inches from hers. It was a nice face, but kind of sad. Or maybe just cranky. His breath smelled like oranges and he was so close that each word he spoke arrived in a citrus puff. She tried not to flinch and break her act.

"You are not welcome at this establishment. Do you understand? This isn't a house of prostitution. This is not Nevada." His voice was quiet and confidential. "This is a family resort, and if you aren't off the property in ten minutes, I'm going to call the sheriff and have you and your scrawny boyfriend removed. If I see you so much as smile at one of my customers, I swear I will remove you myself. You take yourselves down the road and across the bridge and turn whichever way you want. You are never, never to come back here. Do we understand each other?"

"You can't do that—you can't throw us out! We got a campsite. We're customers." Tina didn't even try the sidelong "are you sure" look that sometimes retrieved reluctant johns who were trying to pull away. This whole thing had gone seriously wrong.

"Actually, I can do that. Read the sign," and he gestured to the side towards the cash register.

"What do you mean? I have shoes and shirt!"

His face became even more serious. "The other sign: We reserve the right to refuse service to anyone. That's you. I am refusing you service and kicking your sorry self out. You used the door on the way in, so you know where it is. Now go."

Tina wanted to make a scene, but with the hot bank money in the SUV, she knew it was far too dangerous.

She whipped out of the café, her face burning, shaking with humiliation and resentment. Brad was on the porch where Tina had stationed him, listening to his iPod and jerking his head around, presumably in time to the music, or perhaps just to his own internal twitch. When he saw Tina, he jumped up and popped the ear buds out of his ears. "Wow! Good work, Tina! That was fast! Where's the beer?"

"Get in the goddamn SUV." Tina climbed into the passenger side and hugged her knees tight to her chest. "Asshole. He's kicking us out."

"You must not have done it right! What did you do, bite him?"

"Shut up. He's an uptight asshole and we have to leave. Let's just go."

"But Tina, I'm hungry. Can't you get one of the other guys in there?"

"No, just shut up and let me think."

Brad put his ear buds back in and closed his eyes, moving his head a little bit and letting Tina think.

Tina thought the guy was an asshole, but probably wasn't someone who would let people starve even if he didn't apparently want a blowjob.

"Okay—you have to go in."

"Tina," Brad wailed. "You know I don't trick! I'm not some fucking faggot!"

"Not like that. You tell him that I'm your sister and

I'm mentally ill and I didn't take my pills this morning."

"Isn't he going to freak about you getting high?"

"It's prescription, from a doctor. It means I'm nuts unless I take my pills, so I'm not responsible for acting nuts. You know, like Hoppy's brother. Tell the guy you're sorry and that if we could stay the night, we'll leave in the morning. Try to act totally straight, okay? This is important. And take some of the money to get something to eat. And beer. If he'll even sell it to you."

Tina waited for Brad, aware of a shaking she couldn't control. She'd been in tight places before, but this felt different. He hadn't laughed at her, which was the only thing that would have made it worse. Her mouth wasn't going to get them out of this mess. Maybe they could set up shop briefly, do one or two guys, at a rest stop, but it was so risky with bags of bank money in the SUV and the Highway Patrol going by. It was too risky, but she couldn't think of what else to try. Maybe they would have to spend some of the bank money even though it was almost certainly traceable. Too risky. Maybe they would have to go to Reno tomorrow and try to turn the money over without attracting any attention. But Freddy had connections, he'd have people watching for them, and he would find out before they could get out the door.

Maybe they could contact Freddy and offer to split the money with him if they could come back. It would be hard to sell. And he would lie to them if it suited him. He would still turn her out like Monika, and that was at best. He would never forgive them if he was offended. And he would certainly be offended—in fact, he would be furious about the Escalade, and a furious Freddy would kill them both, or get T-Wah to do it. Everything was too risky. Freddy, too risky. The rest stop, too risky. Prison, too risky.

Brad emerged, bouncing down the stairs, carrying a pizza box in one hand and a six-pack in the other. He was jubilant—problem solved. "He said we could stay tonight as long as we're gone tomorrow morning early. And I got a pepperoni pizza, all hot, and some brewski. Nice, huh?"

"Did he believe you about the meds?"

Brad considered. "I don't think he's the kind of guy who believes lies, so no, it's not like he actually believed me. For one thing, first he'd call you my wife, and then my girlfriend, and then my sister, so it was pretty messed up. You should keep shit like that straight, Tina. It was embarrassing." He turned the SUV on. "Let's go back and get our flexible plates out and eat!" Brad was pleased that he had done so well. He had told Tina he had her back, and here was dinner to prove it.

Dinner was not a great success for Tina, whose stomach was churning with anxiety, or for Brad, who concentrated mostly on the beer. They crept into their luxury sleeping bags, too tired to figure out the pumps on the air mattresses. It was already too dark to read the directions. Although the mattresses and the kitchen gear had been shoved outside to make room for the collapsible table and canvas chairs, Tina and Brad ended up eating in their double sleeping bags braced up by their red pillows, just as they might have eaten pizza and watched TV in bed in their former lives, though here there was nothing to watch but the wan light from the nearest campsites flickering on the blue wall of the tent, and the play of bug-shadows on that screen.

They slept then, each with the dreams that suited them, of strange blind people, of guns, of trees that laughed in Freddy's voice, bowls of sawdust, lollypops, and rivers that collapsed, dangerous machines, the strange calculations and rearrangements that entertain the active mind when the outward circus has closed down for the night. The half-eaten pizza lay in its stained box on the tent floor behind them where Brad had tossed it, still smelling of meat and grease.

5

You never know what you can do until you can't do anything else.

—Anonymous

TINA WOKE TO THE sound of a small, high-pitched screaming, like a teakettle descending into hell, a wavering, hopeless, panicked shrill. The overwhelming smell of festering garbage, rotten fruit, shit, and dirt mingled with her dream. Her first thought was that she had been thrown into a garbage truck and was about to be compacted. But the bumping rumpus in the tent was sideways, not upwards, erratic, not mechanical, not man-made, and there was no grinding engine noise. It was something else.

She felt around in the darkness for a bedside lamp, then, realizing where she was, for Brad, wanting to wake him up out of whatever dream was buffeting him, buffeting them both. She almost fell as she stumbled out of her sleeping bag, but she struggled to her feet, only to be shoved aside, landing with her face on the tent floor. The tent walls were bulging and undulating around her, and the garbage was alive, snuffling, grunting, next to her, threatening to step on her. She rose again in a panic, and when she stood, there, in the light of a new slit where the ventilation panel of the Taj Majal had been, she saw only the glint of an inhuman eye unbearably close to her, close enough that she could have spit in it, and she floundered desperately towards the tent doorway, impelled by the electric adrenalin that flooded her.

Tina's escape was hindered by the extraneous camping equipment in front of the open doorway, the kitchenette box, the pillows, the collapsible table, thrown there by a screaming Brad, screaming so hard his throat had shut down and the sound seemed to emanate from his whole body. She could see him in the moonlight outside backing away in a frenzied dance, his arms flailing and white. She shoved past the lounge chairs, tripped over the table, and as she finally found the open flap, she heard the soft clunk of the car door and the engine turning over. A wave of relief—let's get the hell out of here—yes, good thinking, Brad.

Then she heard the tires crunch over the gravel as the Escalade accelerated, as Brad drove away, as Brad drove away and left her. As Brad drove away.

Kicking aside the pillows, Tina emerged from the tent to see the tail lights disappear, Brad turning the corner to cross the big bridge and speed for the exit and presumably Highway 20 and who knows where after that. Away. Nevada. Safety. She ran, but she knew he would drive like hell until he calmed down, which would take quite a while, and then he would smoke some pot to calm down some more, and then he would probably keep driving.

She raced after him anyway, away from the bear, away from the nightmare that had plucked her from her warm sleeping bag and sent her pelting down the hard road, both escaping and pursuing. She looked back, expecting to see the bear on her heels, but the road behind her was empty and the only noise was her harsh breathing, the rattle of gravel under her bare feet, and the sound of zippers as a few other campers stuck their heads out of their tent flaps cautiously, cast the beams from their flashlights up and down, and then retreated back to their sleep.

The dark wall of trees on either side made Tina feel like she was fleeing down some nightmare corridor, running away from one fear and yet afraid of what might rise up in the middle of the road—another bear, a different wild animal, even, irrationally, Freddy. Or a buffalo, like Brad had always feared. She finally had to stop and lean over, hands braced on her knees, to catch her breath. She saw four dark stripes across her upper arm where the blood was beading up, where the bear had brushed past her in its pursuit of pepperoni. The campground was much quieter now that Brad had left. Left her. As soon as she could, she ran on, still listening for what might come up behind her, and when she came to the turn in the road, peered half hopefully toward the parking lot of the Happy Trout, where Brad might have gone for help or stopped to wait for her to catch up, but the taillights, the SUV, Brad, the money, and everything had disappeared. Really. Sonuvabitch.

The Happy Trout Fishing Resort café was dark. She couldn't find a way in without breaking something, and she wasn't sure if Bill was in there or not. Maybe when the café closed, he went home to his wife and kids in a cozy little house in the nearest town. But probably not. He was probably in there, sleeping safe and sound. Tina found an outside spigot and tried to wash the blood off her arm, but it bled again as soon as she turned off the water. She had a drink, though, and then sat shivering on the porch, leaning against the wall with the chairs as kind of protection in front of her, a big cardboard box she found in the dumpster behind the café braced against the chair backs in an attempt to block out the cold air, vigilant, keeping an eye out for bears, thinking what to do and waiting for her heart to slow down and for Bill to open up. Whereas before her resources had been Brad, the Escalade, about

$250 for present expenses, less the pizza and beer, and thousands to spend later, she now had the red satin nightshirt she was wearing, a striped arm, bruised feet, she realized, the cardboard box, and that was about it. Her fingers itched for a piece of paper and a pen. She wished they had counted the money so she could make an accurate list of all that was lost.

The tent would be wrecked; she had seen the rips and at least one shattered tent pole. Sleeping bag? Pillows, jeans and T-shirt, platform sandals? Had Brad taken her purse? Yes, it was locked up safe in the Escalade. She couldn't remember if Brad had been sleeping in his clothes or if there might be another shirt in the tent she could use, maybe his black hoodie. She was starting to shake in the early, early morning chill, and she drew her knees up to fend off the cold air.

Running from a bear is exhausting, much more exhausting than running a race or running for exercise or running towards a waiting lover. The chemistry of adrenalin is more effective but much less merciful than the serotonin boost of exercise or the dopamine reward of achievement or love. Once the escape from danger has been reached, adrenalin drops you where you stand in whatever shape you happen to be in, but alive, still alive. So Tina dozed off and missed seeing the slow softening of the dark as the sun rose somewhere behind another mountain, sending only a faint rumor of day at first, accelerating to tentative, then full daylight. In her sleep, though, she felt the first ray of sun that picked her out on the porch, the first sign of the widening brightness and returning warmth that made the birds start singing for the day. A rangy black cat with a notched ear and a broken tooth watched her from the porch railing, blinking and humming inaudibly, deep inside.

Bill was not pleased to see her when he came out to sweep the porch, but he didn't seem surprised; he had been expecting trouble in some form. Those two had bad news written all over them. And now here was this scrap of a thing, decked out in Frederick's of Hollywood red, half-naked, really, bleeding and pathetic. He knew he should never have let them stay. This could have been someone else's problem.

Tina woke with a start and the bear marks on her arm woke at the same time, stinging painfully both individually and in concert.

"Jesus Christ Almighty," Bill said.

"It was a bear." Tina avoided eye contact. She needed help and she had to play this right, at least play by his rules, for now. If she made big eyes at him, he'd probably kick her out with nothing but...well, with nothing. She was having a hard time adjusting to her new situation. She couldn't quite believe her plan had landed her here on this cold porch with only this indifferent teacher-looking guy to help her.

"Where's your cousin? Is he okay? Do I need to call an ambulance?"

"He took off, actually. So yeah, he's okay, no ambulance, thanks. But I need you to help me. My arm really hurts and it's bleeding."

Bill shook his head and sniffed the air, looking out towards the river. Not that it was likely to rain any time soon. And the bear had probably gone back up the mountain by now, full of tourist chow. For an instant he imagined ranging along at the bear's shaggy side in the cold morning air, climbing higher into the brush, away from all this people trouble.

"I can't take you into town to the emergency room, you know, and it doesn't look that bad. I've got a business to run, and I'm short-handed and I'm already running late. I guess I can fix you up, though, so you can get on your way. Jesus H. Almighty."

Tina followed him silently, as unprovocatively as possible for a woman in red satin, into the back of the café. Bill led her into a little bathroom marked with a Personnel Only sign, with extra packages of toilet paper and paper towels for the public restroom lining the walls. He wrapped a blanket from the closet around her, sat her down on the toilet seat, gently washed her arm with disinfectant, used gauze and tape to cover the wounds and then tidied up, leaving her with a wide, white armband.

"You could end up with an interesting set of scars there. Should make a good story for your friends back in the city. If it gets red or goopy, you want to see a doctor. I put some antiseptic on it, but bears are not generally clean animals so keep an eye on it." He returned the first aid kit to the shelf and stood back to allow Tina to leave. She was careful not to brush against him.

"Brad will come back, you know. He just panicked is all." Tina wanted it to be true. She wanted Bill to believe it. It would buy her some time.

"I hope you're right, "Bill said. "I don't know the man..." he started, but he stopped. He didn't really see Brad as a man. "I just hope you're right, that's all." He ushered her back out into the café where he left her huddled while he called the Forest Service. They would need to know about the bear. And he would have to find time to post more signs warning the campers to store bear-attractive substances and items in their cars or in bear-proof containers. He had warned Brad, but evidently not very effectively. Brad had not appeared to be functioning like a normal human being.

Tina was pretty sure Brad would keep on driving. It would probably feel good to him to be on his own to do whatever stupid thing occurred to him instead of having Tina telling him what to do all the time. And he would start spending the money right away, and he would talk. Brad would talk with anyone who seemed friendly, and when he started flashing the money around, he'd have plenty of friends. Brad would bring Freddy, and Freddy would be looking for Tina, the bitch that had crossed him, had publicly humiliated him, had refused to whore for him, had conspired to steal his ride, had corrupted his subordinate. No one crosses Freddy Napoleon and lives.

Bill emerged from the office and asked, "Do you want to use my phone, contact friends or family to come get you?"

"Can I have some coffee first? I gotta pull myself together." Tina moved quietly onto the middle stool at the counter to be easier to serve, looking as much as possible like no trouble at all. She kept the blanket wrapped around her, to stay warm and to hide out.

"No shoes," Bill said, pointing to the sign. "Remember?"

"Lend me some shoes," Tina said. "You must have an extra pair around somewhere."

Bill poured her a cup of coffee, then reached down into the lost-and-found box under the counter and handed her a pair of large green flip-flops and an Oakland Raiders sweatshirt, which luckily came down almost to her knees. "Nobody ever claims anything anyway."

"Thanks." She supposed he had noticed that she had no underwear and her nightshirt was pretty short. The sweatshirt smelled of weeds and dirt and fish, but it was warm and comforting. She rolled the sleeves up into doughnuts around her slender arms. The coffee was hot and strong, and it made Tina hungry.

"May I please have an omelet?" Bill's scowl changed her mind. "Just some toast? Brad'll pay you when he gets back."

"*If* he comes back," Bill said, but he went into the kitchen and she heard him break three eggs and whisk them. It seemed like a hopeful sign.

"I'm going to need that campsite later today, you know," he said through the hatch. "Things get busy here on the weekends, especially this late in the season. So see what you can do about clearing out." He fully expected to have to do it himself, but he didn't want to offer. He was short-handed. He had a café to run.

Tina ate her breakfast quietly and then stacked the dishes. She would have taken them back into the kitchen, but she thought Bill wouldn't like that. She was finishing her last sip of coffee when the rangers arrived, like angels, one at each shoulder. Her heart sank. She had been in this configuration before.

"I'm Tom, this is Lee, with the California Department of Forestry. I understand you had a bear problem last night."

Tina turned and looked up at them standing side by side, the same height, the same uniform, the same look on their faces. She didn't know what they wanted.

Bill brought the two of them coffee, which he set on the counter. "Maybe we could take this to a booth?" Tom asked. Tina didn't know who he was asking. She didn't know what a booth would mean, if she would be trapped in the corner. The shock of the bear attack, the lack of sleep, the difficulty of her new set of problems, almost worse than the problem she had been trying to solve, all added up to a swirl inside her head. She could only think one move ahead, like getting breakfast. But she couldn't see beyond that. Who were these guys? They started moving, so she stood up and moved with them to an empty booth. She sat alone on her side, facing them. She felt alone, but she could get out if she needed to. The uniforms made her nervous.

Ranger Lee set a clipboard on the table and pulled out a pen, clicking it nervously. Tina wished he would stop.

"How about if you tell us what happened, in your own words," Ranger Tom said.

Tina had been interrogated before. Apparently Ranger Tom was the good cop.

"A bear sort of scratched me," Tina said, and she pulled her bandage aside for a moment so they could see the lines there. "I wasn't doing anything. I was sleeping."

"Do you have a camper? Or are you tent camping?"

"Tent."

"Okay. Were there any foodstuffs in the tent with you?"

"No," Tina said.

"Did you cook your dinner last night?"

"No," Tina said.

"Where did you get dinner?"

"At the café."

"So you ate dinner at the café last night?"

"No," Tina said. "We had take-out."

"And where did you eat the food?"

"In the tent."

"Okay, did you throw any leftover food or packaging in the trash?"

Tina wished the bad cop would quit clicking the pen. But then she figured when he stopped, he would take his turn at interrogating. So she was safe as long as the clicking continued, unnerving as it was, as it was almost certainly intended to be.

"Was there leftover food or packaging or dirty dishes in the tent, ma'am?" Ranger Tom repeated.

Tina looked away, hoping for some kind of guidance. Bill appeared with coffee carafes in his hands. "Some apple pie maybe? I know you fellas start early, so breakfast was a while back. Shall I bring you a slice?"

"Yes," Tina said, and realized immediately that Bill hadn't actually been addressing her. So she said, "Yes, there was packaging in the tent. Pizza."

They ate apple pie and asked more questions, about Brad, the pizza, the bear. And then Tom, who seemed to be the talker, asked her, "Did the bear have a bright red spot on its back, about as big as a volley ball?"

Tina stared at him. What kind of question was that?

"I know it was dark, but I'm wondering if you might have noticed a red spot on the bear."

Tina shook her head. She knew the less she said, the better, but her curiosity got the better of her judgment. "Why would it have a red spot on it?"

"Well, when we catch a bear in people-territory, we mark it and take it up higher in the mountains where it won't be tempted by people-food. Then, if it comes back down again and raids the campgrounds, we catch it again. And we know it's becoming a danger."

"Like a repeat offender," Tina said. She was glad they didn't paint marks on people.

"Like that," Tom said and smiled.

"I don't think the bear meant to hurt me," Tina said, "to be fair. I think it just shoved me out of the way."

"That may be true." Lee spoke for the first time. His voice was exactly like Tom's, Tina thought. "But a repeat offender bear can become a real danger. We have to take him up to the top of the mountain."

"So you throw him over? You kill him?" Tina said, imagining them throwing the bear over a cliff, his dark shape struggling in the air. She saw from the shocked looks on their faces that she had guessed wrong.

"No, ma'am. Don't worry about that. We just take him higher up, so high that he's not likely to travel back down. We release him, that's all. We don't kill him."

"Okay," Tina said, "because it was basically an accident. You can't kill him just for an accident." She wondered if they were lying to her.

And then, in the silence that followed her pronouncement, she said, "Are we done here?"

The two rangers nodded in unison.

Tina wondered if she had managed the interview okay, if she had saved the bear, as she walked back to campsite #13 to assess the damage to the Taj Majal and see what could be salvaged. Her newly acquired, oversized flip-flops slowed her down, catching on the road surface, threatening to fall off, trying to turn inside out, and scooping up a little gravel with almost every step. It made for a long walk. The black cat trailed along, stopping now and then to play with a cloud of midges or bite at the grass along the roadside.

The tent seemed pretty much trashed, four of the

six poles with compound fractures. One wall had been shredded, one slashed, and only the door, which the bear had not used, was intact. The tent still smelled rotten inside, with a slight nose of honey, mango, and cucumber from the broken jar of moisturizer that had spilled. Most of the camping equipment that had been blocking the way was intact, with only minor scratches. The bear had evidently not shit in the woods, but in the tent where the pizza and most of the pizza box had been consumed.

While the black cat pretended to sleep where the sun made a warm patch in the dirt, Tina stacked the kitchen box, the dishes, the lounge chairs, and the rest of the gear on and around the picnic table and then winkled Brad's sleeping bag, mattress, and baseball cap, which were relatively unpolluted, out of the tent. Further exploration gave up Tina's jeans, $1.54 in the pocket, underwear, super-bra, and T-shirt. Saving the underwear for a more private changing room than the open campsite, she was glad to slip into the jeans, though they felt oddly damp and she was aware that they probably stank of bear. With regret, she spotted her platform sandals directly under the gooey wodge of bear droppings.

It took her five awkward trips to carry the salvageable remains of her camping trip back to the Happy Trout Fishing Resort, where she stacked what she thought she could use in one tidy area on the porch, and the extraneous, which was the majority, against the wall, carefully out of the way so that customers would not be inconvenienced as they entered and exited the café. She went back for one last trip and crammed the stinky tent and its remaining contents into site #13's trash barrel and the barrels of two other campsites that were unoccupied at the moment.

She perched on the picnic table, rested, and took stock. Her arm was throbbing from the physical exertion, but a quick peek under the bandage was reassuring. No white goop, no more bleeding, just four rows of red dots. That was good. But everything was gone now: the tent, Brad, Freddy's Escalade, the money, her purse, her cell phone. Site #13 was clear, returned to its original emptiness, as though Tina had never existed. At least with a hotel room you left wet towels and trash, or worse, on the floor to show where you had been. But the campsite where she had lost everything she had gambled for was blank, and she was alone. She had always been alone, but not like this. The cat jumped up and rubbed against her good arm, and she petted him. Not so alone. Still in trouble.

All around her, on the other side of the road and through the trees, she heard the sounds of other campers, and she saw them emerge from tents, their hair pressed into weird shapes, stretching, greeting each other, cooking and eating, living as though they were in houses with invisible walls. None of them was alone. They were all with families or friends. She saw a woman rubbing something out of a bottle onto the arms and face of an unwilling little girl, who kept turning away to see what her big brothers were doing and having to be turned back. She saw four older men sitting at their cement table, and she saw them laugh together at something, and sip coffee, and laugh some more. The smoke rose from their fire pit, and one of them rose and came back with a speckled blue pot for refills. No one seemed to see her at all, and she found that a little scary, so she hurried back to the café where there would at least be Bill, who could see her even though he might not like what he saw.

Like the campground, the café was full of families, groups of men, moms with little kids eating pancakes and waffles and scuffling their feet under the table. Bill was circulating through the room with two pots of coffee, decaf with the orange plastic rim, and regular (green), chatting, but moving quickly. She hadn't seen him smile before. He had a nice smile. Through the hatch, Tina saw a red-pony-tailed guy in a white cap studying the slips on the carousel, wielding a spatula and frowning. Even at first sight, Tina could tell his heart wasn't in it. He looked like he was debating whether or not to fill each order that he looked at, or considering which order could be filled with the least trouble. Bill returned the coffee pots to the burners behind the counter and asked Ponytail to either pick up the pace or take a turn at waiting tables. Things were moving too slow in the kitchen. Orders were piling up. People needed to be fed, for Christ's sake.

Ponytail pulled off the white cap and threw it on the floor. "I didn't agree to work here because I wanted to work, dammit! I want to fish, Bill. That's the whole point!"

"I know, Pete. Ursula couldn't help it. She said she'd be here as soon as she can get away, for sure before Labor Day. So go ask the nice people what they want to eat, okay? Like a nice guy? Put their orders on the table, take their money, give them change, bus the tables. You can fish when Ursula gets here."

"What about Joe and Angie? Or that skinny kid that was here last year? Why don't you get them?"

"Bobby Haskell is in San Diego at science camp. Then he's going to Washington DC with his school chorus. He's too busy, or maybe too smart, to mess around here. Joe and Angie went to Alaska to work the canneries. Better money, I'm sure. So I'm counting on you."

"Christ, Bill," Pete grumbled, as they do-si-doed through the swinging half door to trade places.

Tina sat on the only vacant stool and waited,

automatically taking stock of the man on cither side of her, on her left a big guy with a mermaid tattoo on the back of his hand, drinking the last of his coffee and picking his teeth meditatively with a toothpick, the one on the right younger, wearing a cloth hat that seemed to have bugs all over the hatband. She caught herself and then tried to keep her eyes on the counter, looking up only when Pete appeared on the other side, notepad in hand.

"What'll you have, miss?"

At least he hadn't called her "ma'am."

"BLT on white toast, extra mayo, no lettuce. No tomatoes. Diet Coke. Curly fries with extra ketchup."

"The condiments are right here on the counter. Anything else I can get you?"

She waited patiently, holding still, and when her plate came, she exhaled, realizing that she had been holding her breath. She kept her eyes down as she ate, especially away from the men and groups of men she would ordinarily be assessing for usefulness and interest. Every time she looked toward the kitchen, it seemed that Bill was keeping an eye on her. She had to stay out of trouble until she was out of the trouble she was already in. She ate her sandwich appreciatively. When Pete brought the check, she told him, "I'm running a tab."

"Sorry, doll. Nobody runs a tab at the Happy Trout

Fishing Resort. That's what keeps it happy."

"Bill started me a tab this morning. My..." Tina started to say, "my Brad," because she was so tired, she couldn't remember who Brad was supposed to be. But that didn't make sense, so she tried again. "My friend, the guy I was with, accidentally drove off with my purse in the car, so I'm running a tab until he gets back. Bill said it's okay. I already had breakfast on the tab. Omelet and coffee."

"Bill? You wanna handle this?" Pete didn't have time to argue. He needed to get drinks to the group of rowdy teenagers in the last booth, reminding them by his adult presence that they were still kids, not quite customers, and he had to clear the tables of departing customers to get ready for the next wave. Bill came out from the kitchen and glared at her.

"I'm running a tab, right?" They were facing each other over the same counter as before, and again he leaned on it so that he could talk confidentially, without disturbing the other customers. Again, his voice was soft but definite.

"No ma'am, I don't run tabs. No one ever pays on them. Breakfast was free. One time only."

"Well, actually, Bill, I just ate lunch, so maybe I'd better run a tab after all. That way, I can pay for my breakfast, too. I have a dollar to put down, okay? You know I'm good for the rest when Brad gets back."

"No ma'am, I don't know that. I don't think your fiancé is coming back. I think you need to make other arrangements for getting home."

"May I use your phone, then?"

Tina saw that his attention was divided—the major part of him wanted to get back to the kitchen and start working on the orders Pete had clipped onto the rack, fry fries, make hamburgers, toss salads, move the business along. A small part of him was mentally reviewing the contents of his office with a view to what she might steal if she were alone in there. Apparently he decided it would be worth losing a few paper clips and pencils if she would call someone who would come and pay her bill and remove her from the Happy Trout Fishing Resort once and for all.

"Help yourself. It's in the office across from the bathroom, which you already visited. Don't run up my phone bill. Keep it short."

Tina entered Bill's office with the same interest and sense of adventure with which she had once, on a dare, invaded Mother Superior's private quarters. You never know what you might find. An office, in this case, and a chaotic jumble. She seated herself in Bill's creaky office chair and looked around. A shelf that ran high around the walls was crammed with rolls of paper, some upright, some threatening to topple, packages of napkins, lengths of pipe, stacks of paper that had slithered sideways and were on the verge of sliding off altogether, a hot pink sleeping bag rolled up and tied with a red belt. A collection of discolored mops, buckets, and cleaning supplies sagged in one corner, draped over a wooden saw horse, topped with an orange safety cone, while another was full of record boxes stacked as high as the light switch with handwritten labels that had been scratched out and rewritten so many times they were illegible. The trash basket had evidently been emptied recently, and it yawned open as if to suck down and swallow the swirl of paper and miscellany. The room smelled of disinfectant, mildew, and French fries, maybe a little whiskey. The sticky dust that comes with frying coated everything. The desktop itself was visible only in the center, where an 8.5 by 11-inch sheet of paper might fit, overlapping slightly with the edges of the haystacks of paper on all sides.

A lighter square outline marked where a bottle of Jack Daniels might have stood, and next to it, a single circle for the glass. Drinking alone, but not from the bottle. Tina ran her hand over the surface. It was smooth, not puckered, seeming like an old mark in the wood. The phone sat on the floor next to the chair in a small island of uncovered linoleum. Tina rifled through the drawers and finally found a stubby yellow pencil and a pad of lined paper with a few sheets left.

She had some planning to do, and that meant a list.

It was Sister Mary Helen who had taught all the second-graders to make lists. She said it was a tool for living, although the lists she had assigned were on topics like "Things I Did Today that Made the Angels Weep" and "How I Can Be a Better Catholic." It had never been about surviving or having fun.

"What if there's only one thing on your list?" seven-year-old Tina had wanted to know.

"Then you know what God wants from you."

"And what if there's nothing, not even number one, on your list?" Tina was the kind of kid who ran a sort of counter-catechism, which Sister Angela whacked her hand for. But Sister Mary Helen was kinder. "It would mean you have died and gone to heaven and your work on earth is done. Now run along, Shatina, and straighten your bed. Inspection tonight!"

Tina had written only the number "1" and was deciding whether to follow it with a period or a dash when the old-fashioned black phone rang and she picked it up before it had quit ringing. She paused for just a moment, stopping herself from automatically saying Freddy's name, "Napoleon event," and sorting through her full name for an alias she could give, since she was now a bank robber on the run. But she had to say something.

"Tina Martin speaking. How can I help you?" She

realized she had forgotten to say "Happy Trout," which was like "River City Florist Service" or "Truchas Brothers Entertainment" or "Casablanca Escorts," and sure enough, the caller on the other end was a bit confused.

"Yes, ma'am," Tina said. "This is the Happy Trout Fishing Resort. Mhmm. Mhmm. Let me look in the book. We have a lot of family reunions this time of year. And they usually book ahead a bit more than this. Just hold on a sec." She was flooded with relief at the familiarity of phone business, the respect and anonymity, but also the pleasure of planning, making something happen. She felt at home.

She found an appointment book under a stack of folders and opened it up, finding a "family campground" page. It was blank. She looked to be sure other pages had something on them. This book could be something Bill had started in an attempt to get organized and then abandoned, but there seemed to be other bookings for upcoming dates, so she took a chance.

"Great, it looks like we're open. How many will there be? Wow! That's quite a gang you have. And how many vehicles? How many of those are campers? And when exactly do you want to book for? Okay, mhmm, morning? Okay, looks great. Now let me run this by Bill to be sure the grounds will be ready for you, and

I'll call you back to confirm. And we're gonna need a deposit to hold the spot, say $200? Unhunh. Okay, I'll get right back to you." Tina tried to think if there was anything else she should have asked, but she could always ask when she called back. It felt good to talk to someone who didn't know how much trouble she was in.

She took her notes and the appointment book into the kitchen where Bill was straining pasta into a sink, his face turning towards her through the steam.

"Leona Gentry called. She said she and her husband Ron have been here before, with their poodles, she says. She wants to reserve the family campground for three days for a family reunion. Four RVs. Thirty-five to fifty people, depending, but some of them just for the day. They say July 30th leaving the morning of the August 3rd. I know that's short notice, but is that okay?"

"Jesus Christ! You answered my phone. What do you think you're doing, answering my phone?"

"I was sitting there, about to make a phone call, and it rang, Bill. And that's what Leona Gentry was calling about. I said I'd ask you and call her back to confirm. So what do I tell her? Is it okay? And how much will it cost"

Bill shook the colander into the sink. "Don't answer my goddamn phone," he said over his shoulder.

"Can I use it to call Leona back and tell her it's on?

She's waiting to hear so she can send out the word to all the other Gentries. She said it's a chance for them to get together now that her son Shaun is back from active duty."

Bill sighed. "Call her back and confirm. $100 a day, so $500 if they're out by 1:00. $200 deposit she can mail to me. Write it in the book. Don't answer my phone again."

After a long chat with Leona, Tina returned to her list, where the number 1 waited patiently for her.

> 1. *Yard sale—low prices, quick sales. Pay tab. Make Bill happy (ha!)*
> 2. *Dinner*
> 3. *Find place to sleep*

This all seemed pretty short-term. It would get her as far as tomorrow, that's all. She turned the page and started a new list, intended as a list of long-range possibilities, though other items that occurred to her as she went got thrown in.

> - *Wash dishes for Bill - free food, $100/day or best offer*
> - *Do whatever Pete does, only cheaper, faster, and better*
> - *Clean up office*

- *Shoes, shampoo, toothbrush/paste, tampons in two weeks (check public restroom for dispenser)*
- *Save money ($5000) and take off—*

1. *Reno showgirl? Probably too short. Probably too old. Casino waitress? Might find Brad. Might find the money. Freddy might find me.*
2. *Air Force? How to stay out of trouble. Too straight? Mean people? Ask Shaun Gentry?*
3. *Nun*
4. *Move to Ohio and get a job.*

Without ID. Without money. Maybe Ohio just sounded like a safe place. She crossed Ohio off the list.

5. *Stay here. Get around Bill. Pete unfriendly? How to stay out of trouble.*

The yard sale that afternoon was a success, though Tina kept a close eye on the café door, afraid Bill would come out and try to stop her. It was probably against one of his rules to hold a yard sale at the Happy Trout Fishing Resort. He probably even had a sign for it. Fortunately, the event went quickly, without a hitch. The prices were more than reasonable, and the goods were brand-new, high-class, and smelled only slightly of bear, a scent that dissipated quickly in the thin mountain air. The lounge chairs and the green pillows were snapped up by a couple of old fishermen, the red sit-up pillows taken by a Winnebago-driving couple who liked to drink themselves to sleep while they watched game shows on TV.

The hardest thing to get rid of was the kitchen box, but Tina managed to talk an older couple into buying it to use as a gun cabinet in their camper, so that the pistols the lady complained about were out of sight, but still within easy reach in the unlikely event of an attack. Plus the top of the box provided more kitchen counter space for whatever cooking she could do in that confined space. "It's like cooking in a shoebox," the lady said, and Tina shook her head sympathetically. At $7.50, it was a bargain. The total take was less than Tina had hoped, but $45 would cover the tab and breakfast tomorrow, with a few bucks left over. And she hoped to figure out another source of income by then.

Tina was kind of sorry when the last of her merchandise had been carried away. She had enjoyed talking with the customers, warning them about the bear and the need to take care in storing food, blaming her departed friend for having been careless. "I fell asleep, thinking he would know to store the pizza box in the SUV, and the next thing I knew..."—she finished her sentence by peeling the bandage back to show her four stripes and explain about the bear's red butt. She liked the attention, and it gave her someone to be—saleswoman, bear victim, safety educator—in this place where she didn't belong.

She spent the rest of the afternoon walking the campground, keeping an eye out for anything that might be useful, trailed by the black cat, who would stop behind a clump of grass, then dash past her, brushing her leg, startling her the first time, and then lie half-concealed behind a rock, where he would look away as she passed, waiting to catch up with her again. Tina stopped at the campground bathroom, peed, had a quick wash, shoved her hair around a little, and noted the Tampax dispenser in the restroom. One question answered. Then a woman came in dragging a shrieking child who appeared to have been rolled in mud and smelled of dead fish, so Tina left. She poked around behind the café, peering through the window of the shed to see dead equipment, spiders, and rusty tools, no room even for a sleeping bag, the door locked anyway, the green VW camper which looked to be inhabited, probably by Pete, the silver bullet trailer, securely curtained and locked up tight, and the red truck camper, locked. Everything locked. She would have to keep working on it.

Dinner that evening was very satisfying—the meatloaf special with apple pie for dessert. Pete was waiting tables again, and he took her order and set down each dish with sarcastic deference. Tina was equally polite in a snarky way, knowing that she had the cash in her pocket to shut him up if he got shitty about it. She was still mulling over her options for sleeping. She had lost the Taj Majal to the bear, and she didn't think there was any point in renting a piece of dirt to sleep on when there was dirt everywhere for free, if she could find a way to stay safe. She was afraid of the bear coming back if she slept in the open. She didn't think she could sleep without some protection.

What she needed was a hidey-hole, a secret place, where no one would find her—not the bear, the rangers, Pete, or Bill. She figured if the bear found her, she was dead, or maybe just mangled. The rangers were an unknown quantity. She was afraid they might have the power to put her in jail. She figured if Pete found her, she'd have to buy him off with a blowjob or something, and Bill would find out and kick her off the place. If Bill found her, he would probably call the sheriff. She decided to check out the VW camper, the truck camper and the little silver trailer in the back again, on the off chance they might have been left open accidentally. At worst, she could slide Brad's sleeping bag under the back porch and sleep with his sweatshirt hood pulled tight over her face to prevent the bugs from keeping her awake. She had slept in worse places.

She was in no hurry to leave the warm café. It would be easier to look around after Bill left or went to bed. She killed time over coffee refills, adding lots of cream and sugar in case it was a long time to her next meal, and settled into a booth with the newspaper to read—the want ads first, in case a job popped out at her, then the funnies, then the news. On page three, Metro section, she found her story.

911 Call Causes Bank Robbery Response Mix-up

Sacramento, CA — A 911 call made by one of the two suspects in the robbery of a Sacramento area branch of Security Pacific Bank caused confusion when the ambulance and first responder team arrived before law enforcement officials responded to the bank alarm.

"It looked like a medical emergency at first, so we assisted the firefighters and EMTs by controlling the crowd," says Captain John Daly of the Sacramento County Sheriff's Department. "It was only later that witnesses reported the robbery. We lost some valuable time."

The 911 call was made when customer Manny Aguirre, 79, suffered a heart attack. Aguirre is in stable condition at a local hospital, where he credits the robber's quick call with saving his life. "It was a miracle," he tells reporters.

Tina folded the newspaper page in two and slipped it into her pocket. It didn't really say anything that pointed to her, but she didn't want to have to talk about it either. Just as well to keep it under wraps. Bill shot her a look from the kitchen as she paid her bill, and she hoped Pete would tell him that she had left a 15% tip, more than generous given the level of service, and she hoped he wouldn't suppose that she had done anything against the rules to earn it and that he wouldn't come looking for her. It was good to have a little money again, though her heart ached and kept her awake a long time as she lay under the porch thinking about the Hello Kitty/Spiderman money that she and Brad had stolen from the bank, and that Brad had inadvertently stolen from her, and that she couldn't get back, no matter how vividly she could imagine it and all the comforts it could pay for. She tried to imagine what those luxuries might have been, a soft bed, a warmer one than the sleeping bag she had used to make her nest, a door that locked out everything dangerous.

When Tina actually dreamed, though, it was not about the money, not about Freddy, but about the bear, who had set up a tea party on the picnic table at campsite #13. On the little white plates were piles of orange crumbs like the ones that crumble from an old, deteriorating foam mattress. She knew what they would taste like. The bear wore a nametag that said "Bear" in big gold letters pinned to his chest. Where the pins had gone through his skin, little trickles of blood ran down and matted in his fur. There were signs hanging from the sides of the table, but when she stooped down to read them, the letters ran down the paper, leaving black streaks like tear-drenched mascara running down a woman's cheeks. The air thrummed in her dream.

When she woke in the middle of the night, she found the black cat curled up next to her, and she moved a little closer to him. She had a funny feeling she couldn't quite name—it was a not-Freddy, not-Brad, alone feeling that made it hard to get back to sleep and made her hope the cat would stay at least until she dozed off.

6

A Dog looking out for its afternoon nap jumped into the Manger of an Ox and lay there cosily upon the straw. But soon the Ox, returning from its afternoon work, came up to the Manger and wanted to eat some of the straw. The Dog in a rage, being awakened from its slumber, stood up and barked at the Ox, and whenever it came near attempted to bite it. At last the Ox had to give up the hope of getting at the straw, and went away muttering: "Ah, people often grudge others what they cannot enjoy themselves."

—Aesop's Fables

TINA CRAWLED OUT FROM under the porch early the next morning, when the light was beginning to seep into the valley and color the sky a lighter dark and the birds were waking from whatever dreams a bird might have. She stretched and took in the scene, her eyes wide from trying to make sense of the strange repetition and emptiness of the forest, tree and tree and tree, and the random flickering of the birds from branch to branch. Her ears seemed to ring in the deep quiet and the quiet rush of the river under that, and the bright notes, repeated and various, that hung in the air overhead. She was the only witness when the rangers' truck rattled down the road from the campground, heading towards the highway, a big cage in the back, in the cage a bear thoughtfully licking its paws and looking around like a bored commuter, and sure enough, a red spot about the size of a volley ball on its back. She hadn't really believed it.

When Pete showed up to start the breakfast prep, Tina was sitting on the back steps, leaning against the wall, listening idly to Bill as his alarm clock went off, he cursed, he stumbled into the bathroom, the toilet flushed, and the water ran in the sink. The black cat was butting his head against her legs, and she petted him absently. She wanted to arrive at the right time, when she could slip into the café's routine without causing any fuss.

Pete stopped and stood with his arms crossed, studying Tina for a moment. She returned his look silently, trying to remember if she had ever been with a red-haired guy. She thought maybe one of the cops, and she remembered the unusual spill of red pubic hair around his cock. That one.

"I know what kind of girl you are," Pete said. "I know little tramps like you. You're out for what you can get, and you don't care what you have to do or who you have to do to get it." It was surprising how friendly he could sound while saying all this. Tina thought for a minute. He probably did know girls like her.

Pete shook his head. "You may be fooling Bill, but you don't fool me for a second, honeybuns."

"I'm not fooling Bill," Tina said. She stepped aside and followed Pete down the hallway and into the kitchen, where Bill was mixing sourdough pancake batter, so it would have time to sit on the counter and get good before the first customers came in.

"Well damn, you're still here." Tina liked it that Bill was busy. It meant he was only thinking about her with half his brain.

"Coffee, please. I can pay. I have shoes, see?" Tina took off one of the flip-flops and waved it in his direction, but he wasn't looking.

"Café isn't open for another thirty minutes. Coffee's not made yet. I'm a busy man. Come back later."

It seemed to Tina like a good sign that he said come back later instead of go away. She went into the front with Pete and watched him make the coffee, taking careful note of how much water, how much coffee, and how the pieces fit together; it didn't look too complicated. When he started laboriously wiping down the syrup pitchers, she took the damp cloth away from him and finished the job, watching him all the time to see what needed to be done next. She wondered why they hadn't done this last night.

When Bill saw through the hatch that she was still there, he stopped what he was doing and gave her his full attention. She found that his full attention made her nervous, so she wiped faster and then organized the condiments on the counter, mustard, ketchup, hot sauce, sweeteners, so that each place was the same.

"Did you call your friends yesterday, or were you too busy minding my business?"

"I don't have any phone numbers, Bill," Tina said. "They were all in my purse. And that's gone."

"Try calling 411."

"I don't have any friends, really. And there's no number for that. The coffee's ready. Do you want some?" Tina poured herself a cup and took a second cup back to the kitchen with a cream pitcher and some packets of sugar and sweetener, in case that's what he liked. Bill added a bit of cream and took a sip. He said thanks, which she thought was really promising.

She waited until Bill was measuring oatmeal into a boiling pot. "Can I work for you?"

Bill didn't even look up. "No," he said, and he began to count out loud so he wouldn't lose his place. "Five, six …"

"…seven, eight," Tina counted with him till he looked up and she figured he was through counting.

"It would probably cost you too much anyway. I bet someone working here would earn about a hundred dollars a day, for a full day, I mean."

"Nothing like it," Bill said. "I can't afford anything above minimum wage. $7.00 an hour. Eight hours and taxes taken out, you're looking at more like fifty take-home, nothing like a hundred."

"Okay," Tina said. It was better than nothing.

"No," Bill said, rattling the lid on the oatmeal a little harder than was probably necessary.

"You're short-handed, you said so. You're over-worked. Ursula won't be here for three weeks."

Bill shot her a look. "Eavesdropping, too?"

"I was just listening. If you don't want people to hear things, you probably shouldn't say them out loud."

Bill didn't answer, so Tina went on. "I'll work hard, and I have a plan once I get some money together. And I'll remember what you said, you know. I won't bother you or Pete or the customers. I can work. It sounds like I could make a thousand or so in a month if I worked every day."

"We're closed Sunday night and all day Monday."

"Okay, so a little less, then. I don't intend to stick around, and I won't steal anything." Tina put her hand protectively over her bandaged arm, thinking of when Bill had been so nice and taken care of her, hoping he would remember that she hadn't caused any trouble then or stolen anything from the office when she talked to Leona Gentry.

"I'm gonna need a discount on food, though. Thirty-five dollars won't go very far if I have to eat out every meal, even here."

Pete, who had stopped working entirely to listen to this conversation, following the negotiations with great interest, chimed in. "Employees eat free. That's how it's always been, anyway. That's what I do. That's what Ursula does."

Bill glared at him, but didn't deny it. "You can't work here. Where do you think you're going to live? Your tent's gone."

"I thought maybe I could stay in the little silver trailer outside? It's locked, but I imagine you have a key."

"That's my sister Ursula's trailer and I don't think she'd appreciate me loaning it out to every vagrant who passes through."

"Not to argue, Bill, but if I had a place to stay, I wouldn't technically be a vagrant. I'd be a temporary resident." Tina knew how these laws worked, having explored the wrong side of them a few times.

"You can't stay there. She'll be here pretty soon and she'll want her trailer empty. I don't think she's looking for a damn roommate."

"Give me the keys to the truck with the camper

shell out there, then, the red one. Nobody's sleeping there. It's not very much space, but I'll be working all day and there's enough room in there for me and the cat to sleep."

Bill turned away from the strips of bacon he was laying out, ready for the grill. He pointed his spatula at her like a nun wielding a ruler.

"Don't you mess with that cat or you'll be sorry. Foster is a mean one. He doesn't like people, for good reason, and if you try to pet him, he'll give you another set of stripes on the other arm. You had best leave him strictly alone."

Pete was still listening, and Tina knew he had seen her with the cat wreathing himself around her calves as she sat on the steps, waiting for things to open up. She hoped he would keep his mouth shut. You don't tell a man his ferocious tomcat is sweet on you when it isn't supposed to like anybody.

"Why is he named Foster?"

"Reminds me of an uncle I had, the one who left me the place. He didn't like people either."

Tina figured that since they were having a conversation about other things now, they had a deal, so she started filling the napkin holders after watching Pete start. It was easy to take work away from Pete.

"Hey, Tina. You know you're going to have to clean the restrooms, right? And do lots of things you won't like—hard, dirty things. Ruin your manicure." Pete teased her as he took silverware out of the dishwasher cage and slipped forks, knives, and spoons into the more or less appropriate slots in the bin under the counter.

"Not a problem, Pete. I've done lots of things I didn't like. I thought you knew girls like me. And it's a job, right? Like any other job."

"And how are you going to like cleaning the trout the customers bring in? Does that sound like it's your kind of game?"

"I guess I can clean trout as well as anyone else, Pete. I mean, how dirty can they be? All they do is swim around in water all day."

Bill and Pete gave her the same long look, as though she had said something puzzling or strange.

"What?" she asked. "What's wrong with you?"

Bill broke the silence that followed, shaking his head and telling Pete, "Show her how the dishwasher works, where the bins are. We're going to need plenty of clean dishes on a Friday. We'll leave the details of trout-cleaning for another occasion."

It was a long day of bussing trays of dirty dishes from the tables, lifting heavy stacks of dirty plates, wads of silverware, and cups into the dishwasher, and then moving the hot clean dishes to appropriate shelves and bins to make room for the next batch of food-smeared plates. Tina knew Bill was watching her, and he was ready to bark orders at her whenever she hesitated or made a mistake. He seemed to be able to read her with his back turned, even when she tried to cover her uncertainty. Between chores, she looked around the kitchen to see where things were stored and what needed doing.

She also answered the phone down the hall and made three more reservations, one a referral from Leona Gentry, who had really appreciated Tina's friendly phone manner. When she told Bill, he grunted. "I'll pick up the voicemail later. Just leave it." But Tina figured he didn't always pick the messages up right away, and a ringing phone was like an invitation, so she continued to look forward to those bright, innocent conversations with strangers. She liked saying "Happy Trout, Tina Martin speaking."

"It's not a happy trout," Pete told her. "The trout is probably unhappy, really, because he has been hooked. That's the idea. He's dead. Probably going to be someone's dinner. So it's not a happy trout. It's a happy resort. It's a trout fishing resort and it's a happy resort. It's the Happy...Trout Fishing...Resort."

Tina shoved him out of the way so that she could wipe down the counter he had been resting his backside on. "Happy Trout!" she thought.

She took a quick break for lunch at 2:00 when the

rush seemed to be over, slurping chicken noodle soup and eating fries doused in ketchup while she watched how Pete waited on tables. Pete was friendly with the customers, joking in a way that would be dangerous for her. It looked easy enough, but she was worried that she would sound sexy when she asked what some guy wanted. "What can I do for you?" She was afraid she would accidentally lick her lips. She decided to start with a blank-faced "May I take your order?" with her eyes averted. If Bill ever let her even talk to the customers, which he didn't seem eager to do.

By 7:30 when the café closed and the cleanup was done, Tina was very tired and very tired of Bill. He had grudgingly given her the keys to the red truck with the camper shell, but it was too light and too early for bed, so she followed Pete down to the river and sat at a distance on a big dished-out rock and watched him cast his line into the water again and again. There was a dreaminess to watching him, the arc of his body as he cast extending into the curve of the line. She watched, wordless, unmoving, her mind blank. Foster sat at her feet, and then rolled onto his back, gazing up at her, as fetching as a skinny black tomcat can reasonably be. She smiled at him and reached over to tickle his tummy. He pretended to gnaw on her knuckle, paddled her hand with his back paws and then scampered away to hunt for bugs.

This was the first time she had really looked at the river. Up to this point she had only driven up and down it looking for the campsite, raced over it in the dark after the bear came, and then trudged over and over it blindly as she cleaned up the ill-fated campsite #13 and looked for a place to sleep. Now she faced it and was still.

Her impression was of untidiness: tumbled rocks, jumbled leaves, uneven river banks, trampled mud, wads of root, messy bushes, like a vacant lot, but no trash, no bedsprings, no paper, no colored wrappers, so that everything she could see was shades of gray and brown and green, even the gleaming surface of the river. The tree trunks lolled instead of standing, but stretched up implacably. The wild grass showed uneven patches of dirt not worn down by human feet. The rocks were strewn like accent pillows without purpose or design, the tiny lavender flowers seemed random and senseless. Where corners of the world should be, the contours were rounded and softened and vulnerable-looking. If she dared to wander into those darkening woods, her path would have to curve and loop and accommodate the shape of the ground and would never arrive at an intersection; everything would be the same, uncontained, individual, and yet the same; strange, then familiar but still strange; safely indifferent to her, but dangerously indifferent. The unnerving thoughts made her shiver.

She breathed in the thin, wet air and the exhalation of pine trees, mud, and something else, something green or brown. She realized that the smell of plastic, exhaust, and people—their sweat, their worry, their passions, their effort—was entirely missing. Instead there was this something else, something she only vaguely remembered from her one time at Red Robin Camp, a smell she could not name then or now.

The air buzzed and clicked and throbbed, but quietly, like traffic a long way away, like everything present was also distant, and the river managed to be both quiet and chuckling, peaceful and lively. She could hear her own breathing, and the whir of Pete's fishing pole and the silence of Pete's line as he laid it gently in the water.

The first big star appeared even though the light was still there but starting to thin. It shone steadily in the sky between the tops of the trees that lined the river, and Tina remembered having seen it before, maybe even the same star, maybe another like it. The very tips of the trees fanned themselves in the little wind that blew up high, that Tina couldn't feel at all, and the smaller trunks rocked slightly.

If Tina had been less tired, she would have been bored. She tried to think, but she had no paper or pencil, and all she could think was that it was probably going to be all right, one way or another. The cat was good, Pete was kind of a pest, and Bill was a hard boss to please, but she really could work hard, she wasn't just saying that. And she watched the first big star and the stars that had joined it rippling on the surface of the dark water and sighed. The first day was over.

The next morning, after Tina had spent a quiet night in the red camper truck with the window slightly open so Foster could come and go, she woke up happy. The bank money was almost certainly gone, she knew that, and she knew it was very sad, but she still felt a lightness in her heart that was right next door to joy. She washed up, scrubbing her teeth with her finger, and arrived at the back door at the same time as Pete. Bill handed her sixty dollars for the day before out of the till, and she celebrated by buying a Happy Trout Fishing Resort T-shirt, giving herself an employee discount price of $10.00. It seemed more than fair since she would be advertising the Happy Trout at the same time she worked there. Bill took the ten and returned it to the till, shaking his head. Tina went back to scrub the café restroom as clean as it could get, stopping to change into her new T-shirt and peer at herself in the mirror while she was there. Her hair was seriously weird. She pushed it around with her fingers, so at least it matched on both sides.

As she shoveled the morning's first batch of dishes into the machine, Bill watched her critically. She knew he was looking for an excuse to fire her, but she didn't think it would happen. He would be stupid to keep Pete and get rid of Tina, who made Pete look like a piece of furniture. The job, dishes, bathroom, phone, it all made too much sense to her, and the Gentry family reunion was set for the weekend after next. He would need the extra help. And she knew Leona was looking forward to meeting her. She had made sure of that.

In fact, two weeks later, the Gentry family reunion went quite well, with only one half-hearted fistfight, which broke up almost as soon as it started. Leona was very pleased with the accommodations. The reunion grove was open and accessible, even to the older folks, and the restrooms were spotless, smelling slightly of paint where Tina had covered over the unimaginative offers of sexual favors, the records of love (Sheila loves LV. Matthew M. rocks!!!!!), and the crude pictures of bodily functions. Leona and her sturdy, handsome son, Shaun, had spent almost an hour in the café having pie and coffee, chatting with Tina and settling the bill in advance. Tina found out about using bone meal for the roses, pruning, deadheading, how to make better potato salad, at least better than Nancy Gentry Hale's poor excuse, which was about fifty percent mayonnaise, and how to keep the fleas from bothering poor old Foster, who had scratched ostentatiously in front of her, though it was the first time Tina had seen him do it. Leona was not afraid to give good advice, and Shaun and Tina eyed each other behind the screen of her chatter. Maybe later, they both thought. Maybe. Maybe not.

Gentrys and Gentry-related kinfolk in various combinations were in buying food all day, taking each other aside for some confidential talk, teasing, telling old jokes on each other, and filling the café with loud talk and laughter. So Tina went peacefully about the chores she had learned to do mostly by watching Pete and Bill, not spying, not eavesdropping, while Bill grumbled and looked worried.

The extra business seemed to make him nervous. Tina made him nervous. But he'd get used to her. And if he didn't, it's not like she was going to stay. She thought she might be asked to leave, again, when Ursula came and he wasn't short-handed anymore, and she didn't know if she could work her way around Ursula. Women could be tricky, hard to play. She realized from listening to Pete and Bill, not eavesdropping, that Bill was planning to take off for his annual September fishing trip to Oregon while Ursula filled in for him at the Happy Trout starting Labor Day weekend. Ursula might be as uptight as Bill. She might be suspicious. Tina had begun to think a lot about Ursula.

By ten in the evening, the Gentry reunion had hushed up a little, the children all tucked into bed dirty for a change, the women gossiping and playing cards by lantern light, or visible in the camper windows setting their hair, the men breaking up into smaller groups with bottles to share, either surreptitiously or openly depending on whether they were from the Church of Christ Gentrys or the black sheep. Shaun Gentry, tired of being slapped on the back, thanked for doing his military duty, and inspected for signs of PTSD, wandered out to the camper where he knew Tina slept, a bottle of red wine and two Styrofoam cups in his hand. He fancied a moonlight walk in the woods with a woman, and Tina had come to mind. The girl he had been dating before he went overseas had gone on to fellows closer at hand, and it didn't seem right to be back and all alone with the moon so full. He knew Tina was older than him, but he thought that might work in his favor.

Tina turned him down firmly and politely. She might have gone, counting on the darkness to hide in, but the truth was she was bone-tired. She still wasn't used to the early hours and the hard work. She really just wanted to sleep. A young man like that could be fun, but he wouldn't be restful.

Shaun was about to give up when Bill stepped out of the shadows.

"What the hell do you think you're doing, young man?" Bill's voice was quiet, as usual, but had an edge to it that sounded menacing in the dim light.

"I am asking Tina to go for an evening walk with me, sir."

"Perhaps you'd better go on back to your campsite. This area is for personnel only."

"It's not posted, sir."

"I'm telling you. Good night."

Shaun was used to being bossed around, but if rank was being pulled, he wanted to know what rank it was. "I'm sorry, sir. I didn't realize you were Tina's husband."

"I'm not Tina's husband. I am asking you to return to the campground. That's the public area, that's what you rented."

"Her boyfriend maybe?"

Bill's hesitation told Shaun that he was pursuing the enemy's weakest point, so he pushed on.

"Are you like her guardian or something? Parole officer?"

Bill thought for a moment. "I am her employer. It is my responsibility to provide a safe and secure work environment." He seemed to like the sound of that.

Tina thought he would probably get a new sign to put up, just so he could point to it.

"With all due respect, sir, I think what you are is the dog in the Bible."

Bill gave that one some thought as well. He had spent enough of his precious childhood hours in Sunday school and Vacation Bible School to be intrigued and challenged. "What dog is that? I can't recall many dogs in the Bible. I don't think dogs were all that popular in the Holy Land. In the ark, maybe? Two-by-two? Is that what you're referring to?"

"It's a saying, sir. Dog in the Bible."

"I don't think there's a dog in the Bible that has any bearing at all on the present situation. In fact, I'd bet a hundred dollars that you've got it wrong somehow."

"You're on," Shaun said. "But you're bound to lose. My mom uses it, and she was raised serious Church of Christ, so it's got to be there somewhere. When we were growing up, she'd always say not to be like the dog in the Bible."

"I'm thinking," Bill said. "Is this the dog that returns to its vomit? Is Tina supposed to be the vomit? That seems pretty harsh."

Tina's voice came from the open camper window. "Could you guys take this conversation somewhere else? I'm trying to sleep here. And I'm definitely not vomit."

"Sorry, Tina." Bill took Shaun loosely by the arm

and steered him towards the café porch, where there were two chairs arranged for just such a weighty conversation. They sat, and Shaun absently poured the wine and handed a cup to Bill.

"I know that's what Mom says. It's like a saying, dog in the Bible."

"Do you think it refers to the dogs that ate Jezebel? That's the only other dog I can think of in the Bible."

"I don't know," Shaun said. "That doesn't make much sense. I thought it was more New Testament than that, like the Christmas Bethlehem thing. Maybe there was a dog in that. And I don't know if Tina is like Jezebel. You would know better than me on that."

"Well, that last is an interesting question."

This led to talk about Tina and her Jezebellian qualities, about particular women they had known, and then about women in general, the way they always wanted to change everything just when you were used to it, wanted to talk about it, wanted some ineffable something that an ordinary man can't fathom. They talked about breaking up, and being broken up with, and divorce and the damned way it felt. They talked about the army, and war, about feeling older than your friends once you got home, even than your own father.

It was a beautiful night for talking, just chilly enough to make the wine welcome, and the singing that drifted over from the reunion, sweet and sentimental, seemed to promise harmony, comfort, and safety for all. After Shaun's bottle had been drained along with the few inches of whiskey kept in the office for emergencies such as this, Bill was fully apprised of Shaun's plans to go to UCLA for pre-law, or maybe start a construction business with his friends from high school, or bum around for a year or two, or maybe re-up for a second tour. He was pretty sure that Shaun was too young for Tina. That made him feel good.

Shaun only knew that Bill was a good guy and that he had a secret thing for Tina even though he hadn't said so.

In the morning, Bill set up for breakfast and opened the café as though nothing had happened in the night, though he was a little bleary-eyed and headachy, and he found himself smiling a little. He had waked up in the middle of the night with the word "manger" in his head, and he had laughed out loud. The Gentrys had left the campground tidy except for the packed garbage cans, which needed to be hauled over to the dumpster and emptied, a task Tina found enjoyable. Leona promised to be back and even booked a single campsite for the weekend before Easter, when the resort would open again for the summer season.

Bill smiled again to see that Shaun had paid off on the bet, leaving an envelope with his name on it on the counter. He slipped the three twenties, three tens, and two fives into the cash register. Who knew that vacation Bible school would pay off in such a worldly way. Onward Christian soldiers.

"I'm taking the camper to Oregon once Ursula gets here." Bill had already started gathering his gear together and was sorting through his tackle box on the lunch counter after the café closed that night. Tina said nothing. She knew he was leaving when Ursula came to take over, and she'd have her stuff moved out of the camper before then. She knew Bill wanted to know where she intended to sleep (with Pete?), but she said nothing. She couldn't afford to ask for permission. She would just wait him out in silence.

"So I guess you might want to be moving on now. You must have saved up enough by now to at least take the Greyhound back to Reno or Sacramento or wherever you're from."

Tina answered him. "I have a couple hundred dollars. That's probably enough." It wasn't exactly an answer. "We ought to get the trailer ready for her, though. Nice clean sheets. Air it out. Put some flowers in a jar. I'll do that tomorrow if you give me the key. Which I will return to you without making a copy. Which I couldn't anyway," she added pointedly in response to Bill's suspicious look. She hoped her efforts would be appreciated.

Ursula finally arrived during an afternoon lull several days later, a tall, rangy, pale-haired Western woman who looked like she would have quite a voice on her and would brook no nonsense, but she entered the café quietly, slipping into a booth. Tina went to take her order: a cheeseburger, well done, and a salad with something besides that orange gook, but on the side, and tell my little brother I'm here and would like a big hug. Tina almost wrote down "hug," but then she grinned. "You must be Ursula. I'm Tina. I work here. And I'll tell Bill right away!"

She followed Bill and watched as he came sweeping out from the kitchen and gathered Ursula into his arms. It was so unexpected and so beautiful, she felt like disappearing. Or like she had already disappeared. She had never seen anything like it. She went into the kitchen and started the burger on the grill. She took a salad out of the fridge and chose ranch dressing, on the side, for Ursula. It was the least orange choice. After she set it on the table, she hovered nearby and listened. Eavesdropping, really.

Bill sat in the booth across from Ursula while she ate and interrogated him about the business, which she seemed to know a lot about. She teased him about being the old man of the mountain.

"Why go to Oregon? Why go fishing? It's coals to Newcastle. You ought to go to Reno and see some shows, meet some girls, have a good time. I know you're not too old to have a good time. I'm four years older than you and I'm not that old. I'm not leaving the party till they drag me out feet first! You need some city fun, Bill. You can fish here all you want."

Bill ducked the question. "How's Benny? I wish he'd come up here again. We had quite a time with that porch. And it's still standing, so we must have done it right. But I guess someone has to mind the store, right?"

"Benny's Benny. That's all I can tell you. He's fine, really, as far as I can tell. His dad died, you know, and the family dynamic there is so strange. It makes us McCreas look like vanilla pudding. With Benny, there's the Navajo side of the family and the Puerto Rican side of the family, and they don't, to put it mildly, see eye to eye about what to do when someone dies. The family meeting to plan his dad's funeral took three days and nights of drinking and fighting and crying. And even then, nobody was happy with it."

"When are you going to make an honest man of him?"

Ursula let out a sigh that puffed out between her lips. "I don't know, Bill. When I want to get married, he cools off. When he wants to get married, I start having second thoughts. So I don't know. Ask me something I know."

"Don't worry, Urs. It'll work out. Forget your worries and just take care of the place. There won't be a lot of business, not this late."

"That's why I'm here, my dear, to wait tables and listen to the customers tell lies. And to get some fishing done myself. There's not much fishing in Hayward."

"We aired out your trailer for you, so it's ready. Back around October first to close down, so don't worry about any of that. I'm off first thing tomorrow morning." Bill shot Tina a warning glance, but she figured she could get moved out of the red camper truck in about five minutes' time. And in the event, that's about what it took.

7

Sometimes you put walls up not to keep people out,
but to see who cares enough to break them down.

—Anonymous

TINA STOOD IN THE damp parking lot in the cold morning air, her box held close with her left hand, paper shopping bag hanging from her right, Foster draped over her feet, watching Bill drive the red camper truck slowly down the dirt road and turn left, over the culvert bridge, and gone. She waited a few minutes in case he came back for something he had forgotten, and when she thought it was safe, she went through the back door and took the first door on the left, to Bill's room. He wouldn't be using it. And she had to sleep somewhere. She dumped her stuff on the bed and trailed apprehensively into the kitchen to see what Ursula was going to do about her. It was too much like meeting a foster mom.

Ursula, who was cutting up oranges for the breakfast plates, turned, rested her back against the counter, and looked at Tina. Tina looked back, trying not to seem nervous, trying to have an honest face. It was like an encounter between two species from different continents, say chimpanzees and penguins. What is this creature? Does it bite? Will it try to eat me? Confusing. Tina didn't know what she had to trade. She remembered this feeling, but that made it worse. It hadn't worked out very well then; it wasn't very promising now.

Into this strange air of encounter, Pete breezed through, late as usual, and gave Ursula a quick, noncommittal, sideways hug.

"Now that the big boss is away, we should all get roaring drunk and party down, what do you say, ladies? Drugs, sex, and rock'n'roll!" He turned the radio up and boogied as he started the daily business of loading the napkin holders and wiping off the condiments at each table.

Tina wished she had thought of the napkin holders and condiments first. It would have looked good, like she was an important player instead of a disposable tag-along, like she knew the routine instead of standing at the counter with empty hands waiting to see what would happen or to be told what to do next. And it would have taken her out of the kitchen, out of Ursula's line of sight. Too late now. If she went to help Pete, it would seem like she was trying to use him or like she was counting on him as an ally. If she stayed in the kitchen, it could mean something else. Men weren't that hard to read. There was no knowing with women unless they were whores. Whores were generally pretty predictable. Unless they were high.

As Tina pulled her hairnet over her wild hair, Ursula put hers on as well, saying "God! I hate these things, don't you?"

Tina tensed up even more. Yes, I hate them because I'm just like you. So you should let me stay. No, I don't hate them because I like following rules. So you should let me stay. Maybe I do, and maybe I don't. Who's asking? She had to answer, so she shrugged and turned to scrape away at the grill, although it didn't need it.

To Ursula, she seemed too old to be shrugging instead of answering a question—that was teenage stuff. Her inability or unwillingness to answer made Ursula ask again, just to see what would happen. "Don't you hate hairnets, Tina?"

Tina kept her eyes on the grill, but even from the side, her face was a study in misery. She turned and faced Ursula like an alley cat facing a pack of dogs, like a foster child on the first day, trying to smile but only able to manage a toothy grimace. She didn't know how she felt about hairnets.

"I don't know," she said.

Again, it was a child's answer, an evasion. But

why? Ursula tried to reassure her. "Don't worry about it. It's just an idle question, anyway."

Tina didn't relax. If anything, she seemed even more freaked out. Her movements were jerky as she began unloading the dishes and cutlery from the previous evening's dishwasher load. She didn't know what an idle question was, if it was important or not. She felt like she had failed the first test and was once again in trouble. All she could do was work hard and hope things worked out. She would get through this day and then plan what to do. What to do next if this went badly. How to hold on.

Ursula soothed herself by turning to the task of having the oatmeal ready, lining up the toast, taking the butter out of the cooler. She hummed to herself, like she did when she was driving or when she was grooming dogs back in Hayward. Maybe it was Mozart, maybe Waylon Jennings. Maybe it was Ursula enjoying herself.

What was it with this strange little woman? Was she suffering from PTSD from some traumatic hairnet-related catastrophe in her past? She reminded Ursula of someone or maybe something. She wondered where she had seen that weird, toothy, defensive half-smile, half-snarl before, that backing away, that sideways glare.

Then she remembered Beedo.

Beedo had been brought in to the grooming shop by her favorite animal control officer, Zack, a blue-eyed all-American boy with a halo of blond curls, freckled. Blessed with a wide, white smile, cute enough to want to tuck into her pocket and take home. She bet herself that he had bitterly resented his sweetly boyish looks in high school, in the not too distant past. She wondered if he had figured out since then that his grin was disarming enough to get him past the defenses women might put up against darker, more threatening men. He seemed so harmless that he could probably put in some serious work in the sack. There was some solid male muscle there. His girlfriend must get a lot of voltage out of that.

In fact, she was so busy speculating about his sex life that she wasn't listening very carefully, and before she realized it, she had agreed to take thc gray matted mess of a dog in the carrier box he had in the back of his truck and try to clean him up. Most dogs just needed a bath and a brush, but this was a Valdez-sized problem, one that called for a professional like Ursula.

"Beedo's probably a really nice dog," Zack was saying earnestly, his baby blues wide and innocent. You wanted to buy a magazine subscription from him so he could go to band camp. "He belonged to an older lady who babied him a lot. And then she died, and the daughter took him, but it didn't work out real well. Abusive boyfriend, alcohol, you know how that goes."

Ursula wondered why he thought she would know how that goes. Maybe she seemed like the kind of woman who had abusive boyfriends. She stepped toward the cage. Beedo backed into a corner and yapped at her frantically, the whites of his eyes standing out as though he were in blackface. He snarled and whipped his head back and forth, which wasn't promising, but Ursula couldn't bring herself to say no to Zack.

"Has he had all his shots? Is he basically healthy? Did he bite anyone?"

"Yeah, the vet gave him a pass, so he's healthy. They had to restrain him pretty hard to get him checked out, but he's okay, they say. Bruised some, and mostly scared. Once he's cleaned up and feeling more like himself, he'll be a real nice little dog."

If Benny had been around, she would have said no. In spite of being in this line of work, Benny didn't really like dogs that much. To him, cleaning up other people's dogs was like detailing their cars or mowing their lawns. It didn't mean you were crazy about cars or grass. So of course, he didn't like pro bono work at all. He called it pro boner. He said you get the hard-on but not the satisfaction.

"Give me four days, okay? It's going to take a while

to mellow him out. And Zack, there's no guarantees. He's in pretty sad shape." Benny wouldn't be back for a week, and it would be a distraction and, admit it, a chance to please Zack. So cute. Woof!

"Take the cage back to the office for me, okay? I can't have him up here. And he needs some quiet so he can calm down for me."

Ursula left Beedo alone in the office all day to chill out, going back between groomings to drop a treat between the bars. The first three treats were greeted with frenzied snarls, the next two with suspicious reserve, and after that Ursula found Beedo waiting patiently for the peace offering, his pink tongue looking oddly clean and fresh hanging out of his matted gray face. It looked like there were raisins embedded in the fur around his neck.

After closing, she took him a plate of food and petted him cautiously while he ate, wearing latex gloves to protect herself from whatever lurked in his fur. Then she clipped a leash onto his collar and took him out back for a nice pee and poop. House trained, so that's good. But still skittish, pulling to the end of the leash and keeping a suspicious eye on her. Back in the office, she sprayed the room with air freshener, so that it smelled less like garbage and more like canned flowers. She sprayed the front room as well, in case the miasma of stink was moving that direction.

She put him back in the cage and before going home for the day, sat at the desk and did some of the endless paperwork of running a business, talking to Beedo the whole time. Sometimes it was, "What a good boy, Beedo!" Sometimes it was, "Why would the phone bill be twice as much as last month? Does that make any sense to you?"

Beedo liked being talked to. He liked Ursula's bold, calm voice and the way she said his name. The clicking of computer keys, of ballpoint pens, the sliding of paper on the desk, all sounded like okay people sounds. He liked being included in the circle of calm sound, the light rumble of pack life, the song of family.

The next day, Ursula lugged the cage into the grooming area, but left it behind a low shelf, shielded from the eyes of paying customers who would have been horrified to see this greasy, gray mop of a dog in the same room as their pampered, much-loved pets. After the early birds picked up their clean dogs, sweet-smelling in the middle, still dog-smelling at each end, the drop-offs were brought in and she found a cage for each dog to wait in. Then she ushered them out one at a time and clipped them in so as to have both hands free to work. As she groomed, she kept up the patter, introducing each dog to Beedo solemnly, to amuse herself.

"Tavish my boy, this is Beedo. Don't judge him too

harshly; he's a little down on his luck at the moment. Someone really made a mess out of him. But we're working on it, aren't we, Beed? Beedo, this fellow here is Tavish. As you can plainly see, he's a Bedford terrier. He's kind of dumb, aren't you sweetie? Obviously overfed, but his owner is crazy about him. Blue ribbon, you think? Maybe the gold?"

Ursula always talked to the dogs. She found that it calmed them down and passed the time. Benny said it was silly, they have no idea what you're talking about, and that was true. But then the dogs were always calm with him, relaxing into his sure hands, gazing with adoring eyes at his impassive face, trying to please. He might not have much affection for them, but Benny had a way about him, there was no denying it.

At lunchtime, she took Beedo out again to what was now his pee and poop grounds, and then for a quick walk around the neighborhood, though she wore dark glasses and took a lot of side streets. Beedo was not a dog to be seen in public with, and he smelled as awful as he looked, but he was cheering up a little and his oily rag of a tail wagged with good cheer, simultaneously fanning and polluting the air around him.

By the third day, she judged that he was ready to wash. She saved it for after hours in case the situation turned ugly. He was no longer freaked out, but you never quite knew what you had on your hands. It would help if he had been groomed before and knew the drill. Beedo stood still in the washtub and wagged as the warm water filled it up. He was an old hand. This was a return to normalcy for him.

She had sudsed and rinsed him three times, emptying out the gray water between rinses, before he began to show his true color, a delicate gold. What a revelation. As the filth and oil was washed away, his coat began to curl a little, then a little more. Beedo emerged from the tub after the fourth rinse as a wet apricot poodle, ungroomed, but clean and perky. Ursula wished she had taken pictures, for a before-and-after display to show Benny. Maybe even do a display on the bulletin board. Maybe include a scratch-and-sniff card to demonstrate the full effect.

"You'd be famous, Beedo! The world's dirtiest living dog!"

She dried him, dodging his affectionate but dog-flavored kisses, cleaned out his cage, gave him new bedding, and put him away for the night with a people kiss on his now sanitary head. She would give him a puppy cut in the morning since that wouldn't require using a razor on his face, which might be too traumatic. Then she could give Zack the cherub baby-doll a call to come get him—the new Ursula-improved Beedo. Someone was going to love this puppy.

Ursula hadn't known how Beedo had become so messed up, and she didn't know what was up with Tina. She decided to talk like she had to Beedo and let the river of her chatter flow around Tina, asking nothing in return. No more hairnet questions. She liked having someone to talk to while she worked anyway. It passed the time.

After a while, Tina lost her alertness for trouble brewing, her hyper-awareness of the possible implications of whatever Ursula was talking about. She quit listening, letting the talk be like the splashing of the river and the talk of birds in the treetops. And by the end of the day, Tina had come to a decision, actually first a realization and then a decision. She turned to Ursula and looked at her. It was time to get real, to take the chance.

"I don't really mind hairnets," she said. "I don't usually know what to do with my crazy hair anyway." It was true. Ursula nodded. It was a start.

The next day was much easier. Ursula worked comfortably in the kitchen, a bit slower than Bill, not aiming for the well-oiled efficiency that seemed to be Bill's goal; she wanted company. Pete was sent out to wait on people, Tina kept in the kitchen to prep and clean up. She had never had so much conversation, a running commentary on the food preparation, the customers, Foster, whatever took Ursula's busy interest at the moment. She found herself filling in an occasional silence herself, and sometimes just letting the silence get comfortable. It was surprising to pass the day with a woman no one had ever told to shut up or hit for talking too much.

Pete spent the first few days after Bill left fishing the river, catching almost nothing, releasing the few little trout that were naive enough to bite, thinking as he slid them back into the water that by the time they were big enough to keep, they would know enough to avoid getting caught. It seemed kind of self-defeating. He was glad when he found Tina's note saying that Melody, an ex-girlfriend, had called. Pete called her back right away, and it seemed that her most recent ex-love interest was kicking up rough. She wanted Pete to come stay with her for a while.

"You don't have to do anything," she said. "Just be here." That sounded like the kind of thing Pete could do. He was anxious to leave, but first he had to make sure Ursula was warned about Tina.

He found the two women in the office trying to balance the bank statement against the check register. Off by exactly $81.00, divisible by nine, so it seemed Bill had transposed some numbers.

"Hey Ursula," he said, and she replied "Hey Pete,"

without looking up. It was going to be hard to get her attention or get her alone for a private talk, but it seemed like his duty before he went to Melody's.

"Can I talk to you?"

"What costs exactly nine dollars?" Ursula asked. "Or ninety?"

"Ursula, I have to take off for a while. Friend of mine. Are you good here?"

"Sure. Not much going on anyway."

"Can you kind of...you know, look after things? Like, be sure everything's okay?"

"We're good." Finally Ursula looked up so Pete could give a nod towards Tina where she was bent over the books.

"Watch out for..." He gave Ursula a wink. "We don't want any trouble. Just keep an eye out." And again he nodded in Tina's direction with a meaningful look.

"Of course," Ursula said. "I'll take care of everything. No problem. You just have a safe trip, okay?" And then turning to Tina, "Okay, it's in the outstanding checks. That's us, not Bill. Kind of disappointing."

So Pete was able to drive away, counting on Ursula to keep an eye on Tina, prevent her from stealing, maybe even kick her off the place. For her part, Ursula was touched that Pete was counting on her to watch over Tina, help her get used to the routines and rhythms of the Happy Trout. Tina wondered if he would come back sometime.

"Why'd Pete leave?" Tina asked that evening, chopping onions for chili and sniffling slightly. "He didn't even tell me good-bye."

"He's likely to take off sometimes. That's Pete."

"Where does he go?" Tina couldn't picture him anywhere but at the Happy Trout.

"He's got friends and family all over Nevada and Utah, but I think it's mostly old girlfriends he visits, really. He seems to have quite a few of those."

"Melody," Tina said. "I took the message."

"Whoa! He'll have his hands full."

"When will he come back?" Tina asked. She wondered momentarily if she would see Brad again. And that reminded her of the bank money, which seemed hazy now, like something on an old list that hadn't happened after all, something left behind.

"He'll be back when he's ready. Pete's not what you would call reliable as a worker, but he's an old buddy of Bill's and he likes to fish, so Bill puts up with him. Not to change the subject, but how come Bill's so put out with you?"

"Bill? We got off to a bad start is all."

"What, he made a pass at you and you turned him down?"

"Something like that." Tina wasn't about to go into

it. It was too complicated anyway. And the memory still rankled.

"He said you'd be moving on pretty soon, is that right?"

"I'm saving up money to go." Tina had $832 saved up so far. It was costing a lot to replace her stuff, more than she had anticipated. She kept running into expenses, a flea collar for Foster, a warm nightshirt that wasn't red satin, shoes she could work in, warm socks, underwear, jeans, bone meal for the roses.

"What's he paying you, if you don't mind my asking?"

"I get $60 out of the cash drawer every morning."

"You're not on the books? Good Lord, even Pete's on the books."

"Well, I'm not. He thinks every day is my last. And I don't have a social security number anyway. Don't tell him that, okay?"

Ursula turned and stared. "How do you get by without a social security number? I thought you had to have one of those to breathe."

"If I have to fill out a form, I just make one up. They usually have little boxes so you know how many numbers you need. And I lost my ID—this guy I was camping with took off with my purse and everything. So even if I had a card before, it would be gone now."

"Men." Ursula broke off to move around to the café

side and pour some coffee for a group of old fishermen who had given up for the day and were taking turns complaining about the cussedness of fish. "Better luck next time, fellas," she said. "There's some fish it's hard to be smarter than." She left them to think that one through.

Ursula was willing to close up the café early one afternoon to go into nearby Pineville and get some business and some shopping done. Tina went with her and spent more of her money on additional underwear, another pair of jeans, tough ones this time, and a rhinestone-studded hair clip to keep the hair out of her eyes when she wasn't wearing a hairnet. She bought flower-scented shampoo and cream rinse and a hairbrush and deodorant. Lip gloss. She was tired of being scruffy. And she'd earn the money back. It was just a matter of time. She didn't want to stink up Bill's bedroom. She planned to look well groomed and normal when he got back.

She took the liberty of straightening up, organizing, cleaning, and then re-organizing the Happy Trout Fishing Resort office with Ursula's admiring approval. Ursula said she wouldn't know where to start. Tina repaired the filing cabinet so that files would stand up straight and slide instead of slumping into a tired, stubborn stack in the drawer, trying to crawl under each other like a pair of oversized flip-flops. She wiped everything down, moved the spare plumbing parts into the no-man's-land of the storage shed out back, and made a nice set of hand-written labels for the folders, though her titles were affected by her lack of business experience. There were files labeled "phone," and "repairs," true, but there were others labeled "old stuff" and "don't know."

Tina found a second phone under a pile of papers and a phone jack in the kitchen to plug it into. She moved phone and appointment book onto a small counter space in the kitchen, which she and Ursula had cleared out, cleaned, and organized to suit themselves. It would make it easier to book customers once the customers started calling again. "Happy Trout!"

"Bill's gonna kill us when he gets back. But it's worth it, isn't it?" Ursula liked the wholehearted way Tina worked, and she had always done some tidying up herself while Bill was gone. But this was beyond tidying. It was right next door to transformation.

Business was always slow after Labor Day, so there was plenty of time on their hands. Sometimes they only had a few customers or none at all camping at the Happy Trout. So Tina learned how to short-order cook, how to do the books, how to knit, how to clean fish, which for some reason made her blush. She was often left to count the cash drawer if there had been any business, and close out for the day so that

Ursula could get her line in the water before the light faded entirely. Tina liked having the place to herself sometimes, as though it were hers instead of an uneasy resting place on loan from the fates. It was like playing house.

Tina would finish up at the café, close up, and then go down to the river followed by the newly accessorized Foster to sit on a log and watch and think and not think. The long evenings were cool and she needed Brad's hoodie zipped all the way up to let her stay the whole time. The same trees, the same river, the whispering and gurgling of the water, the singing of Ursula's reel, the bright rocks under the ripples, the reeds that clicked together when the breeze moved them, the giant trunks that stood and the slender ones that swayed and then stood unmoving, the deep carpet of pine needles, the speckled gray boulders standing halfway in the river, the last purple wildflowers, Foster in her lap, Tina felt as unafraid as she could remember having been. The birds sang out a few last times before settling in for the night's rest. It made her think. It made her want to do things.

"We could have a take-out window and picnic tables outside with little yellow shade umbrellas. We could use plastic baskets for burgers and fries. We should have a really cute sign on the highway. One you can see. Maybe a picture of a really, really happy trout.

The one that's out there looks like he's on downers. I could do that before Bill gets back if we can find some paint somewhere. He'll be surprised."

Ursula listened with half an ear and fished silently and let the river flow. This is what she had come to the Happy Trout for even as a child when she and Aunt Delia had stood on the bank together, casting, their silence contented and complete. The river carried her thoughts away wordlessly.

Sometimes Tina went to Bill's room and sat for a moment on the sleeping bag she had conscientiously spread over his tacky red plaid bedspread, looking around, just looking, not opening anything. She didn't want to invade his privacy—she just needed a safe place to sleep where no one would bother her. He didn't have to ever know. She could get moved back into the camper as soon as he got back. Foster would sometimes watch her from the nightstand, sometimes from the foot of the bed, sometimes would sleep on Bill's pillow, leaving a circle of black cat hair where his warm body had been pressed, so that she had to turn it over for her own sleep. She had rearranged a few things, made more room by moving the clothes hamper into the closet, standing for a moment in the doorway, leaning into the forest of shirts and pants and suits she couldn't imagine him wearing, running her hands along the hangers, letting the fabric caress her cheek, breathing deep. She didn't miss Bill. He seemed more like he belonged to her in his absence.

She missed Pete a little, though, and his smart-ass jokes, but it seemed safer with him gone, since Ursula seemed to like her, not knowing what kind of girl she was, not treating her like a tramp. Tina was breathing a freer air than she was used to, and it filled her lungs with a satisfying lightness. She was off the hook, she was no longer up for grabs, she was in the flow, and she belonged to herself and the Happy Trout, at least for the moment, at least until Bill got back. Then she would have to see.

8

Sometimes you're Demeter, sometimes Persephone, sometimes both.

— *Anonymous*

ONE WARM SUNDAY EVENING, when the last camper had driven down the road and over the bridge, leaving the Happy Trout to itself, Ursula turned the radio to a station that played hits from the 80s and 90s to entertain them while they gave the dining area floor a good cleaning. They up-ended the tables on the counters, piled chairs in the booths and cleared the floor, starting out with a strong intent to do some serious mopping, but the music made them dance, dance, dance. Ursula's dancing style was a relaxed, swooping, side-to-side, hand-clapping move to the music, and Tina's was just plain crazy. When "Funky Love" crashed its way to a commercial break, they stopped, laughing and patting each other on the shoulders—you go, girl. Hip bump. High five. Ursula wiggled her way towards the radio to turn it down. No way to dance to a commercial. So she didn't see what Tina saw, not at first.

Glancing up, Tina was startled to see a frail, dark-haired teenager standing in the open doorway, her eyes bleak and big with trouble, her lips and eyelids black with paint. She drew a quick breath, the apparition was so unexpected, like suddenly noticing that a fox has been watching you, like realizing that you have entered a dream. She might have been a vision or a visitation. Ursula turned back at the faint sound made by Tina's surprise.

The girl's little frame was barely covered by a black T-shirt with the sleeves ripped off and the word "Bitch" in pink sequins across the chest, and her skinny middle was decorated with a belly-button ring. She teetered on black platforms, five-inch stiletto heels decorated with metal studs, her pale little legs rising up like flower stems out of a manhole cover.

"You can't work here, baby," Tina said. "The man here is real uptight." She looked like she could make some serious money, especially with the guys who have it for little girls. The black stuff was probably a mistake. There can't be that many guys looking for straight sex with a baby vampire. They would probably want to hurt her pretty bad. "We can give you some soup or something, but you can't sell it here. Better in Nevada."

"Where's my daddy?" the waif bleated. "What have

you done with my dad?" Then when she saw Ursula, she cried out and ran to be folded into a big hug.

Tina saw with a start that the girl had let a Hello Kitty backpack slide off of her skinny shoulder onto the floor, and for a moment she felt the room swim, as though the money was coming back, as though Brad had returned, like a dream, like a dead future coming back to tease her. This must be what people meant when they said they felt like they were losing their minds. It took her a moment to focus again.

"Rachel, honey, what are you doing here? Your dad's on his vacation. He's in Oregon for another two weeks. What are you doing here?"

Tina sat down on a twirly lunch counter seat and swiveled gently back and forth while she waited to see how it would play out. Not a hooker, then. Just Bill's tricked out daughter.

"I can't stand it at my mom's anymore. It's like being in prison." The girl's sudden tears made soot marks down her little cheeks.

"So you broke out?" Tina had to ask, fascinated with this unexpected arrival. "You ran away?"

"Who are you? Are you my dad's new girlfriend or something?"

"I'm Tina. I work here. Did you run away?"

"What if I did? It's none of your 'fucking' business."

Tina smiled at the careful way Rachel had cussed

at her. "You're a funny girl. Do you like to dance at all?"

"I don't dance. It's against my religion."

Tina laughed and left Ursula to gently scold Rachel and draw her into the café to sit at the counter, where Tina had cleared a space, offering to make her a hot chocolate, an offer which Rachel accepted with a nod and a sniffle.

"Anything else you'd like? The kitchen is a little bare right now."

"No, thank you. Are you my dad's girlfriend?"

"I said, I work here. So, no. I'm not his girlfriend."

"Aunt Ursula, I know what you're going to say, but I'm not calling my mom. She'll just yell at me and make me go back to stupid Hayward. I know, but it's totally stupid. She'll send her icky boyfriend Clive to come get me and I hate him. He has a big stupid mouth and a big stupid nose and he laughs at me. Clunky Clive. I want to stay with my dad."

"Anything else you're avoiding, sweetheart?" Ursula's voice was sweet and persuasive. She was gazing out the window, avoiding the accusing stare she might have leveled at Rachel had she looked at her. "A term paper, maybe? Mean teacher? Piano lessons? What is it, Rache? What's going on?"

Rachel blew her nose into a napkin she had pulled from the holder. "They grounded me because I got a D in math. That's not such a big deal—all my friends got

Ds or Fs. Everybody knows math is way too hard. And now I can't go to the mall or spend time with Carlin, who's my best friend and she's leaving tomorrow to go to Hollywood with her family and they won't let me go with her. To Hollywood! Ohmygod, it's so mean."

"I'm sorry, Rachel. You can't hide out here. We have to call your mom and tell her you're safe. Otherwise she'll have the police and the FBI and who knows what out looking for you. You have to get back to school. You know that's true."

Negotiations went on for a few more minutes, with a frightened Rachel still somewhat impressed by the enormity of what she had done, defensive about her reasons, and emboldened by the justice of her cause. Hollywood! Her debating style was greatly hampered by her inability to run to her room and slam the door, not having a room here, no door. Ursula was imperturbable, reasonable, and persistent, and Tina looked on from her first-row seat. She could see Bill's dark eyes in Rachel, and a delicate version of his nose.

"Who gave you the ride?" Tina asked, knowing someone like Freddy would have been glad to pick her up, but would never have let her out of the car. She was just too marketable.

"Some people. They were nice, like old hippies. They played Grateful Dead all the way. But, Aunt Ursula," Rachel's face grew solemn. "They gave me drugs."

"So you're high now?" Tina felt like this was her area of expertise. "How high? What was it?"

"I didn't smoke it! I said I would save it for later. And there was so much smoke in the car, it was kind of weird anyway." Rachel pulled a fat joint out of her much-bangled black purse and showed it to Tina, who was more than interested, but held back.

"I'll take that," Ursula said. "I think you were lucky this time, Toots. Don't do it again, okay?"

Tina was impressed that Rachel's mother would be looking for her, that Rachel wouldn't be threatened or given real black eyes by anyone, and mostly that Rachel had two places where she was loved enough to stay.

After a bit of protesting and more tears, Rachel made the inevitable phone call, and with Ursula coaching her in the background, arrived at an agreement with her mom: that she could stay for two weeks under Ursula's jurisdiction; that she would use this trip for her Enrichment Project for school, where she was evidently allowed to take random vacations as long as they were "school-related"; that she would help with the work in the kitchen; that her mother and the icky boyfriend Clive would drive up to get her at the end of her visit; that she would never ever do such a thing ever again. All of this, and the promise that she could spend Christmas break at the Happy Trout instead of going to meet Clive's family, a tearful "love you" and "goodbye." Tina had already put the tables and chairs back where they belonged and emptied the mop buckets and put them away while Ursula and Rachel negotiated. Then it was hugs all around, even a cautious wisp of a hug for Tina, and they called it a night, setting up a spot for Rachel to sleep in the back storeroom, cocooned in the pink sleeping bag Tina found for her, surrounded by outsized cans of tomatoes and tomato sauce, the ketchup bottles like sentinels in militant red.

Rachel slept until noon in her storeroom boudoir, emerging cranky and touchy until she had been given hot chocolate and toast. Although she had a tendency to sulk, she was also quick and biddable in the kitchen when her feelings were unruffled. Ursula enjoyed the increase in company, and both Ursula and Tina babied Rachel, calling her pet names, Princess R, Lady Thing, Little Rache, Miss Hotty, and letting her have her way about almost everything. She liked Tina in spite of an inclination to be jealous of this new woman in her dad's life, and she admired Tina's offhand style. Tina taught her how to jitterbug. It's not really dancing.

Rachel taught them both how to play crazy eights, though she said it was really a game for babies. Whenever she was pouting and refused to play, Tina would moonwalk over to her and mutter in an imaginary foreign accent, "Hey babbee! You vant to blay the crezzy ets?" and make her laugh. They all three flirted with the customers, Ursula humorously, Rachel cutely, and Tina very carefully, just to be in the game but not to get in trouble, and they laughed about their shamelessness in the kitchen. Given the average age of the few regulars who fished after Labor Day, it wasn't going anywhere. In the evenings, they made piecrust or soup and talked, sometimes about the Happy Trout, about Bill, about movies, about Foster. And blayed crezzy ets whenever there was a break.

"Why did Bill name Foster after your uncle?"

"Uncle Foster was quite a character, pretty cranky, like Foster-the-cat is sometimes. Also, he's the one who left us the resort, fifty-fifty. So Bill runs it and keeps it going, and I hope I can come up here all the time once we sell the dog-grooming business. Which I hope is soon. I've really seen the back end of far too many poodles."

Tina was thoughtful; it was a line of work she had never considered.

"Why was Uncle Foster so cranky?"

"I don't know. I don't know if his bad marriage made him cranky or if his crankiness made his marriage bad. But he and Aunt Delia used to kick up quite a ruckus. She always wanted to move to San Francisco and open an antique store. Don't ask me why. He was dead set on staying up here with as few people to bother him as possible. Which as you can imagine wasn't that good for business."

"What happened?"

"Oh," Ursula said, "just what you'd think. She moved to San Francisco taking a big chunk of the money, maybe without telling him. It didn't work out, and then she moved back and they fought some more. Then she died, and Uncle Foster was never the same after that. Without Delia to fight with, he kind of faded away."

"Was Foster their cat?"

"No, this was long before Foster, I mean Foster-the-cat, showed up."

"How did he get here?"

Ursula was French-braiding Rachel's dark, thick hair, making two neat rows along the top of her head, down the back, presumably to end with braids that would continue down her slender white neck. "Foster-the-cat got thrown out of a car on the highway and found his way here."

"Why would someone throw him out of a car? What did he do?" Tina scooped him up and held him against her shoulder. "Why would they do that? He could have been killed."

"Evidently they wanted to get rid of him, so they drove out of town a ways so he couldn't find his way home and tossed him out. He had a broken rib or two, and that's where he got that chipped tooth." Ursula patted Rachel's head. "All done, precious. You look wonderful."

Tina, who had witnessed a guy being thrown out of a speeding car, knew how hard that had been for Freddy's guys to accomplish, how he had clawed at their faces and grabbed at the air so hard it should have solidified for him, how loud he had screamed, the sound dying away as the car drove on. She shouldn't have been in the car with them—but she had begged for a ride to the hair salon, and on the way they had spotted Ricky Dick Rivera, such an idiot to steal from Freddy, Ricky Dick walking along the sidewalk as if he hadn't pissed Freddy off so bad that his life was already over. She knew Ricky died, not then, but at the hospital, because she was sent to find out, and the nurse there shook her head and said, "Sorry, he didn't make it." So she knew what it was like, and she promised Foster to take care of him forever, not to let him get hurt again. She lifted him off her shoulder and tried to cradle him like a baby, but he wriggled free.

"How long has Bill lived here?" Tina wanted to ask everything about Bill, but she didn't want to seem like she was prying.

"I guess that's partly Rachel's story, really. He and Barbara broke up when Rachel was eight."

"My mom decided she didn't love my dad. I think

that's so lame, like you can just decide, like whether you want a mocha or a latte today. And he let her decide that because he just liked things like they were; he wouldn't fight. She would start yelling at him, usually about money, and he would just leave the house. And then he left the house and came up here. And my mom was all into doing real estate and going to stupid parties and doing stupid aerobics. I really hate my mom. I mean, I love her because she's my mom, but I really hate her. Can I say that?" Rachel checked Ursula's face.

"If that's what you feel, you can say it. Free country, and nobody listening but us chicks. I didn't get along with my mom either when I was fifteen. I think it's pretty common to feel that way. I surely do miss her now."

"Did you hate your mom, Tina?"

Tina was silent for long enough that it reminded Ursula of the hairnet incident. Something had gone wrong.

Tina sometimes had daydreams about a mom, like a really nice nun without the outfit, just a few kids instead of a dormitory-full, maybe she would be the only one, the only one to take care of. And she sometimes imagined herself as a baby, held close in a brown woman's arms, and there would be singing, she thought, and safety.

"I don't have a mom, actually."

"No, I mean when you were my age, when you were fifteen."

"I didn't have a mom then either. I never knew my mom. I guess I had one, but I never knew her."

Rachel's eyes grew big with concern and even teared up a little.

"You never even saw her, not once?"

"Maybe when I was a little baby I must have seen her. But I was too little to remember it. I don't know anything about her."

"You're an orphan," Rachel said. "That's so cool. Don't cry, Tina You could be in a book! And you could do whatever you want!"

Tina hadn't been about to cry, but being told not to made her tear up. She needed to change the subject. "And your dad? Do you hate your dad?"

"No, of course not," Rachel said. "He's my dad." And then, "I'm bored. Can we make taffy again?"

And they did whatever she wanted, because she was Baby Rache, the Princess R, and a force to be reckoned with, a young woman coming up. Tina rolled the word "orphan" around in her mind for a while, seeing where it fit into the pattern, how the pictures changed, where it opened doors, what tender spots it revealed and soothed.

Sometimes the evening conversations turned to

the matter of men, of sex, of kissing. Tina was mostly quiet, wanting to see what was okay in this world and wanting to conceal what went on and what she had done in the world she had left behind.

The three women were gathered in Ursula's trailer, where they sometimes liked to finish the day, making tea, making plans for tomorrow. It got too cool on the porch now once the sun had gone down, and they had spent all day in the café. Ursula had finished fishing. All the work was done. Sometimes they scattered. Sometimes they drew together.

"Aunt Ursula, why don't you and Benny get married? My mom says you're living in sin."

"So is she, right? Are she and Clive married?"

"They're engaged, so it's okay. He bought her a great big diamond ring, which she waves around all the time, just showing off. I hate it when she does stuff like that."

"Maybe she likes the sparkles," Tina said. Lalo had given her a bracelet once that had sparkling stones in it. Not diamonds, but close. She had loved to watch it in sunlight, candlelight, strobe lights. Then it got lost, probably lifted by someone. Maybe borrowed by Monika and not returned. That's how things get lost.

"Well, I sometimes want to marry Benny, but I feel like I don't know how, and that sounds weird, but it's a fact. I sort of get the Navajo part of him. I almost get the Puerto Rican side. But then he's Catholic, which I don't get, and he's from New York, which I totally don't get. I don't know how I can love somebody I couldn't have imagined. Sometimes I think of him as my significant incredibly other. Or my incredibly significant other. Depends on the day."

"Mr. Turetti says you have to take down the wall of difference one brick at a time. That's in social studies."

"There are some bricks you can't take down, though. They just won't budge. What does Mr. Turetti of social studies say about that?"

"Mr. Turetti has a black belt in karate, at least that's what everybody says." Rachel screwed up her face, trying to remember. It's hard to remember stuff they say in school. "He says if you can't move one brick, you look for one you can move and move that one."

"Maybe I should marry Mr. Turetti," Ursula said. "He sounds good."

"I love Benny," Rachel said. "Not like that, but he makes a really good uncle. He never tells me what to do. He's nice to be around. Do you love him, Aunt Ursula?"

"I do, I do. Love is not the problem, sweetie. That's the easy part. I mean, your mom and dad were in love in the beginning, right? Things just happen."

Rachel nodded her head wisely. She knew things could just happen. They had just happened to her. And now she had her dad up here and her mom down there with a new boyfriend, which was so embarrassing.

Tina listened, feeling like an insignificant other. She and Monika had never talked about love, just sometimes about what different guys seemed to like. She thought of a brick wall as something to climb over on the way to someplace else. She wished she had Mr. Turetti in school instead of nuns.

"Have you ever been married, Tina?" Tina shook her head no, but also in amazement that Ursula would ask. She felt flattered anyone would think that. Marriage was for the movies. For people who lived in the imaginary Ohio she used to think about. Not for tramps, like Pete had called her on her first day. Not for girls like Tina.

Rachel was in a talking mood. She liked that she could say things and not get worried looks like her mom always gave her. She liked having grown-ups paying attention to what she said, but not freaking out about it.

"I like most of the guys, but mostly I like kissing and I like when they make me laugh. That's what I like best."

"Me, too," Ursula said. "I like when they make me laugh, or when I make them laugh. And I do like kissing."

"Aunt Ursula! You're not…you're…."

"I may be older than you, peaches, but I'm not dead yet. I'm not even forty, quite. It's kissing I miss when Benny's not around. Sometimes I think I ought to marry him just for the regular kissing." Ursula shook her head, as if to clear it. "I remember when I was a very young woman lying in bed, never had a boyfriend, not a real one, kissing the inside of my wrist to see what it would feel like." Ursula lifted her heavy braid and let the evening air, seeping through the window, cool the back of her neck. "I may start that up again soon, now that I think of it."

"Aunt Ursula! I can't believe you said that!"

"My mouth, my wrist. I'd go a lot further than that, but I think if I say any more your mom will kill me. She already thinks I'm a bad influence. What about hugs? We all like hugs?"

Tina couldn't remember anyone who had hugged her except Sister Mary Helen. And now Ursula and Rachel. She and Monika should have hugged more, if they had known, not to make a show for a trick or for Freddy, but to feel good. She thought she would like a guy who made her laugh, who hugged.

Ursula yawned. "Well, I'll send you two on your way. I'm ready for bed. Night, Tina. You go too, poppet. Sleep in beauty."

Tina lay in Bill's bed that night and she thought about Monika and their times together, laughing, trying on each other's clothes, calling each other "Sister" and "Sister Girl." They thought of themselves as vanilla and chocolate twins, Monika tall, blonde, and pale enough, but Tina really more butterscotch than chocolate. Then one Friday night when the usual poker game was going on, Freddy's luck was running bad even with some careful play by his guys. Maybe he saw something on Monika's face he didn't like. Maybe her face was the first target that met his eyes. He lunged at her, slammed her against the wall, and then pushed her towards Geron.

"Put her on the street," was all he said, and Monika and Geron were gone. Freddy settled back down into his seat at the table, where T-Wah had redistributed the chips so that Freddy was still in the game. Tina held still and forced her face into a calm mask, blending into the background to avoid Freddy's treacherous attention. Tina had only seen Monika a few times since posing in the neon lights with the other whores while johns eyed them from the safety of their cars, Monika reduced from the laughing party girl she had first known to the burned-out stick of a woman at Freddy's party. Tina knew it was what Freddy, what Freddy's kind of life, did to women. It was what he had wanted to do to her.

She thought about Rachel, so young and unbroken, about Ursula, about Foster, who had gone out for the night, and then about Bill, the Bill who had loved Rachel's mom and loved Rachel and been hurt, thrown out of his life, landing here at the Happy Trout. She wondered if he had clung as hard to his old life as Ricky Dick had done, if he had tried to attach himself to empty air to avoid the crushing impact of the inevitable fall. She wondered how much he still thought about Rachel's mom. Barbara. She wondered if he was thinking about the Happy Trout, about Tina at all, or if he was just fishing, blank-minded and remote. Or if he had gone somewhere like Ursula said and was with a woman. Having fun, Ursula had said.

She went to the closet in the dark and pulled one of Bill's jackets off the hanger, lying down again with it in her arms, like holding the shell of a lover who had melted away, and she tasted the inside of her wrist, and then she gave herself the quiet pleasure of a good orgasm. She dreamed about the bear again, this time asleep curled up in the bathtub, like a black pudding, like a puddle of tar. In her dream, she watched the rise and fall of his breath and smelled his dusty fur; she wanted to touch him.

In the mornings while Rachel was still sleeping, after the breakfast rush, which at this time of year might be five customers wanting coffee and pancakes or the new sesame waffles Tina had added as an experiment, Ursula would look through the paper and read aloud anything of interest—scandals, oddities, human interest. Like, listen to this:

Bank Robber Hailed as Mother of God

Sacramento, CA — Local authorities are puzzled by a recent cult arising from an unsolved robbery at a Sacramento area bank. The female robber is being hailed as the Virgin Mary for her 911 call on behalf of bank customer Manny Aguirre, 79, who had a heart attack during the heist.

According to Aguirre, the Virgin appeared as the answer to his prayer. He credits her touching his chest with his swift recovery.A shrine to "La Santa Ladrona" has been set up in front of the Aguirre residence where it has been visited by scores of adherents from Southern California, Nevada, Oregon, and Mexico.

Luis Aguirre, Manny Aguirre's oldest son tells reporters, "We are asking the bank to let us put a shrine in the lobby to commemorate her, but so far they haven't answered our calls." More than fifty members of Aguirre's extended family are involved in this new sect, petitioning the Vatican to recognize the miracle of La Virgin Maria Bandida.

> Local Catholic priest Father Donovan is dubious. "Of course, we join the family in celebrating Mr. Aguirre's recovery and are grateful to the robber for the emergency call. But there's no way the Virgin Mary robs banks."
>
> Aguirre, a lifetime Catholic, disagrees. "You can be sure the Mother of God has her reasons."

This particular article made Tina laugh until she cried. She had been called so many things, named so many names, but Mother of God was a first. She finally had to take the trash out so that she could quit laughing. She tore out the story later and tucked it under the mattress in Bill's room for safekeeping. She wished she could show it to Sister Mary Helen. She wished she could show it to Sister Angela, watch her face turn red.

Saturday night, Rachel's last night, after a quick supper, the three women drifted apart, Rachel to her little storeroom hideaway to polish her nails, which were chipped from all the work she had inadvertently done, Tina to the front porch where she sat with Foster on her lap, her chin resting on his furry head, rubbing against his velvet ears, Ursula down to fish alone, the best way there is to fish for trout. But at that time when the certain light begins to fail and the crickets pick up the rhythm of the day, Rachel, her hands with newly blackened fingernails held out stiffly in front of her like a sleepwalker in the movies, joined Tina on the porch, draping herself like an expensive woman's mink across the arms of the wooden chair next to her. Foster jumped down to go bug hunting in the weeds by the drive, and then Tina and Rachel walked down to the river to watch Ursula fish and to think night-time thoughts with her, Ursula's circular, sexual, and amusing, Tina's wistful, and Rachel's shaped by that bewildering mix of child and woman that sometimes made her cry, sometimes laugh, on this occasion, just sit there on the cold stone and let her feelings swirl. No one was watching, not even in her imagination. When the darkness and the mosquitoes drove them in, they parted quietly, in peace, with hugs all around.

On the last Sunday, they came to take Rachel away in a black Escalade much like Freddy's. Tina took an instant dislike to Barbara, Rachel's tight-lipped mom, the woman who had thrown Bill away. She was attractive, but too skinny for most guys who buy sex and not enough tits. She was tan, dressed like a Macy's cosmetics saleslady in black pants and sweater with a chunky necklace like a row of ice cubes and a matching bracelet around her stringy wrist. Her long nails were a reddish purple shade, and her long hands were decorated with that ring Rachel had talked about. It sparkled beautifully in the sunlight. She seemed so edgy, so twitchy, so angry, a guy less refined than Clive would probably have backhanded her if only to break the tension.

Tina thought that Clive would be a friendly, straight-sex trick, the kind who likes to pretend to have a girlfriend, probably too naive to go with whores like Freddy's. He would end up getting rolled for sure. He would need to pay big bucks for something more up-town. She was prepared to dislike him, too, but he really seemed pretty nice, a little soft in the tummy, but funny and relaxed. He had an air of kindness and a British accent. He didn't fuss, but he cast a quick, assessing look at Rachel, as if to be sure that she had survived her adventure without any undue mishaps. Tina found it reassuring; Rachel would be okay.

Barbara was surreptitiously curious about Tina, glancing at her sideways from time to time. She must be a new girlfriend. Could she be objected to as a bad influence on Rachel? *Was* she a bad influence? She knew that as soon as the car rolled away, in spite of her better judgment, she would be asking Rachel about Tina and that Rachel wouldn't answer because she never did. She would just roll her eyes and flounce and keep her secrets. But what could Bill see in this woman? Not white, certainly, but not exactly black, not completely Asian or Native American, just a weird mix that came out like that, like this Tina, like a mess.

Of course, Ursula wouldn't see anything wrong with a mongrel like Tina. She's the one who was living with that Mexican dog groomer, washing other people's dogs for pesos. And here, her estimation of the dog-grooming business and Benny's would have been in strange congruence. She turned away to see an amused, pleased expression pass over Clive's face and saw that he was looking at Tina, who was looking at him as though on the verge of telling his fortune. Clive was thinking that Tina was cute as a button. Good for Bill, taking a walk on the wild side. Pretty skin, he thought. Pretty mouth. Inviting.

Barbara decided with a twitch that they should leave now. They had a long drive ahead of them.

As they pulled out of the driveway at last, Rachel having distributed one last round of hugs, gone from view over the culvert bridge and onto the highway, Ursula turned to Tina and pulled Rachel's hippy joint out of her pocket.

"Just us big girls now," she said, and she waggled the joint invitingly. "No Baby R. Let's us dance."

9

Guns don't kill people all by themselves. People kill people and guns are the handiest way to do it.

—Anonymous

BILL RETURNED FROM HIS Oregon vacation looking less than refreshed. True, he had caught fish; he had camped. But the camper was no longer his; he had let Tina in and there was no getting her out. For the whole time he was gone, he had been bothered by the inescapable mango/oatmeal/smoky scent of Tina's skin. He had stopped at a launderette in Eureka to wash the blankets. He had vacuumed the camper the next day in Bend. At a truck stop in Sisters, he had resorted to an air freshener shaped like a strawberry that dangled from his rearview mirror, but he had to throw it out at a rest stop 75 miles along the way, its cloying synthetic smell next to unbearable. Nothing had stopped the tickling memories aroused by the smell with which Tina had evidently infused the camper. Tina brushing past him, reaching over him to get a plate, the scent of Tina's hair as she gathered it up into a hairnet, her little face made more vulnerable by its absence, her golden brown arm with its four pink stripes where the bear had left its mark. He remembered the silky soft feel of her arm as he had bandaged her. He was driving himself crazy.

He resented the hard-on he had every night as he tried to sleep or think about fishing, or at least not have a hard-on. When that proved impossible, he made it a point to think about other women, pale, Nordic, large-breasted, small-mouthed women, as he pushed into his hand. It was a long trip. He persevered. It was his vacation, the same one he had taken for seven years, and he took it again, like a pill.

He had wondered for the last two days, more and more, if Tina would have moved on. He wondered if Ursula had seen her for what she was and chased her away. He wondered if she had slept with Pete while he was gone, or given Pete the blowjob of a lifetime like she had offered to him when she first showed up. He wondered about that blowjob. He wondered if Tina would still be there when he got back. He wondered how she would look when she saw him again. He wondered what she would say, if she would try to sweet-talk him into letting her stay, not that her talk was usually all that sweet; it was mostly her face.

He wanted to hear that she had contacted someone

who was coming to pick her up. No, that's not what he wanted, it was what he wanted to want. What he really wanted was to see her welcoming smile and know she had missed him, had thought about him too, maybe even in the same way. He wanted her to say, "Welcome home."

Tina was thinking about Bill, what he had done on his vacation, if he'd got laid as Ursula had suggested, if he would be glad to see her, if she would be glad to see him. Would he notice all the hard work she and Ursula had done? Would he smell the weed? She hoped not. Would he smile, maybe give her a pat, like Foster, or a hug, like Ursula? Would he be happy with the new sign she and Ursula had painted?

When she heard his truck, she ran out the door, scooping up Foster on her way. She thought he would be glad to see Foster, anyway, and she was feeling shy, like she needed a cat to hide behind.

"Look, Foster, Daddy's home," Tina said from the back porch where she held Foster in one arm and used her other hand to wave his paw in Bill's direction. "Say hi to Daddy!"

"I am not, by any stretch of the imagination, that cat's daddy." Bill tried to shoot Tina a mean look, although he thought she and Foster looked pretty cute.

Tina felt like a fool. She had thought he would laugh. She buried her face in Foster's neck. "I wasn't talking to you," she said. "I was talking to Foster."

Bill whipped past her. "Ursula!" he bellowed, though his bellow lacked the timbre of real anger. It sounded more like a bull stuck in a quagmire. "Where the hell is Pete? What did you do to the kitchen? Why is she still here? What's that sign out there supposed to be?"

Ursula emerged calmly from the storeroom where she had been restacking the paper goods. "You're in a state, you are," she said. "Tina works here. Pete left. I cleaned the kitchen, like I do every year. New sign. I think that's all. Welcome home."

As he laid the suitcase on his bed, Bill immediately noticed the traces of Foster and Tina's presence in his bedroom and it only added to his fever of irritation. She was a thorn in his side, he thought, a perpetual itch, a constant source of trouble and annoyance. She had to go. Surely she would go now that he was back. Maybe Ursula would give her a ride to the Bay Area when she went home. She would have to leave when Rachel came. They would never get along. If Pete had been sleeping with her, she would have left with him. She had probably given herself a raise in his absence, knowing her, and added crepes Suzettes to the menu. What a…what a… he tried to curse her but couldn't find the right words.

Tina hadn't stayed to listen to Bill complain and

get her feelings hurt even worse. She went down and sat on her rock by the river and watched the flicker of sunlight on the moving water. She was disappointed at heart; she had wanted a sign that Bill wanted her there, but what she felt was good and pissed. She had been important when he was gone, but now that he was back, he'd be trying to get rid of her again. He didn't like the sign of the very happy trout that grinned from gill to gill out on the highway. He didn't like the clean office or the organized kitchen. It seemed like he just wouldn't like anything about her no matter what she did. Or didn't do.

Bill thought he was so important, but she would show him. She would take her money, all $750 of it, and leave. She'd hitchhike to Reno and get a job as a nightclub performer. She'd make thousands of dollars and never come back to the Happy Trout Fishing Resort for as long as she lived. Millions of dollars. She'd be driving past in her limo with her high-class friends, snorting a little coke, doing a little ecstasy, and not even stop. It wouldn't even occur to her because she would be so busy having fun.

Or wait. She would have the chauffeur pull into the driveway, cross the wooden bridge and pull up in front of the pathetic Happy Trout Café. She and her friends would pile out and go in, laughing and having fun. Bill would emerge from the kitchen with an apron around his middle and have to take their orders—all with special requirements. Well-done on one side, rare on the other. Hold the mayo, use thousand island instead. Only arugula in the salad. Extra virgin olive oil and wine vinegar. He would have to bow and defer and try to keep the orders straight, and she would laugh right in his face. She would pay with a credit card with her face and her name on it. Platinum. She would tip him fifty dollars, to rub it in.

But would he recognize her? Would she be so dolled up, so partied out that he wouldn't even know who she was? Would he have forgotten her by then? No, he would know who she was because she would have Foster with her, sitting at the table, eating a tuna sandwich off of a golden dish, and he wouldn't even be able to tell her no cats allowed. There wouldn't be one of his stupid signs to point to. She would be wearing a necklace that said Tina in diamonds, so he couldn't forget who she was. He would have to bring her an omelet, and if it wasn't brown enough, she'd send it back. Or too brown. She'd send it back, either way. She'd leave a hundred-dollar tip when they left, laughing about what a dump it was and how ridiculous the guy with the towel around his middle had been. They would drive off and never give him another thought.

Or she could book the family campground under

an assumed name, she could have her personal assistant book the family campground, and she would arrive in a big RV like rock stars have, she would arrive with a bunch of rock stars and they would party all night, and he'd have to put up with it. He'd hear the music and wonder what they were doing. He would walk over in the dark to see, and he would smell the excellent weed, and he would see her in a satiny red dress dancing, so sexy, with someone famous he would recognize. Who would he recognize? Tim McGraw? It would have to be a country singer. They'd have a fire burning, and drummers, and he would be shocked by the half-naked dancers, and he would see her in the center of everything dancing with Tim, but there would be nothing he could do about it.

That wouldn't be the end of it, though.

He would get into money trouble and have to sell the Happy Trout Fishing Resort, and she would be there with the cash and the condition that he stay and run the place, her way. They would serve espresso and gelato, which he would have to learn to make. He would be prohibited from calling them coffee and ice cream. They would have outside tables with girly pink umbrellas. They would change the radio from the country and western station and turn it up. There would be a party every weekend with a live band. He would have to move out of the bedroom and stay in the camper so they could expand the dining room to make room for dancing. He would owe her his job, practically his life, and she would give the orders, or sit by the river and breathe its smells and hear its sounds, because it would be her river then, not his. It would all belong to her.

She finally went back to the café, having worked out a satisfactory revenge and found Ursula beginning to tell Bill about Rachel's big adventure, running away from home. He wasn't taking it very calmly. Tina found this fascinating, how much Rachel was loved, not for what she did or gave or earned, but simply for being a daughter of someone.

Ursula was trying to make light of Rachel's escapade, and failing that, to change the subject. "She was here a couple of weeks, which was evidently okay with that hippy private school they send her to. Barbara and her new beau came up to get her. Did you ever meet Clive? He seems nice."

"Rachel? Here? How did she get here? Is she okay?" Bill wished Ursula would quit banging pans around, getting ready, ostensibly, to cook two little trout for the die-hard fisherman who had insisted on staying to the last good day.

"It's okay, Bill. She's okay, probably better off for the break. Probably they both are." Ursula got out the cornmeal and sprinkled some into a plate.

"But how did she get here, Urs? Did she get a ride with one of those boys she hangs out with?"

"Apparently, she hitched a ride with some nice people. Don't freak out about it, Bill. You and I used to hitchhike up here when we were kids, remember? Nobody made a big deal out of it when we did it. People generally like to help. And besides, she's fine."

Behind Ursula, Bill saw Tina shaking her head at him, her face intent and serious. She knew what could happen to choice young girls like Rachel. She knew it wasn't safe. It could have been Freddy who picked her up, and he would never have let her out of the car. She was way too prime. A pretty young girl like Rachel had no business getting into a car with a stranger. Unless maybe she had a gun, and even then.

"I've got to call Barbara. I need to talk to Rachel." Bill turned in to the office and stopped. "Jesus H. Christ, who screwed up the office?"

After a tense conversation with Barbara, Bill got to talk to Rachel. Tina cleaned the bathroom so she could listen.

"Sweetheart, how are you? You know you can't pull that kind of stunt again. It's not safe. No, not ever, not even then. Even Tina says it's not safe, and she would know. You like her? Well, that's good. No, she's not my girlfriend. Because she's not. She just isn't. If you ever feel like you have to get out, give me a call, okay? Well, yes, I probably will yell some, but I'd rather come get you myself than have you do something so dangerous. Or you can call Ursula. She's not that far away. Call Ursula if you need help. You know she loves you very much. Okay, sweetheart, be good, study hard, and I'll see you at Christmas."

Love you. Love you too. Love you three. Love you four-ever.

Working in the kitchen together was hard on everyone for the first day or two after Bill's return. Tina was silent and resentful doing prep, absent-minded waiting tables, which she had started doing while Bill was gone, and slow and depressed with cleanup. Bill was hyperactive and skittish at the grill, sidling past Tina with unnatural speed and giving directions in a monotone voice. Ursula, who had mostly been waiting tables, finally insisted that Bill take over there so that she and Tina could get some peace in the kitchen together. His spoken orders as he pinned the slips to the turntable, breakfast special, sausage, two sunny side up, wheat, sounded like accusations. Ursula's cheerful flow of talk met with silence from Tina, but at least no one was snorting or growling with Bill out of the kitchen. Ursula's patter began to restore a sense of normality, and both of the lovers, for of course they were lovers, though they didn't know it yet, began to relax into the routine. While they waited for customers, Bill sat in the café and read the paper, and in the kitchen, Ursula and Tina either worked or, if there wasn't anything left to do, played crazy eights. Foster slept.

Bill had been even more unsettled his first night back and subsequent nights when he found that no matter how he fought it, he had the odd sensation as he lay there that the truck out back with Tina sleeping in it was curled into the curve of his relaxed, protective body. When he rolled over, dismayed and cursing, turning his back, he again had the illusion that the truck and Tina lay warmly against him, curling around his back now, relaxed and protective. "I'm losing my mind," he thought, and fell asleep.

In the evenings of her last few days there, Ursula fished, and Bill joined her, although he usually refused to fish the river of the Happy Trout Fishing Resort, claiming that those fish were for the customers. They didn't catch much, but then, they didn't mind much either. Brother and sister traded occasional comments on the water, the light, the bait, the ways of fish, small memories and jokes of a shared childhood. Tina sat on her rock and listened to them, to the river, eyes closed, imagining Ursula as a sturdy little girl with baby Bill at her side looking like a squarish Rachel, letting the images run through her head, of beads, of soft lights, of little Brad, of Monika before she got turned out. She wondered where they were. She wondered, but she let them drift away as night drifted down and the mosquitoes drove everyone inside to fry up the few trout they had caught and hold a private feast.

On the last such evening, after Tina had left to bed down in the camper, Ursula sat her brother down and gave him some sisterly advice.

"I don't know what's going on with you and Tina, Bill, but here's what I do know. She's a good person. She's not out to get you in some way. She's had some bad luck, maybe a lot of bad luck. Sometimes it seems like she's had nothing but bad luck, but she's a good woman. So whatever has been making you act as jumpy as a poodle on the Fourth of July, it's not her fault. You work it out, but don't you be mean to her. She's a good woman." He listened thoughtfully, studying his hands and then meeting her gaze. Ursula pushed it one step further, somewhat against her better judgment. "Tina may be your girl, or not your girl. I don't know. But she's okay."

Bill sighed. "Okay, Urs. No need to chew my ear off. She's not going to be around that much longer anyway."

By the time Ursula had to leave, life at the Happy Trout Fishing Resort had found a happy balance. The dusky evenings down by the river, the bracing smell of the pines had done their work. Tina had cheered up. Bill had calmed down. And vice versa.

"Do you want to come back to Hayward with me, Tina? I can help you find work if you don't want to groom dogs with me and Benny. I don't have a full-time position available right now, but there's quite a bit of turnover. People get tired of smelling dogs, I guess. I sure as hell do. Anyway, Benny and I have room if you're looking for a change of scene."

"Brad might come back for me," Tina said, though they both knew it wasn't true. "I should probably stay here for a while in case he does."

"Okay, suit yourself. Here's the key to the trailer—you might as well use it while you're here. Leave it with clean sheets when you're done and I'm happy."

"Thanks. You know I'll miss you." Tina was aware that once Ursula left, she and Bill would be the only ones there. Except for Foster. "Can't play crazy eights."

Ursula gave her a big hug, and then Bill a big hug, and then Foster a cautious pet, which he received appreciatively, jumping up a little to meet her hand.

Thank you, goodbye, be good, have a safe drive, see you at Christmas, take care, take care of yourself, stay in touch, goodbye.

Bill closed the café and went out to survey the campsites and see what maintenance needed to be done before the next season, hopefully before the first winter storm, to make a list of damaged equipment to replace or repair, lock up the restrooms, and empty the trash for the last time of the summer.

Tina moved her belongings from Bill's camper to Ursula's little trailer. It was like a tiny house with everything she needed, even a shower and a refrigerator. There were nice blue towels in the bathroom and a fluffy comforter on the bed. The refrigerator had bottled water and lemons in it. There was a box of tea on the counter called Sweet Dreams. Tina found that charming. Although there were a few dishes on the shelves, she wished she had saved the collapsible bowls and plates Brad got at the camping store. She thought she would never need to live anywhere else.

She didn't know what she would do if Bill closed the resort for the winter. She had been afraid to ask, but she couldn't see people fishing in the snow. They would get too cold, standing so still. The water might freeze. The fish might freeze. She just didn't know. She didn't know how long she would get to stay in this little nest.

Bill was planning to close down the Happy Trout Fishing Resort on the first day of October, as he did every year. He tried to warn Tina so she could make other plans.

"I don't need any help now, Tina. Mostly I work

on repairing whatever's broken. Once it snows here, there's not a lot to do."

"Okay," Tina said, but she didn't mean it. It wasn't okay. She went to the trailer and dug her list out of her bag. It all seemed a long time ago, Brad, the bank, the marked bear, the yard sale. And now the options she had laid out seemed so childish, so unrealistic. Number one was out—she wasn't built to be a showgirl. She was too short and probably too old. Nice legs, though. She did have nice legs.

She had forgotten to ask Shaun about the Air Force. She figured she was most likely too old to do that too, and she thought she would fare badly surrounded by sex-deprived men. It would only be a matter of time before she was back in the blowjob business, so number two was eliminated. Becoming a nun seemed like the best bet on the list. She wasn't very Catholic, but they probably didn't keep records. And she could always lie about it if she had to. She might like living in a convent, though most of the nuns she remembered had been pretty nasty. But probably only to little kids, not to each other. She still worried that some horny priest would sniff her out.

She wished she had asked Ursula for a reference. She wondered if Bill would give her one, hopefully overlooking her suggestion the first day. Ohio was just a dream, not something she could get to. It was a dumb kid fantasy. She let it go with a pang of regret.

But maybe she could make number five work—stay here, get around Bill, stay out of trouble. Maybe she could help him repair things, maybe things in the kitchen that were dented or coming apart. Like the tray that rolled in the dishwasher. There was something wrong with it that made it stick, jostling the glasses almost to the point of breaking, before it seemed to recover and rolled on in. She borrowed a few screwdrivers, a flashlight, and some pliers from Bill's toolbox in the office and went to the newly abandoned, strangely quiet kitchen. She crawled under the dishwasher counter, and was just beginning her investigation when she heard the bell on the front door, the creak of the screen, and Bill's voice.

"We're not actually open right now, gentlemen. We're closed for the season." His voice was odd. Tina had never heard him sound nervous before.

"You're open if I say you're open." It was the gravelly whine of Freddy Napoleon, a sound that carried with it a load of menace and neck-snapping fear for Tina. She froze for an instant. The impossible thing, the thing she had almost forgotten to fear, had come to pass. Freddy. Then she chose the sharpest screwdriver to use if Bill was in trouble, because Freddy would kill if he felt like it, especially in a deserted resort like this one. No witnesses. No connection. No leads for homicide.

It was a free pass.

"Well, come on in. No need for that. I'll make some coffee, if you like. There's some apple pie in the pantry if you fellows are hungry for pie." Bill's voice was strained. Tina figured that Freddy was not alone, and that almost certainly someone had shown a gun. She heard the familiar sounds of the coffee being measured into the basket, and the trickle of the water falling into the urn from above. She thought she could hear Bill breathing.

"Don't do anything stupid. Just bring me some fucking pie." Freddy always liked sweet things, especially when they were free.

Bill walked around into the kitchen and though he saw Tina under the counter, he made no sign at first. He cut four pieces of apple pie from the dish, and the bottom of his pant legs were close enough for her to touch. He extended his hand below the counter, palm down and patted the air. That means lie low, stay, don't move.

"There we go. And coffee with that. Cream?"

Black, Tina thought. He just likes it black. And whoever is with him won't eat the pie or drink the coffee. They're working. Freddy doesn't want them to do anything but watch his back and scare people. So those three other pieces of pie are wasted. Three, so that means all of them, but not Brad, of course. T-Wah,

Hoppy, and Geron unless he has someone new. Maybe if one of them betrayed Freddy and then got shot for it. Or if one of them got busted and was in jail. But probably those three. Geron might not shoot her, but the other two would. If she killed Freddy first with a screwdriver through the neck, the others might break rank and take off. But maybe not. Not T-Wah. She knew that.

"Anything else I can do for you today? I don't have any money in the till since we're closed for the season."

There was a rustling of paper. "I'm looking for this little whore. She should be out there selling her little ass and making me some money, but she fucking took off. Take a good look, and don't fucking lie to me."

There was a pause as Bill looked at the picture, probably the one where she had won the dance contest at the Monkey Balls nightclub. It was a good picture. It made her look long-legged, taller than she was.

"I am not a man who likes to lie. If she camped here for a while, I would likely recognize her. But there's a lot of folks who stop for lunch on their way to Reno."

"Shut up. Have you ever seen this little cunt? Look again, and don't even try to lie to me."

"Well, sir, you are not a man I would care to lie to, that's for sure. I know she didn't stay here. Did she stop for lunch? Let me just think about that." Tina could tell Bill was buying time, trying to get his story worked out.

He sounded like he was in a movie, wearing suspenders, a character named Doc or Pops. So he wasn't going to give her up. He was going to try to bullshit Freddy Napoleon.

She shifted the screwdriver in her sweaty hand and figured she could scramble out from under the counter and go through the hatch and maybe get Freddy in one move. On the other hand, maybe she would get stuck in the hatch and have to wiggle her way out, which she would probably not live to do. She wished she'd had a chance to practice.

"Yes, I think I have seen that young lady." Bill's voice sounded prim, as though he were consciously correcting Freddy's disrespectful language. "She and several companions were here in early July, just after the fourth as I remember it. Would that be the young lady?"

"Who with?" Freddy sounded impatient and dark with threat.

"An African-American man, I think, though very light-complected. And a very young white man, blond. And another young woman, a very striking African-American in rather skimpy clothing. She got most of the attention, but I think this woman was with them."

"Which way did they go when they left?" Freddy grunted.

"Don't know, sir. I'm sorry, but once they go across the bridge, you can't see which way they turn onto the highway."

"Okay, motherfucker." Tina heard Bill's intake of breath as Freddy did something, probably grabbed his collar or stood on his foot or something else to hurt him. "If you see her, you call this number, you got it? This little bitch belongs to me. This fucking bitch is Freddy's, you got that? And if I find out you're lying, you're gonna wake up one morning with an ice pick through your head."

The bell jangled again and the door closed. Bill locked it behind them, and the café was very quiet. *He's watching them leave*, Tina thought. *That's good.*

After a long while, Bill came back into the kitchen where Tina was still under the counter, her back to the wall, her knees up, shaking and trying not to shake, the screwdriver still clutched in her white-knuckled hand.

"They drove around the campground, but then they drove out. I think they're going to look some place else. Let's stay put for a while."

Tina nodded, and Bill crawled under the counter and sat next to her, shoulder to shoulder. They exhaled at the same time, a long shaky mutual breath. Tina shivered.

"Jesus Christ Almighty, Tina, that's some scary, dangerous business there. That's serious, scary, dangerous business. No wonder you don't want to leave."

Tina nodded. Her heart was still thudding.

"And that's what you're running away from? That's where you've been?"

Tina didn't answer. It felt like that had been her whole life right there, trying to throw her out onto the highway, grabbing at her heels to drag her down to hell. Trying to hurt Bill.

"You lied for me, Bill, and you saved my life," she said.

Tina wanted to ask what she could do for him, how she could repay him, but every way she thought to say it sounded suggestive, like a return to their first botched meeting. "I would like you to tell me if there's a way... like to make things even, to pay you back. Because that really is some scary, dangerous business for you, too."

Bill looked at her sideways. "You want to know how you can ever repay me? For lying to that horrible demonic insane monster for you? For risking having one of his crazed thugs shoot me in the head or break in and sneak up on me and drive an ice pick through my brain?"

Tina nodded. That's what she meant.

"I tell you what, Tina. Clean the grease trap for me. We need to get everything cleared out so we can close up the kitchen. I'd like to go around the campground and make sure everything's okay, check things out, maybe drop a line in the river."

Tina nodded again. She could do that. "Don't call the cops," she said. "It's not safe to call the cops on Freddy. And he won't be back. He'll go on to Reno or Las Vegas, places where he has business connections, where he can stay in a hotel room and send his guys out to ask questions. He checked here once and you got rid of him. I really don't think he'll be back."

"I hope you're right," Bill said.

He crawled out from under the counter and looked down at where Tina was still huddled. "We're closed in the winter, so I'm not making any money and I can't pay you. We don't open again until mid-May, not even then if it's a hard winter. We're basically waiting for the thaw. But you can stay till you feel safe. I've got a space heater I can put in Ursula's trailer for you. And free food, like always."

Tina nodded. That wasn't what she had expected. Most people would get rid of trouble like Tina, bait that brought the big ugly Freddy-fish to the surface.

"Now tell me what I'm supposed to do with the hundred-dollar bill that ugly son of a bitch left under his saucer. It's not money I can hardly stand to touch."

Bill went looking for his fishing pole, and Tina sat beneath the counter until it was almost dark.

She felt as though a whining buzz saw that had been aimed at the back of her head ever since she could remember had been turned off and wheeled away on a little cart into the garage of some nice old man in Ohio who would use it to make bookshelves or toys for his grandchildren. She breathed in the new freedom, not just freedom to do things, not just a narrow escape, but the warm freedom of safety and partnership. She breathed it in, pulled the curtains together, turned on the lights and fixed the jammed roller on the dish-washer tray because she had started to and then cleaned the grease trap because she'd said she would. Still, she couldn't help but resent that the other woman, though totally imaginary, seemed more attention-worthy to Bill. Why didn't he think Tina would be the standout? Just because she hadn't worn skimpy clothing to rob a bank or go camping? It was deflating.

10

O curse of marriage,

That we can call these delicate creatures ours,

And not their appetites.

— William Shakespeare, Othello

LEAVING TINA TO CLEAN the grease trap, Bill grabbed his fishing gear, intending to let the soothing rhythms of the river calm him down, and realized that the adrenalin was still knocking around in him, that he needed to walk it off. So he left the fishing gear leaning against the wall in the storeroom and went out the back door empty-handed, down to the river. He would never be able to stand with his back to the café. He needed to see whatever came over the bridge and into the resort parking lot. He needed to check that Freddy had not left something toxic behind in the campground. But he was fairly certain, like Tina, that Freddy had believed him. And surely a modest little fishing resort would not stand out as a likely hiding place, especially one that was closing up for the winter. Freddy wouldn't be capable of imagining that someone would have enough common decency to conceal Tina, to lie for her. He wouldn't have any way to know how far Bill was willing to go to protect her. To Freddy, she was just a bitch to own, to use, to sell, to hurt. It made him wish, not for the first time, that he was a violent man.

He figured he would walk down the road that ran between the campsites, walking off the remainder of the adrenalin that still fizzled in his brain and his muscles. He would hear the SUV if Freddy came back. And he would do whatever it took to keep Tina safe.

He crossed the bridge, turning to look back at the driveway into the Happy Trout, the café, the outbuildings and vehicles behind it. Seen from across the bridge, the resort looked a little run-down, a little dilapidated like it did at the end of every busy summer season. Needed paint, for one thing, which would have to be next spring as soon as the air warmed up enough. And he couldn't start scraping now without exposing the bare wood to the coming winter moisture. He had painted the whole place seven years ago when he first came up from Hayward, but extremes in weather were hard on wooden structures. Ursula and Benny had come up and they had done it together. Painted the outside all day and when it got dark, drank beer and talked, about Uncle Foster and Aunt Delia, about Mom and Dad, but not about Ursula and Benny. That was too touchy and too present. And not about Bill and Barbara and Rachel. That was too recent a loss. The pain for that was still too easily summoned and too hard to put to rest.

It had been surprisingly generous of Uncle Foster to leave them the resort. It made sense, not having any children of his own, but Bill had been touched nonetheless when the lawyer had contacted him. Somehow Uncle Foster seemed like the kind of guy who would die intestate. Bill had only that week received the final decree on the dissolution of his marriage, his goddamn marriage, as if it had all been a stupid mistake, as if all the love he had poured into Barbara's heart had leaked away or evaporated, as if the years they lived together and shared a life hadn't happened. But there was his daughter Rachel, who clearly had happened, and the awkward visitation arrangement: one weekend a month and half of Christmas, half of summer breaks. Once the bonds of familiarity had been broken, the expectations and habits and daily taking for granted, he found that he didn't know how to talk to her or what to do with her. On her side, she began to find field trips and cheerleading clinics and school dances and parties and other excuses to avoid the Happy Trout and spend time in Hayward with her friends. There was nothing to do at the Happy Trout and she didn't know how she felt when she was there.

The first year of the separation, he took her once to Disneyland, after a series of tense negotiations with Barbara and even Barbara's lawyer, since it required transporting the child more than 250 miles away from her legal residence. He had begun the trip in a bad mood, but Rachel's obvious pleasure in the airplane flight and in his company and in seeing the characters from the movies—look, Dad, it's Pocahontas!—had broken through and, although he was ready to leave the park pretty much as soon as he got there, he was still glad to be with her and go on all the rides with her and share the whole silly thing, down to the last pretend moment. He couldn't have said what rides they went on, but he loved the bright look on her face and the feel of her soft little hand in his.

And now to find out from Ursula that Rachel had been here so recently, could have been here when Freddy came, threatening, dangerous, and chillingly real.

Walking the road between the campsites at the Happy Trout Fishing Resort had a calming effect on Bill, like a stable owner doing the rounds in the evening. Each site had its own personality for him, its own state of health and its own history. The air, though cool, was spiced with pine, and the continuous gurgle and flicker of the river helped him steady his breathing and his heart.

He had never intended to stay at the resort. He had taken his vacation time to get away from the ugliness of the divorce and at the same time to assess the situation, to clear out Uncle Foster's stuff and see what should be done to get the Happy Trout ready to put on the market. He had packed up his little brown Corolla ("Why brown? Why a Corolla?" Barbara had asked when he bought it) and headed up the hill to have a quick look-see.

The Corolla hadn't managed the trip. It started by coughing intermittently, and then catching, and finally stopped outright, taking the power brakes with it, luckily close enough to a turnout and luckily on the downside of a hill so that he could park it instead of rolling helplessly backwards into the mess he was trying to leave behind. The smart thing to do would have been first to call a tow truck and then to call Ursula to come get him. But he wasn't feeling smart. He had left town in a businesslike frame of mind, but every mile had made it clearer that he was running away, escaping the misery of his stupid apartment, his boring job, the constant reminders of his failed marriage. He was running to something better, to solitude, to moving freely in his own skin, to following his own volition, to turning left or turning right or having a nap or cursing the sky or building a teepee, with no one to answer to and no rules to follow. He hadn't realized he needed a vacation so badly, but once he was on the road up through the foothills, he felt like a bat driving slightly over the speed limit out of hell, and he found he couldn't, just couldn't, go back down.

He set the handbrake, took out his backpack, added a jacket, and started walking up the hill. He thought if he stood still, he would break into tears. He knew it was at least twenty miles to the Happy Trout Fishing Resort, but he was moving, that was the thing. He might be sorry later, like when it got dark, or when his shoes started making blisters on his unhardened feet, but he sure as hell wasn't sorry now. Twenty minutes later, when he heard a car coming from behind him, he turned and stuck out his thumb and the car pulled over.

Thirty minutes later, as Bill climbed out of the car at the pull-off for the Happy Trout Fishing Resort, a business card in his pocket (Ronald P. Haskell, real estate, certified estate and financial planning, tax preparation, life insurance), he had already agreed that Ronny, you can call me Ronny, would get his son Fred to bring the tow truck and haul the Corolla to his shop in Pineville, where he would diagnose it and give Bill a call at the resort office with an estimate. Then if Bill wanted, he would do repairs as needed, but no pressure. If Bill wanted it taken somewhere else, to another shop, that was fine, just the minimal cost of towing. Family rate, Ronny said, since Bill was new to the area. Ronny would come by one day next week to give him his straightforward, honest-to-God, no-tricks professional opinion about the possibilities of listing the resort as-is, but it's a sleepy market right now, commercial and residential, so let's not count our chickens right out of the chute.

Ordinarily Bill found salesmen annoying, but he was grateful for the ride, the offers of help and the distraction.

The Happy Trout Fishing Resort sign, seen in the growing dusk of his arrival, was faded and peeling, almost unreadable. The air was growing cold, his jacket was even thinner than he had thought, and the darkness increased with every step. He hoped fervently that the utilities had not been cut off and wished he had thought to bring something as useful as a flashlight. He had packed as though going to the Happy Trout Fishing Resort of his youth, when everything was already there, provided by adults. He was glad he remembered where the flashlight used to be kept. Maybe it would still be there. As he walked across the culvert bridge and around the curve, he saw the vague blurred outline of the café. The windows were blank and unwelcoming, the parking lot empty except for Uncle Foster's red truck. It looked like a place where a lonely man had died alone.

He grasped the key the lawyer had sent tightly in his hand. The porch steps creaked and gave a little under his feet, and he felt a moment of panic, probably, he thought, long overdue. Maybe Ronny Haskell was a serial killer who would double back and sneak up on him in the dark, hatchet at the ready. His shaking hand found the keyhole and turned the key. The door swung open with a jingle, as he half expected it to do. The smell of rotting food and worse was overwhelming in the cold air.

The light switch he reached for on the wall clicked fruitlessly. He shuffled across the rough floor in the dark, running into a table, and then he found the office doorway, where again there was no light. Made sense. No power, no refrigeration explained the smell. He hoped that was all there was to it. In the top drawer of the desk, he found what he was looking for. A flashlight, the same flashlight Uncle Foster had carried when he walked down to the campsites to visit with folks, to find his way around when noises in the night were not easily attributed to skunks or possums. The flashlight. The simple act of turning it on made Bill feel stronger, more like a man in control.

He took a quick tour of the kitchen, which was pretty bad, with food rotting on the counters where Uncle Foster had evidently had time to begin, but not to cook or enjoy, his last meal on earth. He had died here, in the kitchen, so the medical examiner's report had said. Died and wasn't found until four days later when one of his poker cronies had come by to see if he wanted to help swell the kitty at an all-nighter in town. He had taken a whiff and called the county sheriff, who came out to see what was going on and then called an ambulance to take the body away, and the medical examiner, who called the coroner of Alameda County, who had contacted Bill who had called Ursula to let her know. They had driven up to Pineville together to see him properly buried next to Aunt Delia. But he had left quite a mess, it seemed.

Bill took a quick glance around the place, found some extra batteries for the flashlight, checked idly into the cash register where he found several hundred dollars under the tray. It was creepy alone there in the dark.

There was nothing he could do about the stink until daylight, no way to arrange for electricity until business hours, so he went to Uncle Foster's bedroom, closing the door and opening the window a crack to let the cold but clean air in. The room smelled of old man, of whiskey and stained underwear, of sweat and toe jam, but it was better than the kitchen. He piled as many blankets as he could find on the bed, which had a valley running down the center of the mattress, a Foster-shaped valley, Bill thought. Fitting himself into the mold, he pulled the mass of covers over his head and slept soundly for the first time in months.

The morning light revealed a desolate scene; the kitchen was the epicenter of awfulness. Ice cream left on the counter had dripped down onto the floor and into the cracks between the counter and the cooler, turning into a fetid green ooze that reeked almost as badly as the pan of something, maybe stew, that had been left on the stove. Bill knew that the coolers would reveal their own horrors if the power had been turned off more than a day or two. He went to the office and searched for the electric bill to get the phone number, making the call and requesting service as soon as possible. The woman on the other end said if he would come in and pay the deposit in person, they could turn it back on later that day. And she said it was too bad about his uncle, what a character he had been.

Bill called the phone company next, to reassure them that as soon as he found the bill, he would pay it. After any number of buttons pushed and a long wait, the service representative gave him the amount of the outstanding balance and the account number and the address to which he could send that amount, and hoped that he knew that he was a valued customer and they appreciated his call. If there was anything else they could do to improve his experience, he had only to ask and wait while they transferred him to the appropriate department. And they said to enjoy the rest of his day. It seemed unlikely. As a last thought, he called the waste management company and was reassured that they would be emptying the dumpster in two days.

It was hard to know where to start, but it was obvious where the worst of it was, so Bill found some garbage bags and began tossing out the rotting food, containers and all, even a nice cast-iron skillet that held what appeared to be a mixture of dog food, giant fingernail clippings, and gray fuzzy mold. Good skillet, but Bill didn't have the stomach for rescuing it. It was a hard morning, and he was glad every time a bag was full and ready to be hauled outside into the sweet, clean air to be stacked in the dented dumpster in the back. For one thing, it gave him a chance to rest his face, which was otherwise drawn into a permanent grimace of disgust.

He figured it would take him all day and part of the next to get the kitchen passably clean, and more disinfectant than he had seen in the cabinet below the sink. He thought about calling Ronny, testing their new-forged friendship, to see if he would deliver.

Instead, he called Ronny's son to check on the car. Then he found the key to Uncle Foster's truck in the desk drawer. Surprisingly, it started right up, noisy as always and stinky, but in a comparatively clean petrochemical way. So he decided to drive into Pineville to put down a deposit on electricity, buy more cleaning supplies, shop for a camper shell for the truck, and find something for lunch and to bring home for his dinner and breakfast the next morning. As he locked up the café to go, it occurred to him that he hadn't thought about Barbara at all since he arrived. And the only time he had thought of Rachel was to be glad that she wasn't with him; this was the exact opposite of Disneyland.

Four long days later, after spending most of the day filling the dumpster with Uncle Foster's pathetic hoard of belongings—empty bottles, dirty magazines—Bill had called Ursula.

"It's quite a mess, Urs. It needs so much work, it's unbelievable. It's like Uncle Foster hasn't raised a hand for years. I can't just drive up and work on it on weekends. It would take forever."

"Then I guess we have to sell it as-is, even though it won't be worth very much. Basically, we need to get it settled, right? And you don't have to do all that work. You should just lock up and go home and let the real estate guy deal with it." Ursula was sorry she had said "home." She had seen his unloved apartment with its sketchy furniture and blank walls.

"We would only be able to sell it to someone who does HAZMAT work as a hobby. It's pretty bad. We're gonna need to tear out the kitchen and start over. The roof leaks over the storeroom, so there's another repair that can't wait, not another season. I haven't even been out to look at the campground at all. I imagine the restrooms and picnic tables are likely to need some work as well. It's just too much for a part-time handyman like me."

"Okay," Ursula said. There was something about this conversation she didn't understand. Why not make it someone else's problem? "Are you getting hung up over the sentimental value? You'd like to see the old place in good trim before we sell it? Is that what's going on?"

"Not exactly. It needs a lot of work. And Ronny Haskell, local realtor and everything salesman, says it's a sleepy market right now, still not recovered from the sliding trend. The place is going to sit and lose value if we don't do something. We need to spruce it up if we want it to sell."

"Okay," Ursula said. "But you're saying it's too much work. What am I missing here? Can't we get a contractor and have it fixed up? Is there enough money?"

"It looks like there's probably enough money. Besides the healthy savings account, which we should be getting pretty soon from that lawyer, he also left a large, really large wad of bills in the mattress, wrapped in something mouse proof, luckily. That's the second bundle I've found. I know, it surprised me too. I thought Delia spent everything, but evidently not. So money's not the problem. It's time."

"Can't we hire a contractor who will then spend the time?"

"Ursula, you can't hire a contractor and then go away and leave him to get on with it. It'll never happen. Someone has to be here."

Bill didn't usually talk this much. Something was going on. "Give me the upshot, Bill. Quit flirting with it; spell it out for me."

"Okay. Here's the thing. I called in to work and quit my job today. I want to stay up here and get it ready to sell. Ronny says the renovations will pay off in the end."

"Jesus Christ, Bill. You already decided this? You already quit? And don't tell me what Ronny says, okay?"

"I can't go back to Hayward, Ursula. I'd rather be here. I'll just use enough of the money to cover my expenses. I think it'll work out for everyone."

"Especially Ronny? Don't answer that. I'm flabbergasted is all. You really want to do this? You've thought this through?"

"I really do." Bill had thought about it, had imagined packing his stuff back into the brown Corolla, and he had not been able to stand it. He would have been walking away from something that called him by name, turning his back on this quiet life to return to a life of confusion and pain and constant reminders of what he had lost.

"Maybe Benny and I will come up and help. It's the kind of goofy project he likes. And it would be good to see the place before we sell it. Maybe next weekend, I'll have to see. We can bring the Airstream up and leave it there. This whole turn of events seems kind of crazy. Let's talk tomorrow, okay? I need to let this sit." On her end, Ursula hung up and sat with it. It might be crazy, she decided, but if it was Bill's kind of crazy, she would back him.

At first, Bill had imagined that being at the Happy Trout Fishing Resort, he would no longer be plagued by thoughts about Barbara, but after the first flurry of activity, he started to remember things about her, but not like he had in his cage of an apartment, not with chagrin and bitterness and tears. The memories had changed from big-screen, high-def, Technicolor to black-and-white nostalgia, the nagging memories of Barbara now sent to the background by the present tasks of ordering appliances, repairing the porch steps, replacing the roof, list after list of projects, errands, parts, supplies, and tools.

It was only at night that he thought of her at all, often when he went down to the river after supper, to get away from the work and look at the water, which did not break or rot or rust or call for repair. Or change or lie or betray.

He had married young, just a few years out of college, because Barbara was pregnant and Bill wanted the baby to have a complete family. He had been pursuing Barbara steadily for months before she had let him undress her and had been first shy and then shameless with him, but never, he thought in retrospect, never really sincere. She had wanted to be sexy much more than she had ever wanted sex, at least with him. He remembered how troubled she had looked when she came to him with the news about the baby, but he was joyful at the possibility that this was a way to capture her elusive heart and secure her intermittent attention.

He thought at the wedding that he had given his heart away completely. The white gown set off her dark cloudy hair and her dark eyes. In his memory, that was all he had seen during the whole wedding, her face, her eyes, her slender body. He supposed there had been other people there, and a cake, all that folderol that had preoccupied Barbara and bored him for the last several weeks. He had thought then that his heart was completely full. But later, after months of love and misunderstanding, arguments, tears, and pride, when Rachel was placed in his arms, a pink little nothing as light as a potato chip, he realized that his heart was bigger than he had imagined. He realized that there was more to give and no end to it. And then, after a while, slowly at first and then finally, it had ended.

He would stand looking at the river after a day spent in planning and repairs, rattling the stripped screws, bent nails, and odd bits of metal in his pockets, his fingers cut here and there, the skin roughened by months of work with pipes, wires, shingles, lumber, setting his house, his and Ursula's house, in order. Barbara would be repelled by the man he had become, had turned out to be. She had preferred the company of the other real estate agents where she worked, men she hooked up with at sales conventions and agency retreats, men dressed in trendy colors and expensive shoes, whose smooth good looks must have made him appear coarse and dull even then.

After seven years or so, once she got Rachel set up in the school where the children of her friends prepared for success, Barbara started having affairs; he felt sick when he overheard her on the phone, the whispering, the cooing, the seductive purr. She had been discreet at first, but increasingly he saw the signs, her smeared lipstick and tousled hair after getting a ride home from an associate, her endless lunches with friends, and mostly the blank mask of her face, only half-concealing the excitement that bubbled there. She became reckless, and the situation came to a head.

He had tried not to know, tried to be more the man she wanted, until he came home one afternoon to find Barbara and her boss in his bed, not presently copulating, but lying side by side with the sheets pulled up to their armpits like Barbie and Ken dolls tucked in for a nap by a motherly six-year-old, in a state of exhausted contentment not available to the inanimate. He knew he should just leave, but instead, perversely, he walked to the foot of the bed, enjoying their horrified faces, and loomed there, wishing he had something to threaten them with besides his tall body leaning at them and the fact of his presence. He had the illusion of looking down at them from the ceiling, like a wrathful light fixture.

"Well, this is fucking awkward, isn't it?" he said. He watched the play of panic across their faces, receding, replaced by furtive planning, on the spot strategizing in which they, inconveniently, had no opportunity to confer. They would have to concoct separate plans.

Barbara chose to wrap the sheet around her naked body and flee to the bathroom, unfortunately leaving her partner in crime entirely uncovered, a poster child of vulnerability, lying naked flat on his back in a classic posture of submission at the feet of a man who had every reason to be exceedingly, perhaps violently angry. Bill approached the side of the bed, and his wife's lover sat up and pulled Barbara's pillow into his guilty lap.

"Here's your pants," Bill said, standing close enough that the man couldn't swing his legs around to sit up in the usual way, but had to choose between threading his legs between Bill and the nightstand, or scooting down to the foot of the bed to get up. He couldn't flee the way Barbara had without forfeiting his pants. He scooted.

"There's no point in my saying anything, is there?" he said in a brave attempt to preserve his dignity.

"Oh sure," Bill said. "Tell me anything you want. Explain it all away and save my wife the trouble. Tell me a story that will keep me from beating the bloody crap out of you." He was shaking internally and he felt like his heart's blood was draining out of his life. He hoped that his friendly tone came across as unnerving if not downright menacing.

The now dressed man, having regained his Italian wool trousers and his silk twill shirt, was regaining his composure. It was awkward, but not, he hoped, going to turn ugly.

Unfortunately, Bill had positioned himself in front of the bedroom door, blocking the way. "You're not walking out this door," he said. "You're not walking out of my house through the living room where I drink beer and watch football, past the table where my daughter and I eat breakfast, out the door where I walk when I go to work."

"What do you mean?" Bill could see fear in the man's eyes, fear that he wouldn't walk out the door because his dead body would have to be carried out in a bag.

"Go out the slider like the punk thief you are. Or you can try to fight your way past me, but I think you're gonna get bad hurt if you do." Bill was suddenly ready to end the farce, to get the intruder out, and then to get out himself. This was unforgiveable, as he assumed it was meant to be, Barbara's indirect way of freeing herself from his boring, unwanted love.

Barbara's lover slipped out the slider door and trotted around the corner to the gate, which Bill knew to be nearly impossible to open because of a broken hinge he'd been meaning to fix. The motherfucker would just have to climb over, which Bill would have liked to witness. Instead he packed an overnight bag, leaving all his bathroom things in with his wife, and left his house and left his wife locked in his bathroom, waiting for him to knock and call her name so that she could do whatever it was she had decided to do next.

This was a scene he had reviewed in his head over

and over, sometimes imagining what would have happened if he had hit the guy, wondering if he would have beaten him to death or not. If he would have at least ruined his pretty face for him. He played the scene in different ways, gave himself new lines until he couldn't be entirely sure what he had actually said and done, only that Barbara and he were finished and that his marriage had failed. Maybe he had failed. Anyway, it was over. And the thing that hurt most was losing his connection with Rachel.

He had always thought of Rachel as a smaller shadow of Barbara, thinking of them together as his girls, the girls he loved and intended to care for. When Rachel had a hard day, she wanted her dad. When one of her nursery school chums turned on her and bit her on the cheek, she couldn't wait until he got home, so she could show him the tooth marks, could climb into his lap and rest in the crook of his arm while he read the paper, her teddy bear held comfortingly in the crook of her arm. (It's okay, Teddy. It's going to be okay.) As she grew older, it seemed to him that she mostly ignored him, but even lately, she would sometimes bring her iPod and listen to her music on earphones, maybe texting her friends at the same time, leaning up against the support of his shins as he sat and watched a game.

He had been driven to get out of Hayward, into

the mountains, but he knew it was going to be a strain on his ability to love Rachel properly. He needed to be there when she had a bad day, but he wouldn't be. He had come up to this place on the river, to mend it and make it live, and it was good to be out of Barbara's orbit. It would keep him from parking outside the house, hoping to see the two of them, hoping not to see the boyfriends who could now visit openly in broad daylight. He would call Rachel every week, and he thought occasional weekends in the city would give him a break, and that Rachel would like to come up to the Happy Trout Fishing Resort sometimes in the summer. He hoped she would.

That had been his life during his first year at the resort, working mostly alone, contracting out the jobs that required a crew or a permit, preoccupied with the endless details of returning a moribund resort to viability, and experiencing flashes of painful memory like the sudden throb of an almost forgotten wound not yet healed. He kept his promises and sent the child support money faithfully and made his Sunday phone call to Rachel, although she often seemed offhand and uncomfortable. He had always dreaded her adolescence, and it appeared to be coming on strong. It felt like, as he uncovered Uncle Foster's life, he was also exposing bits of his own to be scoured clean by the river and lightened by the sunshine dancing on its surface.

After the major work had been completed on the café and the campground, he called Ronny Haskell to come see what he thought, if the place was market-ready. Ronny was delighted to come around that same day, having taken a fancy to Bill who was much nicer than his uncle had ever been, and give his professional opinion. The market, it seemed, was no longer quite as soft, but was now hollow, with certain sectors having fallen back. Bill had no idea what that meant.

"Would it be easier to sell if it were a going concern?" he had asked, hoping that Ronny's answer would give him a reason to stay. He was already feeling hostile toward the future buyer who would come sliding down that hollow market and make a hash of things. He called Ursula that night and broached the subject, one she had seen coming for quite a while.

"Sure, Bill. Get it up and running if that's what you want to do. That way it'll be lived in and won't fall to pieces as fast. But you need to be sure and send me half of the profits or something. It has to work out financially. For me, I mean. And if it's no go, we have to sell. And tell Ronny I said hey."

So it had been agreed that Bill would take on the work of planning, writing out orders, making menus, buying new flatware and china to replace the bent, scratched forks Uncle Foster had thought good enough and the cracked plates he had been too depressed to replace. Things started looking pretty good. Life was picking up. Bill called Pete to come help him through the first summer season, and fish during the off hours, which Pete thought were pretty few and far between. Ursula came up for a weekend here and there, and Benny came with her for two weeks once, to work and to watch Ursula fish, not fishing himself since he didn't need an excuse to spend time outside and he didn't like the taste anyway. Too fishy.

After Bill's second year there, one year of repair and one of running a marginally successful resort, it was a foregone conclusion that the Happy Trout Fishing Resort would not be sold no matter what Ronny Haskell said, that it was everyone's escape, and that it was Bill's place, his place to care for and operate and live in and be himself. And it was goddammit his place to defend from sickening perverted criminals and thugs who would pull a gun and threaten him and try to abduct his employee and do God knows what with her, he couldn't bear to think. It was his place to share with the people he loved—Rachel, Ursula, Benny, Pete—and to offer as a sanctuary for refugees from the ugly world, like Tina.

It was his place and his intention to shelter Tina.

11

Was this fair paper, this most goodly book,
Made to write 'whore' upon?
— *William Shakespeare, Othello*

It snowed early, in mid-October, big soft flakes settling down out of a kettle-gray sky. Tina had never lived in snow before, had never stood out in it as it fell, falling in on her at the center of the swirling cone, on her eyelids, her cheeks, and her outstretched tongue. It changed the air to a peppermint tingle. She remembered Brad saying that the forest smelled like air freshener, and she laughed. She wished he was here to see this, to feel the tiny weight of each flake on the skin, to be amazed with her. But this whitened sky was a world clean of people, a world for solitude and whirling and falling into a soft bed of snow. She had never been so alone, so cold, so dazed by the blankness, and out of the blankness, feathers of snow that fell and fell and fell.

Bill brought her in, finally, after having looked out

the window seven or eight times. It wasn't his worry, but she looked like she was attempting to freeze to death in full sight of a warm café. When Bill called her from the doorway, she seemed to gesture as though to put him off—or maybe she was waving, he couldn't tell. He had to put on his coat and go get her, bringing her to warmth and safety with one arm around her shoulders, and even then she looked back, then looked up and found that the vortex of falling snow still ended with her. He made her change into dry clothes in the restroom and then sit at the counter with a cup of hot chocolate in her red hands, sniffling, her eyes far away, still swirling with snow. She had never seen it before, not falling. She'd seen pictures and snow globes and commercials and James Bond in the snow, but she had never felt it or smelled it or rolled in it before.

"Does Foster like the snow?"

"No, ma'am. Foster's like me. He likes the electric blanket."

"Can I stay here forever?"

"Tina, you know that's not a good idea. You're still young enough. You need to go and—" Bill shook his head. He had no idea what Tina needed, and he studied her, safe for once from her unsettling gaze, as her attention was still turned inward, snow-drunk, not entirely present. She needed a good life. She needed to be safe from nightmares like Freddy Napoleon and idiots like

Brad. She needed to make things happen. She needed to laugh. She needed to be Tina. He started to think that she needed to be loved, but thought better of it.

"What are you doing here, Bill?"

"I own the place, remember? Drink your cocoa and let me get on with the accounts. Taxes due soon enough." He sounded crabby.

Even through the haze of snow that filled her head, Tina heard him say that she couldn't stay forever, and the thought haunted her later as the snow inevitably melted away from her consciousness and she began to worry again. She wondered if she was in trouble. Bill could make her leave any time he decided and he had said she couldn't stay, that it wasn't a good idea. He could call the sheriff. He could change his mind and call Freddy, though she didn't think he would do anything that dangerous. But still, she had to make sense to him; she had to be needed. The Happy Trout was really the only thing on her list any more.

"We need to open the café for the skiers, Bill. We could serve hot chocolate like this and soup and corn-bread and hot cider and popcorn and grilled cheese sandwiches. We could give them comfort food."

"Skiers don't stop here."

"That's because you're closed. We need to change the sign to say that we're open for the winter. And we could sell chains and antifreeze and mittens—stuff they need."

"They don't need antifreeze and mittens."

"Okay." Tina was ready to move on this. "Food then. If we moved the little store section out, we could put in five more tables."

"I don't have five more tables."

"We could get picnic tables and use them inside for the skiing season and then make a patio outside during the summer for campers. They aren't that expensive at K-Mart if you put them together yourself. You could probably make a patio, couldn't you?"

"There's not enough room for five picnic tables no matter how you arrange them." Bill was still peering down at his account book, answering absently.

"Okay, then just three. We could spend the next week or so getting the menu figured out and ordering food and making the sign and getting the tables and making room for them. Then the sign goes up and the cold, tired people come in."

Bill looked up at her over his half-glasses. "I'm supposed to say no, it'll take at least two weeks, then you agree and I'm committed. I know how you operate. It's why I now have banana pancakes on the menu, to avoid having to pay through the nose for pumpkin out of season. It's why I put out good money for three rose-bushes, because you wanted the whole front area made into a public park. Not to mention all the fertilizer."

He went back to his accounts, noticing that he had put county taxes in the credit column. That's not right. "What makes you think the business is there, anyway?"

"I would stop here if I was cold and hungry and I saw twinkly little lights and a sign. I would want you to warm me up and feed me. I mean, it's what people want."

"Okay, Tina. Here's a deal. You work on this for two weeks for free to get it set up. No more tables, though. Let's go with what we've got. We're open weekends only, afternoon to evenings, say 3:00-8:00, maybe 4:00-8:00. Half pay for you. If I don't break even before Christmas, I close it up. If I make a profit, you get a raise."

"And free food," Tina said.

"Free food," Bill agreed. "How do you know Freddy won't stop in, or someone he knows?"

"Freddy doesn't ski—he might fall down. And his guys and guys like that don't ski. They're too poor. And too scared. They don't do new things like that."

"Okay, then. Pull this off, and I'll teach you how to snowshoe. Now let me finish this in peace. Make a list or something."

Tina woke the morning before they were to open for their winter season to find a layer of fresh snow that came up to the bottom of the trailer and created a cold empty silence in the forest. No birds sang. No insects buzzed. The trees had lumps of white lying along the branches, and even the perpetual river was muted.

Not even one set of tire tracks marked the road between the highway and the Happy Trout, the even white surface marred only by a set of cat prints. Pushing her way through the drifts, she finally stood on the front porch and, looking out, saw that although the road to the highway was smooth and white and lost under the snow, the end of the road was blocked with a tall, dirty white wall where snow had been piled up. No one was coming to the Happy Trout through that.

She unlocked the door with an extra key she had found in the desk when tidying up the office and looked in the Yellow Pages for a solution.

"Department of Motor Vehicles, this is Azalia speaking."

"Oh, sorry," Tina said. "I was calling for the Truitt Snow Service."

"Oh, hang on." There was a ruffling noise over the line, and then "Truitt Snow Service, this is Azalia speaking."

"Hi, Azalia! This is Tina Martin from the Happy Trout out here on Highway 20. Someone blocked our driveway with a big pile of snow. Can you come get it? Or melt it? Or shove it somewhere else, whatever you do with snow?"

"Oh dear, well, most of the resorts and cabins are

closed for the season, so the highway department blocks all the driveways. They're focused on keeping the main highway clear for travelers. Now, we can clear it out for you, but not till day after tomorrow. It's not an emergency call, so it may take Otto even longer to get to it."

"Actually, Azalia, it is an emergency. We're having a special open house tomorrow afternoon—it's the first day of our big winter season. We're expecting a large number of out-of-town bigwigs and VIPs to drop by. Is there any way you can move us up on the list?"

"I can do that, but you should know, it's $150—and we only take cash. I can put you through to Otto if you'd like. He's out with the plow in your area right now."

"Let me talk to Bill and I'll get back with you. And thanks a million, Azalia. You're a lifesaver!"

Bill was not pleased with Tina's initiative. "We can't afford $150 on top of what all those little party lights set us back! I do believe Mother Nature has thrown a monkey wrench into the works. Sorry, Tina, but you lose on this one." He didn't sound sorry; he sounded relieved. She wasn't sorry either; she had heard him say "we" and "us," and she was busy feeling a mixture of pride and caution. Besides, she figured there had to be a way around it. There mostly is.

She waited until Bill had gone out to shovel off the

walkways and called Azalia back to get to Otto and make arrangements. Tina could hear the rumble of big equipment and Otto's voice raised to be heard above it.

"Hi Otto," she said. "This is Tina at the Happy Trout." And they worked out a deal.

Later that day, when Bill heard the roar of the snowplow idling in his driveway, he was furious. He left the comfort of the warm office where he had been attempting to decode Tina's filing system, occasionally letting his eyes glaze over and dozing a bit, to find Otto Truitt, bundled up for the cold and sweating lightly in the bright warm café, leaning on the counter, in close conversation with Tina.

"You sure know how to make a man an offer he can't refuse, Tina." Otto waggled his snow-hat-covered head and winked at Bill. "Quite a gal you've got here." He stopped in the doorway and fluttered his gloved fingers at Tina. "Don't forget—next Thursday, seven o'clock, and lots of candles. Okay? I'll have your drive cleared in two shakes." Then he went out and hopped into the cab of his still roaring machine.

"Jesus H. Christ Almighty God," Bill hissed between clenched teeth. "What have you done, Tina? What do you think you're up to?" His eyes were shooting fire at her and, for the first time, she was afraid of him. But just a little.

"Well, Bill, it gets it done, and it doesn't cost you a

penny. I thought you'd be pleased."

"Oh Christ," Bill said, and his face was pale and tight. "Gather up your stuff, Tina, and get in the truck. You can't stay here. I told you, you can't do that, not here. Get in the truck and I'll take you to Nevada where you can make whatever kind of deal you want with whoever you want to make it with. I'm not having it here."

She stared at him, thunderstruck.

"Get in the goddamn truck! You can't stay here. Get in the truck!" He took hold of her arm, the same arm he had bathed and bandaged, and tried to move her, but she was surprisingly hard to move, particularly when she was in the right.

"Bill, I'm ashamed of you. Let go of me! You don't know what you're talking about. Stop yelling and listen. Just listen. Listen."

Bill stopped yelling and let go of her arm. He sank into a booth, but he continued to glare at her, real pain in his eyes. It hurt her to see it.

"I know we don't have the extra $150 right now, but I remembered the $100 that Freddy left that you said you didn't know how to spend. It's been in the first aid kit all this time. So that was $100. And it turns out that Otto and his wife Azalia are having their thirty-fifth wedding anniversary next Thursday. Her mom died last month, and Otto wants to cheer her up....

Are you getting this, Bill?"

Bill nodded and buried his face in his hands.

"...wants to cheer her up because her mama who was up in Montana died last month and it hit her pretty hard, even though she was in her nineties. Mama was. So Otto's been trying to plan a surprise anniversary date, but Azalia doesn't like Eddy's Grill in town, who can blame her, and the drive to the city is always so tiring that he doesn't want to do that either, plus they'd have to stay in a motel, which is too expensive if it's nice at all."

Bill was shaking his head from side to side, his face still hidden.

"I know, but this is all stuff Otto told me. So here's the deal: he's picking her up from work at 3:30 at the DMV because she's going to close up early so they'll have time to get all dolled up, Otto's words, they're coming here around seven, like you heard, and I'm fixing them a Southern fried chicken dinner, because her mom was from Mississippi originally but moved to Montana to be close to her brother, but Azalia never learned how to cook like that and I know how because a friend of mine had a sister who taught me once." She stopped for breath. "That's the deal. And the truck couldn't get out the driveway anyway with all that snow in the way."

"And," Tina added, "if I have been pushed into a

truck and mistakenly deported to Nevada to work in a whorehouse, since evidently I need to spell it out for you, I can't cook dinner for them. Jesus, Bill, what were you thinking?"

Bill stood up and walked out of the room without looking at her, his face averted. He was more shaken than he could deal with. His heart had fallen through the floor and then cracked open and then been roasted with shame and then returned to him on a plate. It wasn't until the next day, after a sleepless night and his morning coffee that he came to her, having swallowed the bitter pill of having been so wrong while feeling so righteous. He could feel that he was losing his superiority, his moral edge over Tina, and that felt dangerous. But he also knew he was wrong.

"Tina, I believe I owe you an apology for yesterday. I misjudged you and I was wrong." Bill let her see his face so she would know he meant it.

Tina glanced up from the fuzzy blue scarf she was knitting and then back down at the pattern Ursula had written out for her. *Did "knit one B" mean knit one in the row below or through the back loop? Hopefully not through the back—that's too hard, and half of the time you lose the stitch.*

"Yeah, Bill," she said. "You do owe me an apology, but don't worry about it. I'm going to run you a tab. Can you get the ladder out of the storage shed so we can put up the twinkly lights?"

"And by "we" you mean me?"

Tina just smiled at him, so he went out to fetch the ladder, a hammer, a box of tacks, and extension cords to get it done.

In spite of the lights on the very happy Happy Trout sign out on the highway showing the new winter hours, and in spite of the fully stocked and prepared café and the new menu and Tina's high hopes, in spite of the thick file of lists in a folder marked "Plan," opening night did not start out very promisingly. Bill unlocked the door and turned on the OPEN sign at 4:00 on the dot. Soup was simmering on the back burner. Cornbread was staying warm in the pan next to the grill. The new menus, adorned with the Happy Trout picture, were tucked in next to the cash register, ready to be handed out to cold, hungry customers. If only the customers would arrive.

At 4:30, Tina turned the radio to a station that played Christmas carols, thinking that might make a difference. She was jittery and kept stirring the soup, restacking the menus, checking and rechecking the tables.

At 4:43, a car parked in the empty lot, and two men in goofy ski hats came in and ordered coffee. A little pie with that? No thanks, just coffee. They drank their damn coffee, used the restroom, and left. To

Tina, it was like a nightmare where you can't make things work right, like waiting to find out if a patient at the hospital lived or died.

At 5:03, another car pulled in and a family of five piled into the Happy Trout. The restroom was the first stop, while the dad bought some gum, an obvious move to justify the expense of the toilet paper they would use. Bill was looking a little smug, Tina thought. She poured some hot chocolate into a shallow pan and placed it on the pass-through. She put the extra little fan behind it and chocolate aroma drifted in clouds into the café as the kids came out of the restroom.

"We want cocoa, we want cocoa," they shrilled. "Can we sit here?" They commandeered the twirly stools at the counter, in spite of having been told they were just going to pee, that's all. "I'm hungry," wailed the smallest one, a waddling bundle of pink snowsuit, her appealing blue eyes looking up at Daddy.

Tina waited. And Mom and Dad folded, ordering hot chocolate for the kids, then soup since it was so late they would only have time to tuck them in when they got home. Dad went for the grilled cheese sandwich, Mom ordered fries and a hot chocolate, and they were off and running. The next customers, a couple in matching snow hats, sat at a table and had the grilled cheese combo with coffee and pie. They were still exclaiming over how great the pie was when the next group came in, another skiing family with hulking teenage sons to feed.

By 7:30, the place had cleared out and they started closing down. Tina had done it again. And this time with no disasters. "Tina and Bill, high five," she thought, but didn't say out loud.

On the following Thursday night, the Otto and Azalia Truitt thirty-fifth anniversary dinner was a great success. Otto turned up looking surprisingly handsome without his snow hat, and Azalia was sweet and sassy in pink stripes, an orchid (good going, Otto) pinned to her blouse. Tina noticed that they were always touching—hands, hand to cheek—even playing some serious footsy under the table. Otto had brought the music—a little Tammy Wynette, a little Frank Sinatra—and the food, Tina thought, was excellent. Southern fried chicken, mashed potatoes, gravy, green beans cooked with ham hocks, biscuits, and a dessert that moved Azalia to homesick tears. They left, hand in hand, rosy and pleased with themselves and each other. Glancing out the window, Tina saw them in each other's arms, leaning against the car, kissing like teenagers oblivious of the cold, and she smiled.

It was late, but there was time for a quiet celebration and for Bill to be impressed with what was left of Tina's sweet potato pie, made like Geron's sister Juanita, the one who had died, had taught her. It reminded her of Geron pulling her hair when she blew him at the end of Freddy's party. But now she was here and the pie was good. Nothing like it in the world. So they planned tentatively to add it to their pie menu for their skiers, if they could get the sweet potatoes regular, which Bill doubted. Tina went out to the trailer to a well-earned rest while Bill did the last tidying up. She had plans to go out the next morning early to cruise the snowy forest.

Tina had taken to snowshoes right away, although she had to learn for herself, since she wouldn't listen to him, to pace herself instead of using all her energy in the first half-mile. She continued to love the snow, and love Bill for giving her a way to explore the whitened woods. Tina went out almost every bright morning to see the sparkles, and Bill went along on cross-country skis to save her life if she needed it. When the winter storms rolled in, bringing more snow, Tina sat inside and worked on her scarf, read the paper, and missed Ursula a little. When she got stir crazy, she went into the kitchen and cleaned madly, moving shelves, scrubbing behind appliances, or she cooked, trying out new treats for the weekend crowd, who were rowdy, famished, and faithful. They always tried to hit the Happy Trout on the way up, or on the way down the mountain, one or the other.

Mid-December brought Rachel back, glad to be

out of school, somewhat grateful to be there with her dad and Tina, eager to get away from home and back to the resort, though it wasn't the same without Ursula. And it wasn't the same with her dad there. Tina wasn't as crazy or as much fun. Bill and Tina stayed apart, Bill wondering if she was really going to leave, and Tina wondering how she would manage to stay.

The three of them drove into Pineville together the week before Christmas, where they separated for a few hours and met up again at the truck with bags and mysterious bundles that were strictly hands-off, no peeking. Tina bought a little tree and some red Christmas balls and silver tinsel to decorate the café, since Christmas Eve was on Sunday, when they would be open, and the customers they had been getting lately had been in a very holiday mood, singing "Jingle Bells" and "Silent Night" and "Away in a Manger," which reminded Bill of Shaun Gentry.

Just for a kick, while they were in town, they went to Eddy's Grill, an extravagance since they could so easily have gone back to the Happy Trout. But it's a luxury to eat someone else's cooking once in a while. Spaghetti and meatballs maybe a little better than the Happy Trout's, maybe sausage in it, Bill thought, the apple pie not even close. They drove back quietly through the white trees, the white land stretching to the ridge on both sides, where it dropped off into white. The heater in the truck poured hot air like a river into the cab, and Bill opened the window a little to stay awake.

When they got back to the Happy Trout, Rachel slipped comfortably back into her victim outfit, blaming Bill for not even having a TV and satellite, and not even any way to text her friends, so Bill retreated to his room and closed the door firmly. Tina tried to tempt her with crazy eights but was rebuffed. "God, that's so lame. Leave me alone." So Tina went back to the trailer where Foster was waiting patiently at the door, leaving Rachel to work it out for herself. She wasn't sent to her room, because there was no one left to send her, and because she didn't have a real room here. She retreated to the storeroom she had claimed on her last visit, now automatically hers, having chosen that over forced proximity with a grown-up, even Tina, who had offered to share.

She couldn't believe they had gone off and left her alone. Left her all alone when it's almost Christmas. They didn't want her here. At first they acted like they were glad to see her, but now they were taking her for granite, she thought. She did the teenage shrug, but it didn't work as well to roll her eyes when there was no one there to roll them at. If she had been under six, she would have cried herself wordlessly to sleep and been the better for it. Since she was fifteen, almost sixteen, she polished her resentments, then her toenails, and finally her dreams until she fell asleep.

Ursula called the next morning to say that she was on her way, leaving the shop, where business wasn't nearly as busy as last year. Benny could take care of things. She needed a break, she said. She arrived that afternoon with packages for everyone, even Foster, with hugs, kisses, more hugs, just one more hug, pat, pat. The city was driving her crazy, she said, so she had decided to come up in the mountains where everyone else is crazy too. It only took Tina a minute to move her things to the top bunk, figuring Ursula would rather not negotiate the ladder. And it *was* her trailer. Ursula was happy to help Tina decorate the tree, which had languished outside, leaned against the shed, and even Rachel took a lethargic turn or two with the tinsel, not wanting to miss the fun, although it wasn't that much fun. It helped to have Aunt Ursula there. It kept Tina from being so uptight.

Christmas Day dawned bright and beautiful, but Rachel continued stormy. Tina kept watching her, really wanting to see her happy, to see what a lucky fifteen-year-old girl did on Christmas, but it made Rachel self-conscious, aware that she was behaving badly and angry at having to be aware.

Bill sat on a counter stool, the blue plaid flannel shirt from Ursula laid neatly to the side, the fuzzy blue muffler Tina had knitted for him looped twice around his neck, reading the liner notes from the Dixie Chicks CD from Rachel. Ursula meant to take a peek at the first few pages of the mystery Tina had given her, but had lost her footing and was long gone, following the clues. Why was the hundred-dollar bill wet? What was Angela concealing from the detectives? Her ears twinkled with earrings from Rachel, and on her lap she held the black cashmere sweater from Bill, much too expensive, what was he thinking, but so soft, so butter-soft, and a good color for her, her hands stroking it as she read.

Tina sat with her deck of cards from Rachel, with Elvis on the back just for a joke, and her fancy hand lotion from Ursula, and from Bill, a $50 Christmas bonus inside a card with a picture of a black cat like Foster in a Santa hat on it. She opened and closed it, reading "Merry Christmas from Bill" over and over, wishing it felt like something it didn't. Wishing she had a cashmere sweater to stroke and feeling like a fool, out of place.

Rachel sat surrounded by wrapping paper, ribbons, presents from everyone, and she brooded, missing her mom and even Clive, missing the friends who were like her, flighty and self-centered, missing what Christmas had been like when she was little before her parents were divorced, Christmas when she wanted things, and got the things she wanted. Because she was a good little girl. No more.

Tina rubbed some lotion onto her hands for nothing better to do, offering Rachel a dollop, but Rachel bridled as if she had been offered a cockroach.

"God, no," she said. "That stuff is giving me a headache, take it out of here."

"It's nice," Tina said. "Really. It's sweet pea." She sniffed her hands and smiled encouragingly.

Rachel shook her head.

"Show me that jacket your mom sent—it looks cool." Tina was doing her best, but with a fifteen-year-old girl in a snit, there's no do, there's only try. Really, there's only try and fail.

"Why? Just because all you have to wear is a funky sweatshirt? With that freaking trout on it? It's embarrassing. Why are you always so lame?" Rachel hated herself for what she was doing, and the punishing feeling pushed her into punishing anyone else she could hurt.

"Jesus. Rachel. What's your problem?" Anyone else, Tina would probably have pasted in the mouth, but this was Rachel Baby, Princess R, Miss Rachellini, Miss Thing.

"Why are you even here, Tina? This isn't your family. You're not even my dad's girlfriend, so why are you even here in the first place?"

Bill and Ursula looked up, startled by Rachel's raised voice, but Tina was already halfway across the room, leaving her presents on the table. Bill rose to stop her, but she waved him off. "It's okay, Bill. She called it. I'm not in this family. That's the actual truth. I'll see you tomorrow at prep time."

Tina let him see her face, so he would see she wasn't crying or working up a counter-snit and would let her go, and, stony-faced, she was gone.

Rachel burst into tears.

When she had stopped sobbing enough to be able to talk, she was inconsolable, devastated by her own meanness, hurting Tina, getting rid of Tina, but she really, really, really loved Tina. Tina was like the craziest awesomest person, and even Foster loved Tina, and he hates everyone. How could she have been so awful? Tina would never forgive her, would commit suicide, would never speak to her again, would leave and never ever come back. And this was her last night, Mom was coming for her tomorrow, and now Tina was going to hate her forever. Rachel looked up hopefully through her tangled dark curls at the two full-fledged adults for help, though she reserved the right to reject any advice summarily.

Bill cleared his throat, painfully aware of his own blunder when he had suspected Tina of using a blowjob to arrange for the snowplow. "In my experience," he said, "whenever I have hurt someone, it works best to apologize as soon as possible. Preferably face to face so the person can see I mean it. Do you want to try that, Rachel?"

But Rachel cried even louder. She was so ashamed of what she had done. She couldn't possibly look Tina in the face.

"What would you like to be happening right now?" asked Ursula, looking for a less direct way to a solution.

"We'd all be together, with Tina, and we'd be doing something together, like making taffy or something Dad could do too. So not dancing, I guess."

"I'll have you know, young lady, that I am a disco king once I get going." Bill did a disco thing with his hands.

Rachel laughed, as he had intended she would.

"Here's what we'll do," Ursula suggested. "We'll offer an olive branch. And we'll send Dad as our dove—can't you just see him flutter?"

Bill flapped his blue muffler at her and Rachel laughed again. "Okay, how do we make an olive branch?"

Tina, sitting grimly cross-legged on her bed, was out of plans. The paper on her lap remained blank, the pencil dangling unused from her hand. *I never said I wanted a family*, she thought. *I wanted money. I wanted to be safe. I didn't know*, she thought, and she didn't know what she meant by that at all.

The knock on the door didn't surprise her—Ursula would be coming to try to make her feel better, and that was nice of her. Or maybe she was just ready for the comforts of the bottom bunk. Tina opened the trailer door to find Bill there in his Christmas flannel shirt and his Christmas muffler, teeth chattering in the cold.

"What do you want?"

"Let me in, Tina. I'm freezing out here. I have something I have to say, and I hope you will bear with me, because it's not something I've ever said before, I can promise you that. I'm about as embarrassed as I've ever been—I don't talk like this, it's just not my way of doing things."

She pulled him into the trailer, suddenly aware of what a very small space it was for two bodies, much smaller than when she shared it with Ursula. But it was cold outside, and the cold air was invading the trailer. He closed the door and stood there, still shivering.

"You're not making much sense, Bill. What's the thing you have to say?"

Bill blushed and referred nervously to a scrap of paper he pulled from his pocket. "This is from Rachel, but it's also from Ursula and me. Hold on."

He cleared his throat and struck an odd pose, leering down at her sideways and wiggling his eyebrows. "Hey babbee," he read aloud, squinting in the imperfect light. "You vant to blay de crezzy ets?"

Tina had to laugh. Bill was so uncomfortable an actor, and his look so pathetic, like a dog that is being made to walk around in people clothes to amuse its owner. She knew he was playing it up to make her laugh.

"Yes, babbee," she said. "I vant to blay."

So Tina was drawn back into the group on Christmas evening and helped Ursula and Rachel teach Bill how to blay, as he continued to call it. He seemed to be doing it all wrong, and Rachel kept trying to correct him, but Tina noticed that he won more often than not. They played, and then they danced a little to his new CD, though Tina drew back, so mostly it was Ursula and Rachel, then Bill showing them the one easy line-dance he could remember, making up the parts he couldn't. Rachel tried to show them all how the kids danced, but only Tina caught on. They treated themselves to a late supper and told old jokes, though again Tina mostly listened. She hadn't heard very many jokes. She laughed even when she didn't understand, for the sheer pleasure of laughing with them.

And when it was late and they had wrung the last little drop of pleasure from the evening, the good-nights were tender, hugs all around, even a tentative, shoulder-leaning, almost touchless hug between Bill and Tina, the embrace of ghosts, as if they would burst into flames and ruin the evening if their bodies met.

Rachel left the next day to spend the last of the holidays with her mom and the dumb boyfriend, still in a good mood, but Ursula stayed on into January, wanting to see how this idea of keeping the café open on weekends would work out. She wanted to spend some time with Bill, going over the books, hoping there were profits to split, really avoiding another confusing argument with Benny, damn tired to death of cleaning an endless progression of doggie butts and living in a cloud of doggie breath.

"Business doesn't really pick up until February anyway. Apparently, no one makes a resolution to keep their dog cleaner in the New Year."

Of course, it was good to have Ursula there. Her presence kept Tina and Bill apart and oiled the social machine. She provided some ease, but not lubrication that would have allowed them to slide frictionlessly into each other's arms; that's too much to ask. But her presence did keep Tina and Bill from experiencing the kind of awkwardness that tends to arise when lust and love and need and desire and curiosity get all wrapped up with fear and shame, as they frequently do. Tina kept close to Ursula, but kept her distance from Bill. Bill kept close to Ursula, but well out of Tina's magnetic pull. This is a geometry that can't be charted without positing more than four dimensions.

The days stayed bright and cold, so Tina borrowed Bill's gloves when she went out to get the mail. There were usually just bills, junk mail, stray Christmas cards from Bill's relatives, the dentist, the vet. "WE LOVE OUR PETS!" it said, with a picture of a cute little kitten in a Santa hat. So even Foster got mail. Tina was surprised to see that there was a letter for her. The envelope was hand-printed, and it was addressed to Tina Vampire @ The Happy Trout. There was no return address. Tina's first reaction was wariness; most of the unexpected messages in her life had been bad news. But clearly this was not from any part of the network of social agencies, courtrooms, probation officers, or collection agencies she was experienced with. She pulled off the gloves with her teeth and tore off the end of the envelope, the way Bill did. Inside was a letter from Rachel.

Dear Tina,

I bet your surprised to get a letter from me. I am in Keyboarding class, and I have to write a letter to someone. So lucky you. LOL.

It doesn't matter what it says, only the format has to be just exactly like Mrs. Forel says. She's picky.

I hope you are fine, I am fine, and I hop Foster is fine. And Dad. I have a new boyfriend, only I really have two new boyfriends. Tell Ursula that they make me laugh. And the inside of my wrist is getting lonely. You know what I mean, but don't tell.

I decided it's okay with me if your my dad's girlfried, I decided because your awesome. LOL. Mom is her mean old self and Clive is getting better. He said I could not be grounded which is so not what Mom says. Kiss Foster for me, K? I know your not a vampire, jk.

Love from your Princess,
Rachel

It was Tina's first real letter, and she read it over and over, standing next to the pile of dirty snow slush in the afternoon sun, letting the warmth trickle down her body, smiling, caught unaware, surprised by Rachel. Foster rubbed himself around her legs and she put her hand down for him to slide against, over and over, head to tail, then turn around, and back down the other side. Finally, she unzipped her jacket and tucked the letter into her bra and went back in to chop onions, finer, Bill had said.

As she tied on a clean apron and pulled out the box of onions, selected the knife she liked to use, although it was evidently according to Bill the wrong one, she saw through the hatch that Bill and Ursula were in one of the booths, in deep conference, though there were none of the ledgers or tax documents they had been poring over for the last few days in front of them. They looked serious. Tina washed the first onion, made the first slice, and listened with half of her attention, the other half being still on her letter. Probably five onions would be enough to fill the bin. Maybe six since they would be chopped so very very very fine, just to please Bill.

"No, Barbara called this morning. Evidently Rachel's been letting boys into her window at night."

Ursula's murmur, something reasonable or comforting, not to worry.

"You know Barbara never calls me, she hates to call me. But she says Rachel is acting like a little whore, that's her word, and I'm not going to stand for it. I won't have my daughter whoring around with those boys."

More inaudible Ursula, but Bill interrupted her, his voice getting louder and louder, the word "whore" hitting Tina's ears like a blow from an angry hand. Whore. Whore. Tina chopped the onions faster and faster, finer and finer, until they were a fine pool of mush. She slid them off the chopping block into the bin, and went through into the café side, where Bill was still talking. She slammed the bin onto the table, sending onion particles flying everywhere, like a caustic snow flurry.

"Just so you know," she said, in a loud voice, controlled but vibrating with anger. "A whore gets paid. She likes the guy, or she doesn't, she wants to do it, or she doesn't, she gets hurt, or she doesn't, but she always, always gets paid. Is Rachel getting paid?"

Bill dumbly shook his head, the onions starting to make his eyes run, so that he saw a blurry Tina looking down at him through his tears, her anger radiating and adding to the sting of the finely chopped onions.

"No," Tina said. "She doesn't get paid. Then whatever she chooses to do, she is not a whore." Her reasonable tone deserted her and she lifted the onion bin and slammed it down again. "A whore gets money," she yelled into his streaming face, and sailed out of the café, weeping herself, and went down to the river to cool off, leaving Bill and Ursula flabbergasted, dotted with spicules of onion, trying to wipe them off but finding the napkins on the tabletop had also been onionized, finally having to stumble into the kitchen and take turns at the tap in order to get clear.

"Jesus wept!" Bill said.

"Him too," said Ursula.

Bill wet a few bar towels and started back to the restaurant side to mop up the booth and anywhere else the onions had landed, but Ursula took them out of his hands.

"I'll clear things up here. You clear things up with Tina. We can't leave her out there. You have to bring her in."

"Okay," Bill said. He had once thought life at the Happy Trout would be simple. He headed down to the river, Tina's red parka in his hand, knowing that's where she would be. And that she would get cold.

Tina wasn't in her usual spot, but several yards farther down the river, sitting on a log, digging her boots resentfully into the last bit of mushy snow that lined the riverbank. She saw him coming, but looked away. Bill handed her the parka, which she put on, and he sat down on the far end of the log and thought for a minute.

"The crezzy ets thing isn't good enough for this situation, is it," Bill said.

Tina shook her head stiffly and continued to look away, across the river.

He went on. "No, not this time. I'm sorry. I was freaking out about Rachel. It's hard to have a daughter grow up. It's really hard because I'm not there to keep an eye on things. It makes me afraid for her because

I know first-hand what men can be like. That's not an excuse."

Tina just went on punishing the snow, now smashed into icy mud beneath her feet.

"But the real thing is, Tina, I'm sorry for offending you. I have no earthly business insulting you or your life or the people you've probably cared about. I don't know anything about it. I'm an ignorant son of a bitch, and that's a fact." He was encouraged to see that her feet had become still, though she still gazed up the river.

"But I don't think that life was good enough for you," he said. "I think you were mistreated, whether you think so or not, and that you were as happy as you could manage to be only because you're a strong person. But you need to be happier. That's what I think."

She still didn't look at him, but she seemed to have softened. Bill didn't know what else he could safely say. He picked up a flat rock and skipped it across the river, one, two, three skips and it sank. He realized Tina was watching him, so he picked up another and really put his elbow into it. Five skips. After a third one, five again, he picked out another rock and handed it to Tina to try.

"I never saw that before," she said. She had been watching him, the sideways way he was throwing, so she managed one skip before the stone went down with a plunk.

"It has to be a flat rock, and a round flat rock works the best," Bill said. "Uncle Foster used to call that kind of rock a donnick. Here's one that ought to work."

"I never heard of a donnick," Tina said, but she got three skips out of the one Bill had handed her.

"I'm guessing that's some kind of word from Arkansas. That's where he was from." Bill was standing now, to free up his elbow and get a better angle for his throws. Tina stood next to him, reaching down to select a good stone, a donnick, and attempting to improve her technique and better her last one. Six skips—that was the best yet! It was good to see her smile.

The river ran on no matter how many stones danced on its surface and then, all energy spent, descended to rest on its rocky bottom. The river made its liquid noise, water striking against stone, water against air, against water, against time.

It was natural after a while, when they were tired of skipping stones, for the two of them to turn together and walk back to the Happy Trout Café where Ursula had chopped the onions needed for the evening menu, but not really fine enough.

12

Life isn't fair. Just do your best. And stand up straight.

— Your Mother

THERE'S SOMETHING ABOUT SPRING in the mountains, its inevitability in question because the cold nights and the cold days still send us scurrying for shelter if we have any sense. Until the waters rise, spring remains a rumor. All that gives it away is this: the winter sun that can burn our skin even as we trudge through snow, even as we freeze to death on some fatal sunny day, seems now, when spring is in the offing, to warm the air around us, to leave a safety margin, a narrow shell of body heat not stolen. The smell of mud cannot be far behind. The birds and frogs hold their breath, ready to exhale in a million tweets and groans. Respectively.

Tina didn't think about spring coming, but she found herself restive, wanting more things to happen besides the endless, eminently doable rounds of prep, cooking, and clean-up that would begin in April when the Happy Trout was again open as a campground. The skiers were not enough. Foster was not enough. She needed more.

She started going with Bill to the far ends of the campground, slipping silently into the passenger seat of the truck, often with one thermos of coffee with cream, no sugar, the way Bill liked it, and another thermos laced with cream and plenty of sugar. She observed his work silently, sometimes handing a tool to him as he jacked up sunken picnic tables or re-set the bolts, handing it to him like a nurse in the ER on TV. She quickly got the hang of how the different tools worked, when a bolt would strengthen things and when a board had to be replaced. She went along to the hardware store and the lumberyard and helped load and carry. She helped him paint the public restrooms, him in the gents, her in the ladies, which was silly if you think about it.

As Tina swabbed on the creamy paint, she started thinking about the songs they had sung in music class at St. Nicholas Children's Home, or maybe it was at Red Robin Camp, what was it, about running all day and all night. She started to hum, then to sing, "Gotta run all day, gotta run all night. I bet my money on the ball-tail nag, dum diddle dum...."

She smiled when she heard a mellifluous baritone coming through the ventilation panel that connected the male and female compartments. "Going to run all night, going to run all day."

Okay, that made it work out better, no reason you would have to start with day after all, so Tina joined in and they finished together, then sang it again, now that they had the words working. A few more times, then "Old Lang Sign," which Tina had heard every New Year's Eve, including a weird country and western version Bill had played for the skiers, so she knew it even though the words didn't make any sense. Then "When I'm Sixty-Four," with Bill providing the horn section, "Prrp puh prrp puh prrp." Tina wished Ursula and Rachel could hear them.

It made for a cheerful morning, and the painting was done in less time than Bill had figured. When they each emerged from their respective sides of the little building, speckled with paint, Tina held out Bill's thermos, and the two of them sat in the truck, side by side, not singing now, but well satisfied with their work, sipping.

"Did we get Ursula's check sent out?" Bill asked.

Tina just nodded.

"We need to get some orders out this afternoon, or we'll run out of stuff and have to change the menu, which makes us look bad. I'll show you how."

Tina nodded again. She was happy. Happy and kind of sad.

Back in the office, Bill pulled out the suppliers' files, full of lists and receipts to refer to. He had always liked this part of the business, looking at the past and preparing for the future, breaking down the expenses, analyzing the options. Doing the food orders with Tina, though, was not so peaceful, since Tina went at it the same way she used to shop—looking for something fabulous that couldn't fail to impress, something that made her heart sing. After an hour or two of struggle, Bill sent her out to the café, ostensibly to make another small pot of coffee, but really arranging it so he could be alone and get some sensible work done. You don't order crab if it's not on the menu, even if it sounds delicious. Fishermen don't want to eat crab salad. They want burgers and fries and no, not chicken salad with walnuts either.

As Tina lounged behind the lunch counter, waiting for the coffee to brew and giving herself a good talking-to about patience and being realistic because really, she knew better, she unfolded the newspaper and browsed through it. On the second page of the metro section was a picture of Brad, facing forward, and then in profile. He looked haggard but younger, and her first thought was that he had been arrested. Her golden days at the Happy Trout might be about to come to an end. She had $230 left after holiday expenses counting the $50 Christmas bonus from Bill.

It wasn't much get-away money.

But the headline read, not "Bank Robber Apprehended, Accomplice Sought," but:

Fatal Fiery Crash Sends Bank Loot Flying

Reno, NV — An estimated one hundred thousand dollars in cash was blown into the sky Sunday at an Interstate-80 rest stop east of Santuario, Nevada. The money was released when a black Escalade crossed the center divide and collided with the back of a propane fuel tanker.

Dead at the scene were Bradlee Jasyn Hines, 24, and Shatina Mai Wenona Martinez, 31, both wanted in connection with a Sacramento area bank robbery. The driver of the tanker was not in the truck at the time of impact.

The explosion threw $20, $50, and $100 bills from the back of the SUV. Nevada Highway Patrol officer Maxwell Brimm says unburned bills were carried by a freak 30-mile-per-hour wind into the town of Santuario, where Sunday Mass had just ended.

One resident describes the event as "an act of God," but the NHP, working in conjunction with the FBI, states that the money represents evidence in a major felony crime and should be handed over to the authorities.

According to local Sheriff Jack Dodson, a great deal of money is still unaccounted for. "Some of it may have burned in the fire. But this is a poor town. Some unemployed guy finds a hundred dollars in his bean field is not likely to report it. It's just a fact of life," he said.

The bodies are being held in the central Reno morgue pending funeral arrangements. The rest stop has been decorated with numerous memorias, crosses and flowers. Dodson says NHP moved some of these decorations to an adjoining field to allow travelers access to the rest stop.

Tina took the paper down to the river, her river, and there she wept, staring at the picture, which must have been taken, she thought, when eighteen-year-old Brad was busted for a botched auto theft. Little Brad, his eyes so wide with excitement and fear, always saying yes without understanding how anything worked, just wanting to say yes. Baby Brad, so grateful to be picked up and held. So clinging. So terrified. So foolish. And now so dead. She took the page with the pathetic face, the stupid headline, the dumb jokiness, and tore it into pieces, which she dropped, like tears, into the dark water, which carried them far away to where all waters merge, the end.

Brad gone, as though he had just that moment driven away screaming, leaving her to be eaten by bears. Whatever hot young girl he had picked up, lured no doubt by the promise of money, coke, a good time, gone now, party over, and held in the morgue under the wrong name. Double gone. Tina released from the past—first Freddy, then Brad. And in some obscure way, it felt like maybe even Tina herself was gone, a life lost, a gamble that was never going to pay off, finally lost and gone, forgotten. Freddy would think she was dead along with Brad. He would be glad, would laugh when someone made a stupid joke about her. But he would quit looking. Because she was already dead.

Tina wished Brad could have played in the snow with her, skipped stones across the water and called them donnicks, that he could have seen those spiders that look like they're stuck to the surface of the stream, unable to get down into the life below with the fishes and unable to rise and fly. She would have shown him how they walk on water. He wouldn't believe it. He would think at first it was some kind of trick.

When she went back in to the office where Bill was anxiously waiting for her, thinking she might have given up, that he had been too impatient with her about the walnuts, he saw the tears standing in her eyes, turning them from their usual shiny to a glistening black. Tina told him that she was just tired, that she had seen in the paper that an old friend had died, trying to make it sound like she had been thumbing through the obituaries instead of reading crime headlines.

"Cancer," she said, lying. "I knew him a long time, since I was little. I don't know anybody else who died." Not true. She had known a lot of people who died, one way or another, including Ricky Dick, who had flown out of the Escalade, flapping like a rag and screaming.

Tina was glad in one way that the newspaper page with Brad's haunted face on it had floated away on the river in pieces, safely carried away, gone from sight. Bill hadn't known Brad for long, but he would most likely recognize him. It was a pretty good picture, for a mug shot. She had been tempted to keep it, to remember. But she had decided, in the event, to let it go, and she imagined it now as though Brad were floating down the river, playing his hands in the water like a baby and laughing his goofy laugh.

Bill took her small hand and held it for a long moment in both of his, smoothing the golden skin with his thumbs, then released her, and she went to the trailer and had a really good cry, this the second time she had cried since Freddy turned on her and his guys had treated her like she was nothing. She wasn't counting the tears shed during the bear attack.

Foster jumped up next to her on the bed where she had collapsed and curled up against her body. And she cried from relief that maybe she could stay at the Happy Trout, that Bill wouldn't find out about the bank robbery and make her leave or call the cops, and maybe all would be well. And she cried for poor little Brad. And for all that money gone for good. Good-bye.

That night, she dreamed about Brad sinking into the water. She could see his lips moving, but she couldn't hear him. She knew he was in danger, that the bear was in the river. She had to warn him, to get him to listen. She struggled to shout at him, and the shout came out as a strangled cry that woke her up. She knew immediately that she had been dreaming and that Brad was safely dead where no one could hurt him. Ursula had said to help herself to whatever there was, so Tina turned on the bedside light, plopped a Sweet Dreams tea bag in a mug, plugged in the electric kettle, and waited for it to whistle.

Outside, Bill had found himself without slippers or robe, standing in the cold night with his hand on the trailer door latch. And then he woke up the rest of the way. He thought he must have heard Tina scream, and here he was. But when the light went on in the trailer and he heard her moving around, he pulled his hand away and went back to bed, his feet now freezing cold, and he tried to dispel the continuing sense of

Tina's presence, a haunting sensation that still filled the curve of his body when he faced one way, and curled around his shoulders when he turned over. He tried to convince himself that it had been a reasonable decision to walk away, maybe even a narrow escape. If he had knocked, anything could have happened. And everything might have changed.

Tina was in a subdued mood for the next few days, quiet and withdrawn, not, as Bill assumed, out of grief, but lying low, needing the Happy Trout more than ever, her escape routes, however illusory, cut off and the options on her list now seeming even stupider and more childish. She didn't want to be a nun. She wanted to stay with Bill and learn the business and be so useful that he couldn't do without her. So she was lying low, keeping her ears and eyes open, watching how things would go.

Bill was surprised to realize that she could do the orders just fine, even though they had left off his lesson at the point where she was wondering what they could do with "flaked coconut."

"You don't do it that way," Bill had said. "You order what you need to order for the menu, not the other way around." And now she evidently got it.

He even trusted her to drive into town in the truck sometimes now that the roads were clear of snow and black ice to pick up things they needed, plywood or fresh lettuce, or even to drop off the week's earnings at the bank, which Tina cased with the dispassionate interest of a retired professional. Young security guy with his attention focused almost exclusively on the cute little girl in the second cage. Low counters. A shifty manager who looked like one of Freddy's friends she had done at Freddy's request. As she remembered it, he had expected a lot out of a freebie.

When she came into the Happy Trout after one such jaunt, she could see by Bill's creased forehead that something was troubling him.

"I got a call," he said, "and it didn't make much sense to me, frankly. Some girl who kept describing herself as 'the great-granddaughter' wants to reserve the family campground two weeks from now, which is fine because it's open and the only bookings we have are a couple of fishermen who won't want anything much."

"What about the Gentries? Did they cancel?"

"They moved it up. Coming in a few days. And they just want one spot, not the family grounds. But Azalia Truitt called. They want to camp here while their house gets painted, same weekend the great-granddaughter is wanting to book. More fun than a motel, she said. And there could be more."

"So let the great-granddaughter reserve the site. What's the problem?"

"They're going to have live music, for one thing, amplified as near as I could tell. There was a lot of background noise, like a flock of birds chattering, like she was calling from the zoo. And she called it a fiesta, but evidently it's also some kind of pilgrimage. I don't know. Do we even do that here? It sounds like a cult."

"Give me the info, Bill, and I'll sort it out. It would be great to have the family site rented out so early—be a good start on the season, don't you think?"

"I don't want to get involved in anything too weird, that's all. I'm not going to have my customers harassed to join some crazy religion. Name is Jennifer Aguirre." He handed her a post-it. "And there's the number."

"Hi, Jennifer. This is Tina Martin at the Happy Trout. Bill says you are looking to book the family campground weekend after next. Is that right? Something about a zoo?"

Not about a zoo, after all. What Bill had heard was Jennifer's grandma and aunts trying to help her make the phone call. Luckily, someone had shown up to take them all to Denny's for Senior Discount Day, so that level of confusion was removed. But there was more to come.

"You're having a fiesta, is that right? Can you tell

me about that, just for starters?"

"Short version—and this will sound a little weird, I warn you—my *bisabuelo*, sorry, my great-grandfather had a religious experience that saved his life. And then the money got all spread out over the town where his *primo*, sorry—my family speaks mostly Spanish and I'm having a hard time switching gears." Jennifer took a deep breath, let it out with a sigh, and continued. "Okay, so, where his favorite cousin Ernesto, lives, so they're having a pilgrimage from Sacramento to Santuario where there will be a mass, and then halfway back to Sacramento, which is about where your place is, so it's perfect because then everyone has the same distance to go home after the fiesta. Does any of this make sense?"

"Okay," Tina said, her mind spinning with the realization that this wasn't just a big event. It was dangerous. Was this really that *Maria Bandida* thing? She had assumed the excitement would die down, that there would be no more miracles to feed the religious passions of the Aguirre clan, but it seemed that Ernesto, damn that Ernesto, had made the connection. She didn't understand it. The robbery had gone so well, but the complications of the getaway never ended. Could she keep the miracle, and so the crime, from getting back to her? At the same time, it would bring in the big bucks, maybe take a wrinkle off of Bill's forehead.

"Will your great-grandfather be there?"

"He's the one who had the vision, plus he's the oldest so he'll be right in the middle of things. Probably sleep through a lot of it. He's in a wheelchair, but we'll get him settled where people can pay their respects and he'll be fine. Have the time of his life. Shouldn't be any problems there."

"Okay," Tina said, feeling her way. "How many people will attend?"

"The Sacramento family is about fifty people plus the kids, and I don't really know how many from Santuario. Lots, I would think, since it's their miracle too. Maybe another hundred?"

"Oh Christ," Tina said.

"We don't need anything but the space," Jennifer said. "We can pay for more spaces, if the big site gets filled. And we can pay up front, if that helps. If you can take cash, which there seems to be a lot of. If you need to get a rider on your insurance, we can pay that premium for you. The thing is, we really need to be right there. Where you are. At the Happy Trout. It's the only place that works."

"Bill says you'll have amplified music, is that right?"

"My cousin Mort has a band that's gonna play, *norteño* and some *mariachi*, but the accordion player isn't very good, so he won't play the whole time, especially since it's going to be a *mariachi* mass."

"There's a mass?" Tina could see why Bill had been confused. "I thought it was a party."

"Yeah, a fiesta. The mass is in Santuario. Mort says he and my cousin Randy are writing a *corrido*, a song for the whole fiesta. The good thing, though, is that we'll only be there for the afternoon. And evening, though lots of people will go home after the *comida*, sorry, the picnic."

"Well, it sounds like quite an event," Tina said. "I imagine we can work out the details. I'm a little concerned about the other campers. It's just me and Bill up here, and with that big an event, we'll have to close the café so we can service the restrooms and keep the trash emptied. Plus things come up. That could be a problem for the other campers, you know?"

"Send them over," Jennifer said. "Listening to my grandmother and her sisters, there's gonna be a mountain of tamales, all kinds, and a barbeque and Aunt Dee's chicken molé and all kinds of food, enough for ten times the number of people."

"Really? Send them over?"

"It's a fiesta. The more people that come, the more respect is paid to the saint. That's how it works."

"There won't be preaching, will there? Because that wouldn't sit right with Bill. He doesn't want our regular customers bugged."

Jennifer laughed. "No preaching. Just music, beer,

food, dancing. A great big party. What do you say, Tina? I'll be up that way on Tuesday. I could stop by with the deposit, see the place, and we can make plans."

After hanging up the phone, Tina sat for a moment at the desk, her hands flat on the desktop, mind working on two tracks. First, a mental list of all the things that would have to be done, the details she would have to iron out, with Bill, with Jennifer, with the insurance company. What had Jennifer meant by "a rider?" Second, she was fervently praying for an end to miracles.

But that was silly. There are always more miracles: a baby born, spring again, a timely rainfall, love and sex and robin eggs. The age-old list is long and softened by the touch of human hands and the mist of human tears, and it circles back on itself endlessly, twisting into a Moebius strip braided from the inevitable, the possible, and the improbable. Love and sex and robin eggs, a baby born. And so it goes. Spring again.

Tina and Bill worked it out, with Bill calling his friend Ronnie about the insurance. Leona and Phil Gentry arrived in their travel trailer, pooper scooper on the ready like the good citizens they were, with their two mild-mannered poodles, Jack and Dandy, and with a baffled Shaun, coming back to the Happy Trout, not certain where else to be.

Shaun had expected to be readjusted to civilian life by now, but everything around him looked thin and slightly translucent, as though cut out of isinglass. He found he hadn't wanted to travel; he wanted to be home in a way he couldn't quite achieve. He found that he couldn't stand his high school buddies anymore, their beer drinking, their devotion to punishingly brutal music at high decibels, their general grogginess until well after noon. Going into the construction business with them, as undisciplined and feckless as they were, was out of the question, a losing proposition from the get-go. School? Maybe. He had been accepted at UCLA and Uncle Sam would foot the bill. It would be okay, but he knew his parents were starting to worry a little. It was only a matter of time before he got The Talk. Son, what are you going to do with your life? He wanted to talk to Bill. He wanted to see Tina.

So he was sitting in the café, teasing Tina about her attempt to do the crossword puzzle, ("'spic and blank' is 'span', Tina, not 'dago',") when Jennifer Aguirre walked in, as beautiful as the first new morning—dark star-filled eyes, a cap of silky black hair with tendrils curling down around her slender neck, lips like the petals of fresh roses, her breasts like pomegranates swelling her black Los Lobos T-shirt, oh vision, tell me your name that I may conjure you.

"Hi," she said, glancing at Shaun. Cute guy. "I'm Jennifer. You must be Tina."

"I'm Shaun."

"Oh—spelled how? Are you a S-E-A-N? Or a S-H-A-W-N?"

"S-H-A-U-N."

"Oh, of course. That explains everything," she said, and smiled up at him through her endless curving lashes.

"Sure, hi," Tina said, not sure she would be heard. "Just let me bring the papers out here, okay? Bill's out and about right now so I'm on my own." She left Jennifer and Shaun and went back into the office. By the time she got back, they were deep in conversation, Shaun mostly listening and Jennifer explaining her pre-med program at Fullerton and her plans to work at a barrio pediatrics clinic.

"Or family practice. I don't really know yet."

"You'll be a great doctor," Shaun said. "You have the hands." He touched her hand with one finger, to see if she would let him, to get started, to see how her smooth brown skin felt. "You have the dedication. Do you have a serious boyfriend?" Shaun figured anyone less than serious could be swept out of the way. Serious would take more doing, but it would be worth it.

Jennifer looked at him for a moment, seriously,

taking his measure. "Not really. I don't have much time for going out or doing clubs or all those LA kinds of things. I have to keep my grades way up or my chances for another scholarship go way down. You know how that is."

"Um," said Tina, who had been standing there unnoticed. "Here's the paperwork. Let's take it to a booth. Do you want some coffee or anything?"

"Sure." Jennifer slid into a booth, and Shaun escorted Tina into the seat next to her, so he could sit across from them and gaze.

"I'll bring the coffee," he said.

"I'll take some cream with mine," Jennifer said. Shaun smiled at her approvingly. Of course she would. Just right. Then the coffee would match the lightest highlights in her dark hair. Beautiful.

"Creamer in the little fridge thing," Tina said.

So for the next hour, Tina explained the setup, took notes, and they talked it over, Jennifer always aware of Shaun's gaze on her face, tracing every angle and curve. She turned to him often, to ask his advice, to explain her family, and sometimes just to smile. He looked across at her proudly, as though she were his own invention, which, in a way, she was.

"You're probably going to want to see the site, see if there are any problems we need to tackle," Tina said, though she was a little concerned about turning them loose in the woods, where they might vanish into the springtime or bed down on the patch of tentative wildflowers that graced the riverbank. She had certainly been around sex before, but this was love-at-first-sight, like in the songs, which she had always assumed were lies to get women hot, like wine or coke.

Of course, Shaun went with them to look. The family campground was still damp and a little dispirited, but the picnic tables were all level, the trashcans had been scraped and cleaned out, and the restrooms were freshly painted. It looked like fairyland to Shaun in his altered state, and Jennifer was pleased with it, liked the openness where couples could dance and the space for the band. The smaller campground sites around it were empty, so it looked like plenty of space to expand.

"We should probably go ahead and reserve all the sites around this area. Can we do that?"

"Sure," Tina said. "It'll cost you more, of course." She couldn't wait to tell Bill about this cash bonanza, so early in the season. He would be pleased, she hoped. Shaun, predictably, walked Jennifer to her car. When Bill got back an hour later, Tina was looking at them out the café window, Shaun and Jennifer standing right where Otto and Azalia had stood, talking, looking, but not touching, not kissing, not yet.

She wasn't jealous. She could have had something

with Shaun the last time he was here, could have enjoyed his smooth, muscled young body. He had asked her, after all. But there was Bill. She sighed and started wiping down the kitchen counters. Bill heard her sigh and thought she might be tired, still grieving for her dead friend, so he took the cleaning cloth out of her hand and took over. She stood there, unsure of what to do. Had she been doing it wrong? She picked up another cloth, and together they made short work of it.

When Tina glanced out again, Shaun and Jennifer were gone. She and Foster trailed down to sit by the water, tired of all the coming and going. She sat in her spot, her coat wrapped around her tightly against the cooling air that flowed from the forest and the damp air that rose from the river. The snow, her beautiful snow, was almost all gone now. She wished she had gone out every day, every minute. She wished the white magic of it back, a bootless wish, though the snow did in fact come again six months later. But now the few remaining drifts were dirty, collapsing into themselves, dried out, returning to earth. The river, fed by the first melting snows in the mountains above, ran high, flashing in the slanting sun, dark and bottomless-seeming in the deep holes where the fish slept a little longer. The trees that had dropped their dry leaves even before the first snow were sprigged now with shiny green new ones, and even the pines were decorated at the tips of the branches with bundles of soft young needles. The damp ground, the glorious mud of spring, squished under her feet as she shifted on her hard seat.

This place, this Happy Trout, where lovers embraced or refrained from embracing in the parking lot, where even a cat thrown out of a speeding car could land on all four feet, could fall in love, where the currents of time washed in, bringing Tina, Brad, the bear, Freddy, Ursula, Rachel, Shaun, and then washed them out again, the bear, Freddy, Ursula, Rachel, Shaun. But not Tina. And then they came back to the Happy Trout where she was waiting for them, Rachel, Ursula, Shaun. She let their faces play across her memory, out and back. Not Brad back, though, and she hoped not ever Freddy. It made her dizzy to hold still and let life swirl around her. But there was always Bill, Bill unmoving, Bill at the center, Bill the heart of it all.

13

Holy Mary, Mother of God, pray for us sinners,
now and at the hour of our death. Amen.

Tina enjoyed the planning meetings with Jennifer, with Shaun now inevitably in tow, and she felt confident about the plans, as far as plans for a big event like this—like the party that had catapulted her away from Freddy—as far as plans could be counted on at all. She remembered the mess-up at Freddy's party, the fireworks insulting him in big red letters, and she vowed to think of everything this time. She set up a schedule for her and Bill to service the johns, empty trash, sort the trash into the recycling bins, and generally monitor the festivity from the sidelines, and she took on most of the rounds herself. She wanted to witness the fiesta, the most exciting event the Happy Trout had ever hosted, at least while she was there, but she was also afraid that Manny Aguirre, the great-grandfather who had seen the Virgin Mary rob a bank with his very own eyes, would spot her and everything would tumble apart—the vision, the fiesta, and Tina's life at the Happy Trout, which meant Bill. She would have to see what she could while staying out of sight as much as possible.

The day of the fiesta was fair and cool, with only an errant cloud or two floating idly across the sky. Tina made tour after tour around the fiesta grounds, making sure that everything, every last thing, was perfect. Bill watched her come and go, ready to help but also ready to let Tina take the lead. It was so clearly her thing. She was bright with excitement. She came back into the café, closed for this one special day, and consulted her lists, which spread over Bill's desk in the office and had started a little outpost on the kitchen's stainless steel counter. She had already watered the roses in front, which, in the loveable manner of roses, had chosen this day to open, red and pink and fragrant.

"It's just a big family picnic, Tina. You didn't do all this when the Gentries were here, and they stayed for two days."

"I was new then," Tina said. "And it's not just a picnic, Bill—it's a fiesta. And if it comes off right, it's supposed to be an annual event every year. That's good for the Happy Trout, good for business."

Tina was there waiting when the cars and trucks and low-riders, scheduled to arrive at 1:00, pulled in at 2:30, music pouring out of a loudspeaker held steady in the back of a pick-up by three old men. The music poured, and the people filled the campsite, the papas greeting each other with loud shouts, as though they had not parted in Santuario an hour earlier, the mamas setting out the food, teasing and quarreling.

"See how you are! You want to seduce the good-looking young men with your green tamales, you shameless thing!" and they would all laugh and continue to set out and rearrange the dishes until either everything was right or maybe they got tired of the exercise. The papas brought out large tubs of ice with beer bottles and cans thrust in deep, joking that the young men wouldn't find them that way. They laughed and pulled the tabs, helping themselves to cut lemons and salt set out on an overturned tub, to keep the beer company on the way down.

Tina stood sheltered behind a pine tree, a plastic garbage bag hanging limp at her side. This was more commotion than she had imagined. It was a bigger deal. She hoped it would come off all right since it was her thing, not Bill's. She wanted to show him that she could make this work, that she was good for the Happy Trout.

She saw that a tall pole with a newly painted image of *Nuestra Señora Ladrona* fastened to it was driven into the ground so that the saint could enjoy her party along with everyone else. She was a bright Madonna, smiling sweetly, her face golden, her eyes a darker gold, to symbolize the money. On her lap where the Baby Jesus might have been lay a pistol with a halo around it, its edges jagged, almost like the corona around the word "POW!" in a comic book. The wooden frame around the Virgin's image was painted skillfully with angels toting loot bags, and between them, dollar signs and coins falling into upstretched hands. It had taken Ernesto's youngest grandson, Robert, four days to complete. Pinned to the frame were little tokens and pictures—a bicycle, a TV, a prescription bottle, all the things *Santa Ladrona's* bounty had paid for. Tina was glad to see that the Mother of God looked well pleased. She also looked a lot like Tina.

A careful young man wheeled Manny Aguirre into the center, next to the Saint who had healed him and blessed his people. He seemed smaller than Tina remembered him, pale and drawn in, but his smile was wide and glorious. Tina ducked back behind a tree and hurried down the path, glad to see Manny again and glad to avoid being seen.

The old people had dressed in their Sunday clothes to honor the *Señora*: bright dresses and black shawls for the women, the men in clean trousers and white shirts rolled up at the sleeves or unbuttoned to hang loose when their wives weren't looking. The young people gathered at the other end of the campground, separate except where the sheer numbers made the two groups overlap. They were dressed in jeans and T-shirts, the girls with flashing gold earrings and high-heeled sandals making it hard for them to walk steadily across the rough ground, so that they had to hang onto each other and laugh. They talked and teased and shoved each other, sometimes out of the group, but Tina noticed that the outcast always circled back and found a spot next to a sweetheart or a favorite cousin. The girls with regular sweethearts stood with their backs against the boy's chest, his arms wrapped around her protectively, and they rocked with the music, not yet dancing. Santana, Los Panchos, Perez Prado, Celia Cruz for their parents, old music from Mexico for the really old people.

Ronny Haskell and his friend Bob Hatch, regular customers who always came early to the Happy Trout to celebrate the end of tax season, had caught the limit and were walking back to their campsite, down the road that ran between the official fiesta grounds and the adjacent sites. None of this had been there that morning when they had headed out. It had been quiet and deserted then, with the occasional screech of a jay to break the silence. They had been told there was going to be a party, but this was more than they had envisioned. They tried not to stare, but a fiesta in full swing, one you have to walk through, can't be ignored.

Tina tried to intercept them in case they would be irate with the people and the noise, but she couldn't get to them through the crowd, and she kept getting distracted by the vibrating excitement all around her.

The center area was alive with colors, movement, music and the outside picnic tables were occupied mainly by families with small children, the mamas making sure the little ones ate their *tacos*, talking to them in stern voices, trying to keep them from running wild underfoot like little crazies. The two fishermen, rods in hand, full creel banging against Ronny's knee gently at each step, meant to stop and watch for just a minute, so they stepped back when Ernesto gestured them, come on, come on, come on to the party. They demurred by gesturing back, hands held up to say, "No thanks," but they looked to Ernesto like they were being robbed, and that made him laugh. *Santa Maria Ladrona*. Clearly they were honored guests, whether they knew it or not.

"Come everybody," he said. "*Fiesta* for everybody! Have a beers! Good for your health. Make you strong. So you can catch more fish!"

"Oh, no, thanks," Bob said, looking nervously at Ronny. What did he think? Should they? "We're just passing by. Besides, I have to say, I'm not even Catholic."

"No problema!" Ernesto said, having taken a great fancy to them. He took Bob's sleeve and pointed into the crowd. "See this two guys over there? Both Seven Day, both of them, brothers. Nice guys. Maybe they end up in hell, who knows. But they come to the fiesta. See that fancy guy in the red shirt, the one standing with the big woman? That's my cousin Jorge and his wife Celia—both Baptist. No kidding. But everybody loves the Virgin, no? Everybody likes *tamales*! Everybody likes a beer! Come, my friends!" So they were pulled into the party, and Tina saw that Ernesto was introducing them to all his friends and family, his arms across their shoulders, steering them gently towards the beer.

Tina didn't know what to do with herself in this fiesta she had first accidentally inspired and then carefully coordinated. She felt like a spirit, like she was a holy ghost floating around the fiesta blessing people. But with a big black trash bag in her hand.

She moved quietly to the table where Jennifer's mama was setting out paper plates, and automatically started setting out cutlery and napkins with her. Mrs. Aguirre had liked Tina's way of doing business right away. And she took advantage of Tina's presence to talk about her worries, thinking that Tina might have some insight into how she could control those daughters of hers. Oh, those daughters.

It was clear that she was proud of both of them. Ariana was following right behind in her big sister's footsteps just like when they were little, but neither one of them married yet, and so no grandchildren to love. Her cousin Patty had already five. What is a mother to do with such girls. But there was hope. Ariana was bringing her *novio*, the boy she met at nursing school, so the family could meet him for the first time. Mrs. Aguirre started to complain that Ariana's boyfriend was black, though Ariana described him as *moreno*, dark-skinned, but she caught herself. Tina herself was the color of a beautiful, light beef broth. She might take it the wrong way.

On the phone, Ariana told such nice stories about Dante, how he gave her presents, how he helped his sisters, the funny things he said. Even if she exaggerated, it had to be better than that Lopez boy she dated in high school. No one could tell a nice story about him, good riddance.

"Mami!" Ariana had arrived, pulling Dante by the arm, and Tina watched carefully to see how Mrs. Aguirre would be. Dante looked a little like Geron before he lost his eye and got scarred up. A pretty brown boy, Tina thought. Seeing his rounded lips and nose and eyes made her realize how long it had been since she had seen a black person, and it made her a little homesick. She thought how pointy all the Happy Trout customers were, nice, good people, but pointy and white.

"This is my sweetheart, Dante. I told you, he's in nursing school with me, one year ahead. I told him to come and meet my family, who are all very nice, very friendly people—and the fiesta is for everyone, right? Grab yourself a beer over by the truck."

"*Mija*, think what you are doing! I pray for you every night, that you will not end up in shame with a crowd of little black children to care for."

"Oh Mami, you're just saying what Papi says Here's the big news! We're engaged as of today! So you can start going crazy now, trying to plan a big wedding where no one will notice what color the groom is. Oh, this family." Ariana turned her hand so that her diamond solitaire flashed in the sun, sending a defiant signal to any onlookers. "And besides, they'll be dark brown, like Tia Claudia. And they'll have flashing black gypsy eyes like you, their beautiful *abuela*. And bowlegs like Papi and all the *tios*."

"Oh, *Dios*, what have I done to deserve such a daughter?"

Dante returned, beer in hand. "Ariana, quit teasing your momma. This girl you raised, Mrs. Aguirre. What a trial she is, a trial and a tribulation!" He put his hands on Ariana's shoulders and shook her tenderly. "Someone needs to keep this girl out of trouble!"

"See, see how he understands you! Even your *novio* knows how you are! Go, enjoy the fiesta. Find your sister and her Anglo boyfriend. Put your wicked heads together and plan how to break my heart some more, eh?"

Mrs. Aguirre shooed them away, not entirely displeased with Dante after all. And besides, young people are flighty. Sometimes they change their minds. Oh, but not Ariana. Head like a stone, that one. Oh, *Dios*, what to tell her papa.

"Sorry, Dante. It could have been worse. Mami is doing her best. They're going to love you to pieces, once they see that you're not going to get me pregnant and then leave me." Ariana took his hand and glanced up at him sideways, a look of uncertainty. "You aren't, are you?"

"Not me," said Dante. "I'm in for the long haul. They can safely start loving me anytime now."

"Good, because otherwise I would have to follow you around whining, and you don't want that. I love you, that's all."

And in the prescribed manner and because it was true, Dante said, "I love you, too. You know I love you. You're my beautiful girl."

"Okay then. Let's go look for my sister. You'll like her. She is only slightly less beautiful than me."

Tina had already connected with Jennifer and Shaun to take a rest, regroup, and to be sure that the fiesta was going as it should. In all the swirl of music and people, she was having a hard time keeping her head on the lists they had so painstakingly written out. Jennifer and Shaun had made themselves hard to find, sitting on a picnic table at the very edge of the fiesta, thighs in tingling contact, his right arm curved around her, his left hand captured between hers, to keep it from wandering too far. Her head rested against his chest, and she could hear his steady heartbeat. They greeted Tina as an old friend, someone who had played a role in their love story and deserved a share of their happiness.

"Do you believe it?" Shaun asked her. "Do you believe the miracle, that the Virgin Mary healed Jennifer's grandfather, robbed a bank, and gave the money to the poor in some little town in Nevada? I'm not making fun, I'm just asking."

"I don't know," Tina said. "Things happen sometimes. Things do happen."

"My great-grandfather, Manny," Jennifer tenderly corrected him. "Not my grandfather. My grandfather is Tomas and my other grandfather is Martin. And I don't know. I do know my great-grandfather doesn't lie. He doesn't lie even when he probably should. They tell about when my great-grandmother asked him about some woman in Stockton he was seeing, and he told the truth. All that generation talk about it like it was World War Three. She beat him with a broom and locked him out of the house for weeks. He had to sleep in the chicken coop, that's how they tell it. They don't tell how he ever got back in the house, but it shows that he doesn't lie."

"I like that song they keep playing," Tina said. "I like the part that goes 'dron.'"

"That's my cousin Mort's *corrido*. I'm glad you like it because they're probably going to play it a hundred times before the end of the day. And it'll get stuck in your head and you'll keep humming it for weeks."

"Help me out," Shaun said. "My eighth-grade Spanish doesn't stretch that far. I know *ladron* is thief and Maria is Mary. What else is going on?"

"Okay," Jennifer said, settling her head more firmly against him, but otherwise reminding Tina of a nun giving a catechism lesson.

"Here's the song. It says that the Mother of God, Queen of Heaven, went to the biggest priest in the world. She says, 'My son, the people suffer with no work, no food, and the children are sick. You should help them.' And the big priest says 'Oh, those damn poor people, they are always bothering me. Tell them to say five Our Fathers and five Hail Marys. That will shut them up.' So then he goes back into his big house and shuts the door and eats a fat dinner, a big dinner, leaving Mary on the porch with nothing in her hands."

Jennifer stopped. "I don't know what the priest

in Santuario made of that. It's kind of a slap at the Pope. Maybe his eighth-grade Spanish doesn't stretch that far either. But anyway, then we have the chorus, '*Ladron, dron, dron*,' the part you like, Tina. Which as you know means thief, but then the guitars do the strum that sounds like the *dron* part. And *ladrona* is a female thief, meaning Mary. Are you sure want to hear this? Am I boring you?"

"No." Tina said, "It's like hearing a bedtime story, only better." It reminded her of being tucked in bed in the dormitory when the nun in charge felt like reading to them, if you got a nice one. The mean ones said to say their prayers, be quiet, and go to sleep or the devil would grab them by the toes and drag them down to hell.

"Okay. It follows kind of the same pattern, like they do. Mary goes to the highest *jefe* in the land, which I guess is the president, and asks him for help. But he says he'll have his army catch them and send them all back to Mexico to shut them up. And then the chorus again. Then Mary goes down to Hell to find Gestas and tells him the same thing."

"Who's Gestas?"

"He's the bad thief, the unrepentant thief who was crucified with Jesus. The other thief, his brother Dimas, repented, so he went to heaven, but Gestas didn't, so that's why he's in hell."

Shaun shook his head, like he was trying to get water out of his ears. "Why don't I know this stuff? I thought with my mom's family, I'd know stuff. But I've never heard of Gestas."

"Right, he's in hell. So Mary tells him that this is his lucky day. She pulls him out of hell and together they go to the biggest house there is in the entire world, the bank where the money is sleeping."

"Aha!"

"Yes. Getting to the miracle now. They take the money and give it to a gang of angels to take to the poor people, and they scatter it all over the land. So that's the miracle of the fiesta."

"Then what? Is that the end?"

"Then Mary and Gestas, hand in hand, rise straight up into heaven and explain everything to God."

Shaun laughed and then stopped himself. "I'm sorry. That strikes me as funny."

"Of course it's funny, silly person. It's supposed to be funny. It's serious, but it's funny. And then the *corrido* ends with that long bit that says Mary the Bandit, *Saint Mary*, *Maria Bandida*, *Santa Maria*, over and over. And then someone else starts singing it from the beginning, usually. It's a catchy tune."

Having rested her feet, knowing that the two of them were going to start kissing pretty soon whether she was there or not, Tina decided to move on to policing the restrooms and renewing the toilet paper supply. She was glad to know what the song was, and she liked the idea of Gestas. She thought she would like to name something Gestas someday. Maybe it could be Foster's middle name. She imagined rising straight up into heaven, but she knew she wasn't ready. Still the image was appealing, the refreshingly cool clouds parting over the top of her head as she rose to see the flocks of pearly-winged angels and little cupids that would be flying around. And now Gestas would be there, and he would surely welcome her.

Jennifer and Shaun remained sitting at the table, their bit of solid land in the sea of fiesta, their island, their cloud above the future, their bubble.

"Do I need to be Catholic to marry you?" Shaun had been worried about this.

"No, my darling dear Shaun. You just have to do a few Catholic things at first and talk to the priest, and then you can be whatever you want."

"Let's get married here. Now."

"We can't do that." She half-turned and shook her head at him, and he wanted to plunge his hands, again, into her dark, dancing curls. "We don't have a license. My mother would truly kill me if we eloped. She would hunt me down and beat me to death with a tortilla press, no kidding."

"Soon then," Shaun said. "Before we leave for LA.

Before August."

"Your folks kind of want us to wait till we finish school, you know."

"That's not going to happen," Shaun said.

Otto and Azalia Truitt waited as long as they could at their downstream campsite, wanting to do the polite thing and not arrive too early. Azalia had always wanted to travel to Mexico, ever since she got her youngest off to college, but something always came up at the last minute—the furnace went down and the whole system had to be replaced, Otto's automotive business folded, their son Bob's wife got so sick that time and Azalia had to look after little Pam and baby Garth for three weeks, until Bob and Laurie returned from getting all those tests in the big-city hospital. It was worth it, of course, but the Mexican vacation had never happened. She had doggedly driven fifty miles round-trip to attend weekly "Spanish for tourists" classes, to keep her hand in. When Tina called to warn them about the fiesta, she had been thrilled to pieces. "¡*Que bueno*!" she had thought, remembering about the upside down exclamation point, the one that lets you know ahead of time how excited to be.

Azalia would have come to the Happy Trout for

this even if they hadn't needed to let the paint dry and the fumes clear out of their house. She dressed carefully in a puffy-sleeved white blouse with red embroidery that she had bought from the United Nations store in Reno and a full black skirt that would flare out when she turned. Otto had not tried for anything so exotic, but to please Azalia, he had dressed in good trousers, a blue shirt, and a tie, which he promptly took off and stuffed in his pocket when he saw the open-necked shirts of the rest of the men at the party. There is a reason neckties have to be required. Otto was very glad to see Azalia so excited. It boded well for their evening together. He'd go easy on the beer and hope to get lucky later on.

Tina saw them arrive as the dancing began, Azalia beaming with excitement. They stood for a moment, hand in hand, to get their bearings. The young people were dancing together in the middle of the party, their youth and heat and passion, their pleasure in supple bodies, smooth skin, rich desires, forming a burning center. Around them danced the *viejos*, sedately, their faces stolid, in perfect step, moving gracefully through the dances they had danced together all their lives, danced for forty, fifty, sixty years, at every fiesta, every wedding. The old men and women danced without the smiles and invitations of youth, without the flourishes and ornaments of seduction and display, but seriously and perfectly, two by two, passions spent, perhaps, but well spent. The Truitts took a breath and slipped into this stream without a splash.

Tina had never seen old people dance before. She really hadn't been around old people very much, she realized. Neither Freddy nor any of his guys, nor any of the girls who worked for him, would ever be old, not this old. They would arc and spiral and die like fireworks, but nothing so beautiful, of course. They would shoot each other, and shoot up, and fall down, and vanish into the ugly dirt of the city streets. They would never be old. But the young people at the fiesta, Jennifer and her sister and cousins, they would go on and someday do this dance like their parents and grandparents before them, maybe here at the Happy Trout, maybe for the robber saint that wore her face. It gave her shivers, like she had stepped through the membrane between two dreams.

When the old people had had enough, they retired to the peripheral campsites, sitting at the tables with their grandchildren, worn out themselves from running around underfoot like little crazies. Some of them napped, both old and young. And the parents took their turn at the dance, their style falling somewhere between the physical desire of the young and the physical serenity of the old. The party was winding down. The air was cooling, the sun slanting down on the fiesta, and it was time to take *Nuestra Señora Ladrona* home to the church in Santuario, to take up the everyday business of caring for the poor and loving them.

Tina continued to circle the fiesta, pulling full-to-bursting trash bags out of the cans, lining the cans with new bags, sorting and carrying the trash, some to the dumpster, some to recycle. She spotted Dante leaning against a tree outside the restroom, no doubt waiting for Ariana, and decided to stop and talk to him, drawn by the familiar look of him, brown skin, soft round features, crisp hair. It almost made her miss Geron or T-Wah, just to look at, though.

"Hey Tina," he called out as she veered off the gravel to approach him. "What's up with you?"

"Hey Dante," she said. "Nothin's up. Just doin' my job, keeping the trash from taking over the place."

He smiled at her. It was surprising to see a sister here. "This is a very nice place you have here," he said, "a very nice place. This is your place, isn't it?"

"Yes," Tina said, and then "No." But saying no was like seeing the Happy Trout vanish, a sudden jolting drop, a heart-stopping loss. "Yes," she said. It was her place whether she could stay or not. It was her place, not because it belonged to her, but because if she had to leave, she would always want to come back. She would remember and grieve for it and struggle to return, no matter if she was sent away by Bill or stolen away by Freddy. No matter how far away it was, she would turn around and start working her way back.

"Yes," she said again.

And Dante, who had been watching the clouds and shadows cross her face, said "Well, glad we got that settled, then," and was given the benediction of her brilliant smile.

"Be careful leaning on that tree, by the way," she said. "It's one of the sticky ones."

Tina greeted Ariana and went on down to replenish the supplies in the restroom, ignoring a stall on the men's side with two sets of feet, one in high heels, the other in high tops, and the murmurs and rhythms of sex that emanated from it. Not her business. She didn't know exactly what Bill's rules would be, but Bill wasn't here. Men and women. What you gonna do, she thought, sounding to herself like cousin Ernesto. She refilled the toilet paper holder in the empty stall and the paper towel dispenser, and moved on.

Wherever she was, she tried to keep her face turned away from Manny Aguirre, who sat at the front of the crowd of onlookers in his wheelchair with a brilliant blue and gold blanket over his lap, receiving the respects due to him as the head of the family, but also as the lucky one, the one who had been touched, the beloved *hijo*, the son of the Virgin herself. He was happy to shake the hands of all his relatives and their relatives and neighbors, but it tired him out so that he dozed off and then awakened slowly, moving back and forth between the two worlds, the party invading his dreams with color and voices and music and his dreams inhabiting the fiesta with a second holy vision.

In this second vision, he saw Her again, the blessed Mother, *La Santissima*, *La Santa Ladrona*, *La Maria Bandida*. She stood there holding a black plastic bag, full of money, full of blessings, he thought, and she looked right at him. No one else seemed to see her, and she raised one finger and held it up to her lips, counseling silence. He returned the gesture, and her face flooded with happiness. He was filled with a joy that sat on his ailing heart like a flame on a candle, and when he died a month later, surrounded by the same people who surrounded him now, he would die in the absolute conviction that the Mother of God was waiting for him and would lead him straight to Paradise. As the noise of the fiesta swirled around him, he sat in his wheelchair silent, overwhelmed by the blessings and goodness of his beloved saint. This was their secret, the last miracle, the reward for a lifetime of devotion and faith.

14

The one thing that can solve most of our problems is dancing.

—James Brown

After the excitement of the fiesta, the season flattened out. The effervescence seemed to have disappeared into thin air, all the bubbles popped and the music silenced, leaving the smell of dusty service roads, canvas, sun block, and kerosene behind to temper the pleasant smell of pine and the harsh cries of jays to accompany the buzz of insects. The usual customers and the usual kind of customers, even when they came because of reports of the fiesta, offered so little to fascinate. They wanted bug spray. They wanted sun block. They wanted pancakes. They wanted their children to quit running and their wives or husbands to hurry up. They wanted more service and less contact. They were white and flat and pointy. Or maybe that's just how it seemed to Tina. Maybe seeing Dante had made her lonely for people more like her, like Geron.

But not Geron or T-Wah or Hoppy. Maybe she was spoiled by having a party thrown, however indirectly, in her honor. She knew that, obviously, she was not the Virgin Mary. She was not the virgin anything. But it had pleased her deeply to see an image that was so like her face as the icon ruling over the party. Compared to that, life at the Happy Trout was hard work.

Bill was made cranky by the increase in customers. He knew it was good, and the books, when he got a chance to do them, would show a nice profit. But he was tired of working too hard, like Tina.

"I haven't done anything but work since the great-granddaughter's shindig and that's just the café. No more parties, Tina, they bring in too much business. We're not going to get a chance to breathe until Pete shows up, and who knows when that'll be. I'd hire someone else, but I don't have time to think about it."

They both rose at early dawn, sometimes earlier. Bill started the day's chores by driving the truck through the still sleeping campground, cleaning the restrooms, collecting trash, keeping an eye on things. Tina got the kitchen going, prepping for the breakfast crowd. It had become habit by now, but even in the doldrums Tina took pleasure in the life of the Happy Trout and the minutiae of its doings. It was her place, after all. Dante had said so.

Foster had taken up the habit of sleeping in, curled

in a bun of contentment in his basket under the table where Tina occasionally sat to use the phone. So he was, in a way, not sleeping in a working kitchen at all, which would have been against county health regulations, but instead in a very small business office, which was okay.

Sunday was another hard day, the sixth day in a row of a full campground, made harder by the arrival of a group that had been regulars during their winter ski season and seemed to expect the same jolly attitude, leisurely conversation, and prompt service. But summer isn't winter at the Happy Trout. Summer has its own pace, and the pace is fast for forest-dwellers. Summer is when the business of the world gets done—the raising of young ones, the finding of food, the building and replacing of shelter, the work that has to be set aside when the iron hand of winter tightens into a fist and shuts everything down, giving you a chance to think. Summer isn't winter, folks. No time for Christmas carols. No time for crezzy ets. Hardly any time for thinking.

To add to Tina's sense of life out of tune and to Bill's discontent, it seemed like the fish had not been biting for days in the river that ran through the Happy Trout, at least to hear the customers complain. It was the wind, or the water temperature, or the forest service. It was the other fishermen or the kids or the cars or the radios. It was something upstream, or in the water, or in the air. Something was keeping the fish in the river; someone was tipping them off.

"It's a license, fellas, not a guarantee," Tina would say, like Ursula always did when the grumbling went on too long. And she would zip by, one coffee carafe in each hand, orange for unleaded, green for Ethel. That was Bill's joke. She didn't get it, but she repeated it sometimes, just to happy up the breakfast scene. She was getting used to not understanding things, to being in this foreign, but increasingly familiar world. Like Ursula's significant totally other, or whatever she had said about Benny. This was Tina's beloved other, her Happy Trout, her place, however out of tune it was at the moment. But summer doesn't last forever. This is one of the few true things, though it can be hard to believe.

Tina was relieved when she saw Pete pull into the parking lot and slide out of his van, a yellow bandana tied around his head, his ponytail now twisted into a braid. She liked it when people came back, as they seemed to do at the Happy Trout. He was Pete, true, and he only had one gear, but he was better than nothing. And she knew him from before.

"Pete's here," Tina said through the hatch to a beleaguered Bill, trying to cut more potatoes while he kept an eye on the burgers browning on the grill.

"Goddamn cavalry," Bill said. Tina didn't understand why he said "goddamn." She thought Bill would be glad to see Pete. He would be another hand in the kitchen, so she hoped he wasn't there expecting to fish. Bill needed some relief, and you can't cook and serve at the same time, not unless there's only one or two customers. She stepped out onto the porch to greet the fresh troop, the carafes still in her hands.

"Tina?" Pete was surprised to see her, thought she would have been on her way some time ago, having scooped up all the loose cash she could get her hands on, having hitched a ride with some horny fisherman. But here she was, cuter than ever.

"Hi Pete." Tina was glad to see that he looked perky enough, ready, she hoped, to chop and fry and clean. "Nice to have you back. How's Melody? Did you run out of girlfriends?"

"Wow, Tina, you're still here. You look great! How are you doing with the boss man in there? Do you have him wrapped around your little finger yet? Got him where you want him? Doing the horizontal mambo?" Pete twiddled his index and his middle finger together, obscenely suggesting limbs intertwined in sexual abandon. Tina stared at his hands. She'd never seen that one before.

"No, Pete. I just work here." She didn't want him to see that his digital pantomime had created an image of her and Bill together in the semi-dark, touching everywhere, caught up in a bubble of mutual desire. It was none of his business. But he saw more than she intended, reading her wistfulness as an indication of a woman in need of a man, and not, in this case, him.

Pete followed her into the café and was pressed into service immediately, reluctantly putting on a clean apron and chef's hat and staring in dismay at the bag of onions on the counter. Really? Couldn't Tina do it? He sighed dramatically. He liked being hailed as a savior, but not having to hang around and work.

"You can fish tonight, damn it. I don't know what's wrong with those people out there; they're like piranhas. This is the third guy in a row ordered two burgers. Who needs two burgers? And two orders of onion rings?"

"Besides," Tina added as she clipped another order to the turntable, "the fish aren't in the mood to get caught anyway, so you might as well make yourself useful."

Monday morning, when the Happy Trout Café was always closed so everyone could catch a break, Pete dragged Bill down to the river with him, ostensibly to fish, but standing close enough to talk, too close for serious fishing. He cast his line and then turned his head to look at Bill. His manner was severe.

"What the fuck, Bill?" he asked in a conversational

tone.

Bill glanced over at him, but mostly kept his eyes on the moving waters of the river where his fly had settled and floated temptingly, he thought, though the fish were apparently unmoved. "What do you mean?" he asked. "What are you talking about?"

"You heard me, Bill. What…the…fuck?" Pete was starting to sound angry, or at least disgusted.

"You mean why is Tina still here?"

"No, Bill, I mean what the fuck? What's the hang-up? How long do you have to listen to the sizzle before you pick up a fork, man? How long do you let the engine idle before you get it in gear? How many roads must a man walk down, for pity's sake?"

Bill shook his head. "Can you just tell me what's wrong? Leave the metaphors and hippy-ass lyrics out of it?"

"If you've still got lead in your pencil and you leave that little woman there untouched, you're out of your mind. What makes her out of bounds? What's the problem, Bill? I mean, what the fuck?"

"Well, Jesus, Pete. Not that it's any of your business, but Tina just works here." Bill studied his fly, squinting into the glare of the sun reflected on the moving water. He wished he had brought his sunglasses. "You know, she's turned out to be a surprisingly good worker."

"Bill, I didn't ask you about her freaking job

performance. I said what the fuck is wrong with you. Why aren't you doing the natural thing, getting it on with that little woman who is *right there*!" Pete stabbed his finger in the direction of the Happy Trout Café. "Look, man, you don't have to drive anywhere. You don't have to get dressed up or pay for anything. You don't have to explain it or sneak around. Maybe she has better taste than to put out for a numbnuts like you. But you've got to be in there pitching if you want to make a home run. Stands to reason. I know you're a Boy Scout, but it's time to earn your Tina merit badge."

"Shit, Pete." Bill quit casting and gave Pete his attention. "It's not that easy. I mean, it's complicated."

"Of course, it's complicated, Bill." Pete's heavy-handed patience was starting to crack. "It's always complicated. They're women."

Bill sighed. He couldn't begin to explain.

"Is it because of Barbara? I know she trimmed you pretty good, but I didn't think she took your cojones as part of the settlement. Hey, Bill, you used to be quite the guy with the ladies. Mighty Bill McCrea. William the Conqueror. You succeeded where better men were thrown out the window." Pete cast again. "Remember Heather Mills?"

"I do," Bill said, smiling a little. "I do remember Heather Mills."

"She was so fancy and so rich," Pete said. "She was

like a movie star."

"And so good-looking," Bill added. "Blonde hair down to here."

"And stuck-up," Pete said. "We all thought you were crazy to go after her. She was so damn shocked when you dumped her. She left campus at summer break looking like Marie fucking Antoinette being hauled away in a tumbrel."

"A tumbrel," Bill repeated.

"Yes, Bill, a tumbrel. I'm a French major. So don't be so surprised if I remember a few things. Marie 'Eat My Cake' Antoinette in a tumbrel."

"I just couldn't stand her after a while. The sex was great, but I couldn't stand her attitude," Bill said. "She was always showing me off like some exotic wild animal she'd bought and paid for. It was embarrassing."

"But you are a wild animal, Bill. That's exactly what you are, my man. So why are you still sniffing the air for danger? Why are you still goddamn hibernating? Which takes me back to my original observation. What the fuck, buddy?"

Bill said, "You don't understand. With Tina, I don't know. It's just not a good idea."

"Of course it's not a good idea. Sex is not any kind of an *idea* any more than food is an *idea* or gravity is an *idea*. No, it's a fact of life. Hell, when people talk about 'the facts of life,' that's what they're talking about, right? So what is it? Do you find her unfuckable in some way I can't begin to imagine?"

"Jesus, Pete. You know damn well she's more than attractive."

"Good," Pete said. "Now we're making some progress. Would you say beautiful?"

"I don't know. At times, maybe, when she's fooling around with Foster, or in the snow, or when she looks serious, like when she's pouring coffee for someone or chopping onions. Or when she's excited about something, like that damn fiesta that I personally think started all this trouble. So yeah, attractive. Beautiful. Whatever. Her skin. . . ." Bill quit pretending to fish and reeled his line in. Not going to catch anything anyway, most likely.

"There you go," Pete said. "Tell me about it."

"She has this silky-smooth brown skin. And she's cute, she has that darling little face. Sexy, well, that doesn't take any eyesight to see." That didn't make sense. Bill shook his head like a horse beleaguered by midges. "I'm not doing this, Pete, just because you say so. I'm not running my sex life based on your advice."

"What's the best word for her, Bill? Where is her face in the dictionary?"

Bill looked down at the mud between his feet, then studied the opposite riverbank, visions of Tina flooding his mind. It was a relief to quit holding them back, for once, to let them come. "Adorable," he said. "I guess the correct word is adorable."

"There you go," Pete said, and resumed casting into the bright water that glinted like a window in the sun, adjusting his stroke for the breeze that had sprung up, making the fly skip lightly against the current. "There you fucking go."

Bill turned then and saw Tina running toward him, rosy and excited, and he thought for an instant that she would throw herself on him and they would tumble together to the ground. He held his arms out in a gesture that might have meant, like Pete, "what the fuck" or perhaps, "come to me, my love."

Tina stopped short.

"Bill, guess what!"

"Can't guess. Tell me."

"Mrs. Aguirre, Jennifer's mom called. They're getting married, both of them!"

"I thought Mrs. Aguirre was already married. To Mr. Aguirre."

"Bill. Both of Mrs. Aguirre's daughters, Jennifer, known to you as the great-granddaughter, and her sister Ariana. They are marrying their boyfriends—Shaun Gentry, who you know. And Dante, the black guy. Jennifer and Shaun, Ariana and Dante. Double wedding. And the best part is, they want to have the wedding here!"

"Really?" Bill said, realizing that he didn't much care what she was saying as long as she stayed close by. He wanted the conversation to last. He just wanted to look at her and enjoy his new-found appreciation of her adorableness. "Really? Another big party with noise and cars parked all over and going through toilet paper like it was cheap beer. I don't think we can handle another one of those Aguirre parties."

"No, wait. They're having the whole thing catered, including all the cleanup and maintenance. So all we'll have to do is block out the space and the time and interface with the caterers. It's great, Bill! Right here!"

"Interface? We have to interface?"

"Talk to, meet with, make arrangements, show them the site. You know, interface."

"I think we were damn lucky with that first wingding. Something is bound to go wrong if we do it again."

"Bill, of course we'll do it again! The pilgrimage is an annual event, and that means it's going to happen every year. Nothing will go wrong. And we'll get a rider like we did before."

Bill sighed. "When is this disaster scheduled to strike?"

Five weeks, only five weeks to get it set up. When the Truchas Brothers Pyrotechnics, Catering, and Big Top Company showed up to check out the place, Tina was strangely missing, hiding in the women's restroom. She recognized the guy in the Truchas Brothers truck, and she was pretty sure he would remember her, given the way she had earned a really good discount on the fireworks for Freddy's party.

Bill looked around for her, but in the end he did the necessary interfacing from the notes she had set out neatly in the center of the desk. The site for the big top tent was chosen, though it turned out that for a wedding, it's called a pavilion. Together they worked out where to put the musicians. The Truchas brothers would also handle the extra porta-potties, the refreshing of all facilities, the garbage pickup, and the cleanup at the end of the event. But no pyrotechnics. Not at a wedding. Not in the forest.

"You come out here the next day," said Danny Truchas, not an actual Truchas brother, but a nephew who did sales and public relations, "you won't even be able to tell Columbus discovered America, that's how clean it's gonna be—Priss Teen."

Bill planned to hole up in the office the day of the wedding until the commotion died down. But when Tina picked up the mail, she found a stiff ivory-colored envelope addressed to "Miss Tina Martin and Mr. William McCrea." Inside was another envelope. Inside that was the invitation. Tina had to make a phone call to confirm, being a little confused by all the envelopes.

But Jennifer was happy to explain. They were invited to the wedding.

After arguing with Tina about it, mostly to tease, Bill agreed to attend. Really, because he was fond of Shaun, he wouldn't have missed it. And Pete could keep an eye on things, the café would be closed, and the other campers could look out for themselves for just the one day.

At first he dug in his heels at wearing a suit. "They're not going to stay married any longer because I'm wearing a suit. It's outdoors! They'll probably all be in shorts and tank tops anyway."

Tina gave him a look compounded of disbelief, derision, and frustration, just a hint of pity, conveying with a gesture that involved letting her mouth fall open slightly, rolling her eyes, shrugging and, head slightly tilted, turning as though to an invisible audience who totally agreed with her that no one in the history of the world had ever been so lame. It was a complex move, and not even Rachel could have done it better. Bill recognized it and laughed.

"Okay, Tina. I'll wear the damn suit. I'm afraid all my dress shirts are kind of wrinkled because of someone having shoved that hamper in there, so don't expect *Esquire* magazine."

"Bill," Tina said, holding the thick paper invitation against her heart as though it could heal a hurt there.

"I've never been to a wedding before in my whole life. I've seen them on TV, but I never was invited to one. With a white dress and flowers and little mints and all that. So I will iron your shirt for you, Bill. But if you mess up this wedding somehow, the only wedding I've ever been to in my entire life, I will save myself some time and just iron the front. That way you can wear it in the coffin at your goddamn funeral."

Bill held up his hands in surrender. He liked seeing Tina fired up like this. It made him smile.

"And what are you going to wear, Miss Tina? Gonna buy a brand-new Happy Trout T-shirt?" Bill secretly wanted to see Tina dressed up, like in that picture Freddy had shown him, Tina in red satin.

"I need to go into town, Bill. Azalia's going to close down the DMV a little early since she's the only one working tomorrow afternoon anyway, and she's going to help me."

"Jesus, that woman does play fast and loose over there with the government's time. It's surprising anything ever gets done."

Tina wasn't listening. "And we're going to find something for me to wear. She knows where to go, she says. The colors for the wedding are turquoise and forest green. And they have bridesmaids, twelve of them, and they'll all have matching dresses. And flowers. And there's going to be dancing, Bill, so I need to get something I can dance in."

"Turquoise and forest green?"

"No, Bill. That's what I thought, too. But Azalia says the colors are meant for the wedding party, not the people who are invited to the wedding. So maybe red, if I can find anything. Or gold."

"Red," Bill said. "Do you have enough money for a fancy dress like that?"

"I've got $50 at the moment, which might not be enough. Maybe I could get an advance?" Tina was preparing to bargain. She figured she needed at least $100, and maybe she could find some shoes at the Goodwill.

Bill disappeared into the office and came back with a nicely filled envelope to hand to Tina. "Don't feel like you have to spend it all. But get what you want, okay? Otherwise I'll never hear the end of it."

Tina took it and thanked him with a smile, and he thought for a moment she was going to throw her arms around him. That made the second time recently he'd had that sensation, first when she came running towards him to tell him about the wedding and now, as she accepted the money. And each time he had been stopped from taking her in his arms by the fear of upsetting the delicate balance that had kept her there at the Happy Trout. Where he could keep an eye on her. Where he could see her every day.

Four weeks later, on the appointed day, the Truchas Brothers workers showed up at dawn, and for several hours, everything was a riot of forklifts and trucks, beeping together as they backed up, roaring as they went forward. The porta-potties were set up, the big top rose, an amorphous, flapping cloud of canvas that snapped into shape all of a sudden to become, surprisingly, a pavilion, the serving tables went down, and the rest of the tables were stacked, to be quickly placed and set once the rows of chairs for spectators were vacated. After the infrastructure was in place, the food catering crew and the florist moved in, and white linen and white flowers blanketed everything, as fresh as snow.

Tina and Bill walked down to the wedding together, Bill looking handsome and surprisingly comfortable in his suit and tie, Tina in a red satin *cheongsam*, fitted and short, with a short red satin jacket over it, embroidered with black dragons. She had had her hair cropped in what Ursula would have called a puppy cut, short all over, making the most of the elegant shape of her head. Bill had thought he might have to carry her when he saw the height of her heels, but she was nimble and practiced, and her legs were fabulous to see, slender, curved, round. That's what high heels are for. He walked with his hand behind her, not touching, but ready to catch her if she stumbled.

The priest arrived, the groom and his party came

in two SUVs, swelled out to twelve groomsmen by the addition of a number of Jennifer and Ariana's cousins to match the twelve bridesmaids, who could be seen flitting around a smaller tent set up behind the restrooms, where Mrs. Aguirre had set up her command post. The musicians played background music, a string quartet that went nicely with the birdcalls and gurgling of the river. The guests chatted affably in the folding chairs and waited for the brides to come so the ceremony could begin. Presumably having marshaled the bridesmaids and given her daughters one last hug, Mrs. Aguirre bustled in to take her seat in the front row next to the empty seat her husband would take once he had played his role. It was going to happen. Everyone was seated, everyone looking cheerful, both Leona Gentry and Dante's mom a little weepy, but in a very good way. Tina simmered with excitement.

The music changed. The two grooms emerged from the forest and stood at the front, looking down the aisle, and it was time to begin. First the flower girl, a dark-eyed poppet who threatened to steal the show, unsmiling, conscientiously scattering flower petals from her basket, going back once to where she thought she had spread them too thick to grab a handful of petals and redistribute them more evenly. Then the ring bearer in his first suit ever, his hair strictly parted and glued down, his tongue held sideways to keep him on task, then the first of the lovely bridesmaids, escorted by the first handsome groomsman, followed by eleven more couples, who parted at the altar to make a row of twelve young women waiting for the brides, and twelve young men backing the waiting grooms.

The music changed again, and the audience stood and turned. Bill could feel Tina holding her breath at his side. The brides. Well, the brides were everything brides are supposed to be—beautiful, tender, strong, and happy. Their father brought them down the aisle, one on each arm, his girls, his little sweethearts. He watched them join their new partners to stand before the waiting priest. The mass was celebrated. Songs were sung. Vows were made and rings exchanged. The marriages of Jennifer and Shaun, Ariana and Dante, were consecrated, witnessed, and sealed. And then the party began.

Tina knew from Freddy's party that the Truchas Brothers put on a good spread, and now she saw that they were even better cooking the food they knew best—tamales, enchiladas, little empanadas with cinnamon, cream cheese, and fruit in them. After the dinner and the toasts, the band began to play an old-fashioned waltz, and the newly married couples led the dance. Bill looked across the table at Tina.

As good a time as any, he thought. Make your move.

"Bill," Tina reached across and took a firm hold of his hand, emboldened by a few glasses of champagne, the elixir of high spirits. "I hope you're going to dance with me. That's what I hope."

Bill, who had had quite a bit more champagne, led her to the edge of the dancers, held out his arms, and she walked in, confidently placing her arm across his shoulders. He knew there was no turning back. And there wasn't.

They were both good dancers, and they would have danced together until the music stopped, but Shaun, having danced with his bride, his mother, and the other bride, and with the bride's mother and with at least some of the bridesmaids, cut in and whirled Tina away. Cousin Ernesto, who had driven in from Santuario for the event, had brought a few dozen bottles of tequila in case there wasn't enough to drink. When he saw Bill standing there, watching Tina vanish into the crowd, feeling the sudden emptiness of his arms, he motioned him back behind the pavilion and urged him to drink with the international invitation, a thumb-and-little-finger rocking gesture aimed at the mouth, where the drink goes.

"Come on, my friend. Some guy takes your girl to dance, you need courage to take her back from that one. Have another. Man and woman, what you gonna do."

Bill found that sufficiently persuasive and stayed to drink with other cousins and friends who brought flasks of their own to hand round. Even the grooms came by for a quick snort. Shaun was touched to see Bill there, dressed up, looking handsome. In an obscure way, it made him feel like he was joining something worth joining, the ranks of men who loved.

When Bill was finally able to reclaim Tina, the music had settled into a slow foxtrot, and many of the couples on the floor were hardly moving at all, shamelessly embracing, saved only by their verticality and their wedding finery from outright intercourse. Bill pulled Tina closer, erasing the final quarter-inch that had separated their bodies, and like the others, they rocked and nestled.

Tina felt him hard against her belly and she had five thoughts. First, she was pleased. That's the effect a woman in a red dress should have. Second, she was nervous. This was new territory with Bill, and she didn't know what to expect. Third, she was excited, an excitement that filled her body and made her press back against him. Fourth, she was deeply happy to be here, with this man, this very one and no other. Fifth, she was angry. What was she supposed to do with this?

Just then Bill murmured into her ear, hoping to lighten things up, "I think I'm about ready for that blowjob now."

He knew immediately that, though true, it was exactly the wrong thing to say. Tina stiffened in his arms, drew back, and hit him in the face, rocking him back on his heels. She was surprisingly strong, no doubt the result of all the hard work she had done at the Happy Trout.

Then she felt a sixth thing that entirely drove the other five feelings away, something she hadn't felt for a long time; she felt panic. She had never hit a guy before, not Mickey, not Lalo, not Freddy, not even Brad. She had seen what happened to girls who fight with guys; they lose. They lose their teeth, they lose their looks, and sometimes they get lost themselves and you never see them again. She turned and walked stiffly away, hearing Bill following after her, his feet crunching on the gravel. She walked faster. And then her nerve broke, and she began to run. It was worse than running from a bear. A bear doesn't break your heart.

Bill called out to her, but she ran even faster. "Oh shit," he thought, and he took off after her, feeling his left knee click at every step, catching up just as she put her hand on the door of Ursula's silver trailer. He leaned on the door, trapping her, and frankly, just trying to catch his breath.

"Tina," he said. "I'm sorry. I'm so damn sorry. That was a stupid, stupid thing to say." And he stepped back, letting her open the door.

Tina felt three new things.

She was relieved that he wasn't going to beat her up. It occurred to her that this man, Bill, her Bill, would never slap her or shoot her or beat her with a coat hanger or make her do things that hurt, no matter what. Just never. Even when he had misunderstood about Otto's snowplow, he hadn't hurt her. It was more like he had been hurt.

The second thing she felt was confused about what had just happened and how they would get along, how she could stay at the Happy Trout after this. She had gone to considerable trouble to please him, or at least to stay out of trouble, and now she could give him something he really wanted, which might be sweet, but it seemed for the first time like it would turn her back into a thing, a Kleenex, a scrap of nothing that could be used and thrown away and never missed. She didn't want to drop to her knees with him; she wanted to see his face.

And that led to the third feeling. She wanted Bill so much her body ached. Even more, she wanted to belong, not belong to him as she had belonged to Freddy and the others, but belong with him, take her place in his arms, in his life, in his Happy Trout resort, and belong there forever.

"Maybe you should just marry me," she said, and went in and closed the door firmly. She waited for him to knock, but he didn't. She laughed. And then she cried.

15

We that are true lovers run into strange capers.

— William Shakespeare, As You Like It

Bill went to his room in the Happy Trout, his face stinging where Tina had belted him, dazed, more than half-drunk, sorry, and wondering how he could keep Tina around after his stupid blunder. He didn't cry, but he surely felt like crying. He sat on the edge of the bed, head in hands, and cursed himself for a fool. Then he smiled. Then he laughed. And then he kicked off his shoes, peeled off his wedding duds, climbed into his solitary bed, and went to sleep.

Tina woke early the next morning with a singular feeling of dismay like a block of ice or a car battery or a big black dog on her chest, right over the heart, pressing down, immoveable. She wanted to sink down and disappear, to melt into the ground, to be relieved of the burden of her own miserable self and the trouble she couldn't stay out of. She was too disheartened even to make a list. If option number five, stay at the

Happy Trout and work things out with Bill, didn't pan out, there was nothing left. She had tried so hard and she thought she had done pretty well. She had made friends with Pete and Ursula and Rachel. She had left the customers alone. She had learned how to clean fish and not to lean on pine trees. She knew that a blue jay, although blue and a bird, was not the same as a bluebird. All of that and her hard work all wasted now. She would never go to another fiesta or another wedding. She would have to leave Foster behind, and he would be so sad, in a cat way. She would have to leave Bill, and he needed her whether he knew it or not.

She struggled wearily into her work jeans and Happy Trout T-shirt and slipped into the café, tiptoeing past Bill's door, where, if she had tuned into his dream, she would have seen her own face. Adorable.

She figured he wouldn't fire her while she was cleaning the grease trap, at least until she finished, so she opened the trap and started paddling the spent, solidified grease out into an empty half-and-half carton, not caring how messy she was. She had nothing to lose. She had already lost it all.

Pete came in, whistling, and started filling up napkin dispensers and making coffee like always. He set a steaming cup next to her, gently so as not to be jarring in case of headache, but Tina didn't even thank him. She just scraped another slurry of grease off the paddle with a listless slap.

Hung over, really hung over, Pete thought, diagnosing her silence, her bleak face, her dispirited movements. *But why is she here alone? She wouldn't crawl out of a well-used bed and start slinging grease all by herself. Where's my man Bill?* After a wedding, it was natural to mate. But it seemed like something had gone very wrong.

Bill, meanwhile, woke with a start, shimmied into his jeans and Happy Trout T-shirt, and barged into the kitchen, full of energy, a man with, finally, a mission. His eyes, though slightly bloodshot, were bright with intention. His cheek was a little discolored.

"Okay, Tina, leave that and get in the truck. Let's go to Nevada today and get it done."

She turned, resting her butt on the counter, not caring that she would have a stripe of lard there all day. She was past crying, too sad for tears, she thought. The last item on her list was crossed off, the list crumpled and burned, the ashes blown out onto the highway, and she didn't know which way they went from there.

"Is that your solution to everything?" she asked. "Go to Nevada?"

"You made me a proposal, and I'm accepting. And Nevada seems like the obvious place to go."

"Really?" Pete said. "You're going to have this conversation in front of me? Hello?"

"Bill," Tina said, trying one last time like a man falling out of a car, grasping at what isn't there. "It isn't fair if someone asks someone to do something and then something happens, and then the thing that happens means that you have to do something you aren't supposed to, and then you don't, and the next thing you know, you're going to Nevada. It's just not fair." By the end of this speech, she was crying so hard he couldn't quite tell what she was saying. It took him a while to work it out.

"What's wrong? I thought it's what you wanted." He patted her turned back and was aware even in his concern of the soft feel of her, the smooth skin under the T-shirt, the stretch of skin down her backbone.

"I wanted to stay here, damn you. I don't want to go. I didn't do anything wrong." Tina smacked some more grease around, but her movements were jerky and purposeless.

"Wait," Bill said. "Tina, listen to me. You remember you said we should get married, or I guess what you said is that I should marry you. And you're right, I should. And doing that today means going to Nevada. But then we'll come back here. If you want to wait, I'll understand. But I think we should just go."

Pete was amazed. He had been wondering what was going on between the two of them, but this was more information than he had bargained for. "Really?"

he said. "You're going to talk about this? Even though I'm right here, listening?" He perched on the steel worktable, his heels kicking. He felt sure they would go somewhere else or at least ask him to leave. He was so close he could have reached out and touched them.

"Or maybe you don't think you should marry me?" Bill said.

"If I don't marry you, does that mean I have to leave the Happy Trout?" Tina turned from under his hand and stood twisting the grease paddle back and forth in her hands.

"No, Tina. No, if you don't marry me, you can still stay as long as you want. You'll just have to get used to hearing me cry myself to sleep every night. Very loudly, I might add. Marry me if you want to, but you don't have to. I'm willing. It's your call."

Tina regarded him solemnly, unmoving. This was a new one. She had thought last night about what it would mean to put herself in Bill's hands, as though he were a cruising john who had pulled up to the curb, looking for action. He wouldn't hurt her, she knew that. Then she started to figure in things Ursula had said, how sweet Jennifer and Shaun had been together, how Bill had lied to Freddy to protect her, how much he loved Rachel, how it would be to step into Bill's sphere, to take him into her heart, to claim him as certainly as she claimed Foster, to be folded into the

Happy Trout and held there in his arms.

Bill watched her think. He was a patient man on the verge of success.

Pete picked up a ladle and starting slowly spinning the circular rack overhead, watching the pans and skillets swing past like streamers on a carousel. No one told him to stop.

"Do you know how to get married?" Tina asked. She hadn't planned the double wedding, just attended, or she would have had lists to refer to. She didn't know which parts mattered.

"Sure," Bill said. "We go to Nevada, stop at the first wedding chapel we see, do some paperwork, and then a judge or someone does the deed. Then we're married."

"Then what? Do we have to go to Las Vegas like Jennifer and Shaun?"

"Then we come back here and open up for lunch, and do like always, only married."

"What kind of paperwork? Do you need a social security number?"

Pete spoke up again. "You need ID, like a driver's license or something. And you need a witness. An old friend is a very good choice," he said. "That would be me." He didn't want to miss out on this. Having gone this far, he didn't want the rest of the story to take place without him.

Bill and Tina both glanced at him fleetingly then

locked eyes again.

"Do I need a special dress?"

"If you want one. But no, it's not something you have to have."

"Can I wear red instead of white?"

"You can wear whatever you want. You're the bride."

Tina stayed with that for a moment, thinking of Jennifer and Ariana, how beautiful they had looked as they walked down the aisle to join their lovers.

"Okay," she said. "And we can take Pete, right? Does he come, too?"

"Right," Pete said. "And we don't even have to talk about him in the third person any more."

"But you will *be* the third person, Pete." Tina turned her strong, happy face toward him, and it made him a little dizzy. "Just wait till I get dressed and we can go."

She started out to the trailer but turned back, at first because she didn't want to leave the place where things were working out so well, as though when she returned Bill would have changed his mind. But his face was steady and loving. Then with a second thought. "But I don't have a driver's license, Bill. I know I take your truck to town sometimes, and I do know how to drive, but I don't have an actual license."

"We'll stop and get one," he said, and as she left to put on her wedding dress, he called Azalia Truitt and made arrangements. For once, he was grateful for the flexibility with which she fulfilled her state-paid function.

Pete made a "Gone to Get Hitched" sign out of a cardboard box to tape in the window. He was the best man, after all. They piled into the truck, Tina in her red satin dress and heels, Bill in suit and tie, and Pete with a borrowed tie around his neck over his Happy Trout T-shirt, Bill looking seriously happy, Tina incandescent, and Pete like he always looked. It seemed to him that the air in the truck cab was warmer than usual, and the air was sweet except for the smell of old truck.

First they took a quick detour off the highway to town to get Tina a driver's license in the name of Tina Martin. She was grateful to leave the other names, the ones listed on her birth certificate and then her rap sheet, behind. She wondered why her mother had given her all those names, as if she didn't know what kind of life this baby would have and what she would need to be. She only needed to be Tina, as it turned out. Tina was enough.

Azalia Truitt was thrilled to pieces to help them. They could come by any time with their certificate, she said, and she'd change the driver's license to say Tina McCrea for them. After the ceremony when it was official. It seems like if one wedding brings another, a double wedding must bring another one the very next day! If Ronny Haskell hadn't come in at that moment wanting to register a speedboat and change ownership on an SUV, she would have climbed into her car and come too. She did make him wait while she called Otto to share the news. She rushed Ronny's paperwork through, took his money, and then hustled him out so she could shop for a wedding present. The part-time clerk could open up again when she came in at 11:00. Not a toaster, of course. They must already have plenty of toasters.

The wedding party drove away from the DMV, the lovers holding hands now, Tina's head resting on Bill's shoulder, where it fit like an egg in a spoon, Pete whistling through his teeth, but unable to irritate anyone enough to silence him. He might have been inaudible for all the impact he was having. He might have been invisible for all the attention he could get.

"Will Foster be my cat now?" Tina asked, her voice soft and dreamy, as though she had just come in from the snow.

"Foster has always been your cat. No change there."

"Do I get a raise?"

"Tina, you get what I get. You become a co-owner along with me. Ursula still owns half, but the other half is ours, yours and mine."

"So I don't get a raise?"

"No, sorry, no raise. But you share the profits. The Happy Trout is one-quarter yours."

"Free food," Pete offered, but he knew he would be ignored.

"Is Ursula going to mind?" Tina wished that Ursula was there to tell her how to do this. Even though she wasn't married to Benny yet, she would know some things about common sense. About what people do.

"I expect Ursula is going to be very happy for us. And not surprised. She saw this coming a long time before I did." Bill figured they could work out the logistics and the numbers with Ursula. The important thing was to get Tina, to have Tina, and to keep her safe. To keep her.

"Rachel said she was okay if I was your girlfriend. So maybe she'll be okay with this too. I wish she was here."

"Rachel will be happy for us. In a Rachel way, of course. She'll be glad to have a totally awesome stepmom like you."

Rachel would probably be okay after a while to get used to it, maybe to grow up some more. It was hard to worry about it, with Bill's warm, solid body next to hers. Tina sat with that for a moment, watching the trees fly by and enjoying the way the momentum of the car on the curving road snuggled her against Bill, and then on the next curve moved her body away with the promise of a return to contact. She could smell him; she smoothed her face against his sleeve. Mostly she wanted to throw herself on him, but she could wait. They would keep the car on the road. They would arrive. She was on her way.

"Where do I sleep now?" She knew, but she wanted to hear it.

Pete, having tired of humming, shook his head and pretended to cover his ears. "Just stop it. Please, Bill. *Pas devant les enfants.*"

Bill kept his eyes on the road, but he could still see Tina. He remembered being in love before, but this felt better, warmer, safer, and sexier.

"You sleep with me, Tina. Right there next to me so I can hold you. You can keep the trailer if you need some space, because I know it's a little cramped in my room. But I'm hoping you will join me in my bed. I only snore a little."

"Can Foster sleep there too?"

"Foster sleeps wherever he wants to. And so if you're there, I imagine he'll be there too. Could get a little crowded, I guess."

"Count me out," Pete said. "Don't be looking for old Pete to bunk in with you."

Tina gave him a quick glance, and then she smiled and took his hand and held it softly for a moment. It occurred to Pete that he didn't understand her at all, and he wondered if he should have made a play the first day or if something precious had been batted away by his own careless hand. He was silenced.

"Okay," Tina said. "This is good."

Then they came to the state line and the trees thinned out on the granite outcroppings, presenting a landscape Tina had never seen before except in cowboy movies. She pressed her head back against Bill's shoulder, Bill, and that was enough. More mountains, the end of the ridge, welcome to Nevada, and then Rev. Wally Buck's Wedding Chapel of Dreams, license and ceremony, credit cards/cash/ATM, same-day service, drop-in okay.

"Welcome! Welcome to the Wedding Chapel of Dreams." The Rev. Wally Buck hailed them as he emerged from one of several trailers parked in the gravel lot in front of a converted garage with "Wedding Chapel of Dreams" lettered on the door in elaborate Victorian script. Rev. Wally Buck spoke in a voice so sonorous as to be almost singing. Had he been a baritone instead of a tenor, he would most likely have been consigned to doing funerals instead of joining living people in holy matrimony. His long, flabby face was split by a wide smile. Business had not been good so far this month and he was delighted to see them.

"Welcome to the Happy Couple! Welcome to the Wedding Chapel of Dreams!" He shook hands all around until he could get things sorted out, to make sure he didn't congratulate the best man and miss the groom.

"Let's just take care of the business end, shall we, and then we at Rev. Wally Buck's Wedding Chapel of Dreams will give you a ceremony you will always remember for your entire lifetime of wedded bliss."

He pulled out his licensing book and his cash box, ready to do business.

"And you are the lucky man? Congratulations! Cash? That's fine. Allow me to see your identification and we'll get the forms filled out properly. That's right."

"And our beautiful bride?" He shook hands with Tina.

Together, Bill and Tina filled out the forms, although Tina's side was a little skimpy. "What if I haven't been married before? How do I fill out that part?"

The Rev. Wally Buck was reassuring. "Not a problem, Miss..." he craned his head to read the name she had entered. "Miss Martin." He started to say, "Not to be Martin much longer," but that was a joke from an earlier time. So many brides now kept their maiden names, a shame, but one must keep up with the times. Not to mention those that kept a name from a previous marriage. "Just fill in those lines about previous marriages with 'NA,' meaning not applicable."

Bill was amused to see that Tina had filled in "mother's name," "father's name," and "place of birth" the same way, as though she had somehow arrived unparented in an unspecified location. She was so Tina.

Rev. Wally gave the form a quick look. "Fine, fine! Let me just give a call to our wedding planner and second witness," with a quasi-bow towards Pete followed by a warm handshake, just in case he might ever be looking for a good wedding chapel experience for himself. "I'll just give Miss Anya Niedzewicz, former Miss Virginia, a call so that she can help prepare for the ceremony." It sounded as though she were a head priestess decorating a lamb with a crown of marigolds, ready for sacrifice. "She is my guest in the second trailer back there, so she'll be with us presently. Miss Anya will help you design your ceremony and choose from among the flowers in our large selection."

He pulled out his cell and turned his back tactfully, speaking in a muted but still musical tone, and summoned her. Evidently Miss Anya's preparations were short and she would be on her way, he told them.

"What kind of music will you be wanting for this auspicious occasion?" Rev. Wally Buck did not rub his hands together, but he seemed to be restraining them from making that creepy motion by clasping them tightly in an attitude of quasi-prayer.

"No music," Bill said, "unless you want music?"

"No music," Tina said. "But flowers. I wish I had brought some roses."

"Miss Anya will help you select a bouquet. Here's a chart if you want to see what we can provide. And how about the Memory Lane photo package?"

Bill shook his head after a quick glance at Tina. "And we don't have rings yet either."

"I see," Rev. Buck said, trying not to sound disappointed. "Just the basics. We will still need Miss Anya as a witness, however, so please be patient. Now, what kind of ceremony did you want? Do you have vows written out? No? Would you like to choose from our exclusive anthology of wedding vows? There's Whirlwind Romance, Commitment (that's a nice one, very serious), Second Chance, Sacred. No? Okay. Maybe just the basics on that as well, then."

He led them ceremoniously into the Wedding Chapel of Dreams, turning off the thundering organ music that sprang up as they entered.

"Light show? Very romantic images, very popular." But he didn't sound optimistic. And it wouldn't be the same without the soundtrack anyway. "Sunset, ocean, clouds, rainbows." He didn't wait for an answer.

Bill shook his head. Tina held onto him, afraid to even run her hand over his arm, afraid for a moment that he would change his mind, afraid the Wedding Chapel of Dreams might turn out to be a front for a hot escort service.

Pete was surprised to find that he was feeling teary and sentimental. He sniffed and blew his nose on his red bandana.

"And here's Miss Anya now!"

Anya Niedzewicz, former Miss Virginia, immensely blonde, beautifully made up, tightly corseted, sweet-faced, and dressed in fluttering ribbons of lavender and apricot, made her entrance. She greeted the happy couple with all the hospitality of a Virginia upbringing and a lifelong career in femininity, including Pete in her gracious smile and warmest congratulations. Pete was plunged into a flash fantasy of removing the firm foundation garments from her full, round body, and sinking into the cloud of a willing Miss Anya. She would probably be grateful, he thought. He was having quite a sensation-filled day.

After conferring briefly with the Rev. Buck, Miss Anya drew Tina aside to confirm. She knew grooms were sometimes in a hurry to get it over with and get straight to the honeymoon, and she saw herself as a staunch advocate for what she believed to be the universal desire of all females to have a fuss made over them.

"Maybe some violins, honey? Just to set the mood? It's part of the economy package, so it doesn't run anything extra."

"Red roses," Tina said. "And no music. There isn't any music for this. But thanks."

Miss Anya pulled a bouquet of red paper roses out from under the altar and tucked it into Tina's hands. She stood back and cocked her head. "Beautiful. You are a truly beautiful bride. So radiant," she said, as she usually did except when it was a patent lie. After moving the players up to their marks, gently, like a kindergarten teacher attempting a Christmas pageant, she nodded gracefully at the Rev. Wally Buck to begin. Dearly Beloved. I do. I will.

The following Friday, former Miss Virginia Miss Anya Niedzewicz leaned back over the sink at Hair's Looking at You Salon and sighed, leaving herself entirely in Mario's hands. This was her time to let down, to exhale, to escape from and also prepare for the production that was Miss Anya Niedzewicz. Mario had been her hairdresser ever since she had hooked up with Rev. Wally Buck and moved to this nowhere corner of Nevada. It had been a hard decision at the time, but she found it suited her. Rev. Wally was deeply appreciative of her title and her good looks, being himself a man with coarse, irregular features, blessed only with the beauty of a preacher's voice. He openly admired her. He was proud of her, and she found that endearing after a career that went from its high point at nineteen, through a series of showgirl jobs, not dancing so much as standing around, and then the expo circuit. Her last job had been as hostess at The Hot Spot Grill, a third-rate steak house and bar where she had not been admired or appreciated at all. The men weren't so bad, but the younger girls were merciless, calling her Miss Vagina of 1827 and refusing to share their tips. Wally Buck was her Sir Galahad.

Mario slowly poured the warm water over her head, watching the blonde strands melt into a dull beige, almost white at the roots.

"Sweetheart," he said. "I'm seeing you as a champagne blonde. We're going even lighter than last time! I'm going to add the tiniest bit of lavender tone to bring out the highlights and get that blonde gleam. You'll look fabulous. What am I saying? You always look fabulous!"

"You do make me look good," Miss Anya said, having almost drifted off, lulled by the warm water and the strong security of Mario's hands under her head, the scratching sound of the round plastic brush on her scalp.

"So tell, ducky. Who married who this week? How's the wedding business?"

"Well, first there was a December-May wedding; we know how that ends. Although the girls always seem so sweet at the ceremony. The groom's son looked like he was going to be the trouble at this one. But you know, love is a mysterious thing. And we always wish them the best."

"I know you do. That's because you're a classy lady"

The crème rinse smelled of elderflowers and lavender. She relaxed even more.

"Okay, my pet, then what was the most best wedding, most likely to succeed?"

"These two came in on Monday morning, no music, just roses, no photo package. They hadn't brought rings. So it seemed kind of spur-of-the-moment. But they were dressed up pretty nice for that. She was a little thing, sort of Black or Asian, or maybe Indian. You just couldn't tell. She was a whole walking United Nations, is what Wally said after they left."

"Who was the other witness?"

"Sort of a hippy type with a braid like Willie Nelson. I don't know where they picked him up." So much for Pete's fantasy.

"Romantic, was it?" Mario said, wrapping her head in a maroon towel, tucking it in to make a turban. "Over this way, now. Watch your step."

"Not really romantic, Mario. After all, no music. They were so serious about it, though, and all lit up like it was Christmas and New Year's and Easter all at once, all shiny."

"And the bride wore…?"

"Red satin Chinese dress, you know with the…" She made a gesture across her full bosom to indicate the diagonal. "It looked really cute on her. She had the figure for it. But they were so…." She looked up at Mario, and the glow in her eyes was impressive. "I can't explain. But the way they held onto each other, like something had clicked into place."

Mario trimmed a few bits from the sides, studying her in the mirror to be sure it was even. He feathered the top a little more, spreading out the hair to cover her pink scalp completely.

"Okay, precious, now you relax and let me work my magic." Mario took a tiny, almost invisible strand of her wet hair, set it on an aluminum foil square, daubed it with gray mud, and then folded it up, and then on to the next until her head was covered with packages, ready for the hair dryer. He helped her up and walked her across the room to the drying station.

"It was beautiful, Mario. They belonged together," Miss Anya said as he tucked her into the hair dryer and put a *People* magazine in her lap to look at before she dozed off. "And the kiss! Oh, Mario, it was perfect!."

And in a short while, after a brief visit with the lives of the beautiful and famous, lulled by the heat and the dull whirr of the dryer, Miss Anya closed her eyes, just to rest them for a moment, and dreamed about rivers, dreamed about fish.

Epilogue

EIGHT MONTHS AFTER THE wedding, when winter had come and gone, Foster's health failed. He slept all day on the bed. He quit eating and drinking. Not even fresh trout from the river could tempt him. Then he went out one day to die in the forest where he had hunted, holing up in the shelter of a fallen tree where he had rested many times before. Tina called his name for hours before he managed to stand up and walk unevenly toward the sound of her voice. She lifted him, no heavier than a handkerchief, and cried into his dull fur. When she took him to the vet, there was nothing to be done. She had him put to sleep to end his suffering, though he was already so close to death that the shot merely nudged him over the edge. He died with his eyes on Tina, his first, his only love. Then the light went and he was gone, so quickly. She and Bill buried him by Tina's rock so that he could be with her when she sat and listened to the river.

A few years later, Miss Anya Niedzewicz, diagnosed with advanced cancer in both of her magnificent breasts, scarred with surgery, burned with radiation, blasted with chemotherapy, became herself for the first time since she was six when her mother had decided she was the ticket out of poverty for both of them. Sitting in front of her mirror, she carefully removed first her false eyelashes, then her cancer wig, and her rouge, her lipstick, and saw in the reflection the sweet old face of her beloved grandmother looking back at her, compassionate but not alarmed. She put away all her makeup and her foundation garments, put on a plain gown, wrapped a shawl around her shoulders, and lay down on her soft bed, where several months later, with Rev. Wally Buck sobbing at her side, she met death, not like the former Miss Virginia at all, but like a little Polish girl a long way from home.

Pete died in a blizzard, driving down Highway 50, the loneliest highway in the world. His van conked out, and he had to get out and open up the back for a look-see at the engine. He was sure he could get it going again, and he would have, but when he started to get his toolbox, he slipped in the treacherous snow, struck his head on the trailer hitch, and fell there, unconscious. In ordinary weather, he would have come to in half an hour or so with a ringing headache. But the sun was almost down and the snow kept falling, drifting against his cooling body, glistening white in his graying red ponytail. The cause of death was listed as exposure.

Freddy Napoleon died of a gunshot to the back of the head, and the Russians took over his business, employees, contacts, and profits. T-Wah died as part of the take-over, also from a gunshot. Hoppy had already gone to prison on aggravated assault charges that resulted from his work for Freddy, and he died there of neglect and age. Geron died in a bus crash. His nephews sued the transit company for sixteen thousand dollars and won.

Monika Lindberg died alone in a run-down motel room from bad judgment and whore's luck. The heroin, all she had been able to score that day, was under-cut, of much better quality than she had supposed it to be. Her body was claimed by her sister Elsa, who flew in from northern Ohio to settle her paltry affairs. The funeral was attended by nine hookers and Elsa, who set up pictures of Monika as a flaxen-haired baby, child, and young woman, Tuesday's child, full of grace. White roses were placed on the closed coffin, symbolizing beauty, the loss of love, absence, and a life unclaimed. The minister was tactful. The women wept together, ate little waffle-shaped cookies with coffee, and then went their separate ways.

Ursula died during surgery for uterine cancer in

Florida, where she had moved with Benny after they sold the pet grooming business and retired a few years later than she had hoped. She was supposed to survive the routine surgery and live for years, but the family heart gave out. She was cremated as she had requested, but her ashes were accidentally switched with those of another deceased, a ninety-two year old woman named Ida Pesh, so Ursula's remains still rest in an elaborate urn on the closet shelf of a complete stranger. She would have found that amusing.

Benny started drinking immediately after he sprinkled Ida Pesh's ashes into the Atlantic Ocean. He drank all that day and didn't quit until he died three years later of acute alcoholism in another town.

Bill had always said he would work till he dropped, and that is what he did. One winter day, at the age of sixty-five, he went out to clear the parking lot. He told Tina, as he did with every snowfall, "I'll be out shoveling your snow in the parking lot," as though she had drawn the white feathers out of the sky by sheer force of longing, and it was left to him to clean up the mess. But on this occasion, the snow was too much for him; his heart burst and he fell. Tina didn't find him until an hour later after she had done the next week's order, and he was lying curled up with his shovel flung aside, dead and cold and gone. She sat down in the dirty ice next to him, calling his name, feeling guilty for an instant because her snow had killed him, but really, it was everybody's snow. And it comes whether you call it or not. She hoped she would die with him, but her constitution was too strong to release her just on her say-so. Bill's grave can be found in Pineville in the cemetery across from the DMV. The tombstone gives his name, the dates of his birth and death, and reads: "Beloved Bill. Always and Forever." On it is a carving of a very happy trout.

Tina ran the Happy Trout Fishing Resort by herself for seven years after Bill's death, but it wasn't the same. The river was a little shallower, the trout less lively, the trees darker, the snow less brilliant, the spring too quick to come and go, and the work harder with only temporary help. No one who showed up at the Happy Trout seemed to stick like she had. In the end she sold the place, knowing the café would be torn down and the Happy Trout Fishing Resort would be replaced by a national chain with honeymoon cabins on both sides of the chuckling river, where lovers would still do the natural things they do, and the seasons pushed each other through the years as best they could. Tina moved into Pineville where she lived frugally on the proceeds from the sale, then into a nursing home closer to Rachel, where she died of a series of strokes as her 89th birthday approached. Her last cogent thought before she became not Tina, became just the animal, struggling to let go, actively pursuing the business of dying, was gratitude for it all.

Rachel dies. Rachel's daughter dies. This is how all stories end, even Tina's. Even yours. Even mine.